KILLER TRANSACTION

CATHERINE BRUNS

∿

KILLER TRANSACTION
a Cindy York Mystery

by

CATHERINE BRUNS

∿

❀ Created with Vellum

ACKNOWLEDGMENTS

There are so many people who played a part in this book being published. First, a debt of gratitude to retired Troy, New York Police Captain Terrance Buchanan for sharing his wisdom and knowledge with me. Special recognition goes out to my former real estate manager, Mary Peyton, who always had the answers to my questions concerning the trade. Critique partner Diane Bator was a huge asset in shaping this story. Beta readers Constance Atwater, Krista Gardner, and Kathy Kennedy were nothing short of amazing with their support and great ideas. Thanks to my family, especially my husband, Frank, for his infinite patience and belief in my ability. Last but certainly not least, a profound thank you to my publisher, Gemma Halliday, and her talented staff of editors, especially Danielle Kuhns and Kristin Huston, for helping to make this book a reality for me.

CHAPTER ONE

his was a new one for me. I'd never had a client fall asleep while signing a contract before. I blew out a sigh. Was I really that boring? "Mrs. Hunter?"

There was no answer.

"Mrs. Hunter, can you hear me?" I glanced anxiously at my watch while she dozed. It was after 11:30 on a brisk Tuesday morning near the end of April. I was hosting an open house in less than an hour and really needed to be on my way. The caterer would be arriving soon with the sandwiches and expected me to meet him at the front door.

Again, there was no response, except for a faint whistling coming from the mouth of Agnes Hunter, a tiny and sweet, white-haired, eighty-year-old woman. In the two weeks since I had come to know Mrs. Hunter, she seemed to have shrunk more with age. She needed to sell her home at 6 Partridge Lane in order to pay for the upcoming expenses of going into assisted living. A friend of a friend had recommended my services, and Mrs. Hunter had finally decided to let me come over to tour the house and, after a week of running personal errands for her, agreed to sign a contract. She didn't even argue about the seven percent commission fee my agency charged since she needed the money desperately and was anxious to proceed.

Fred Hunter had built the white, raised ranch-style house specifically for his wife about 60 years ago, complete with cute red shutters and a white picket fence. They'd lived there their entire adult lives, until Fred passed away two years ago. There was no way Mrs. Hunter could keep up with the repairs alone.

The sun shone through the wood-framed windows adorned with handmade lace curtains. There was peeling wallpaper and worn carpeting in every room. The clapboard siding had seen better days and was cracked, splintered and faded. Cosmetic issues could have easily been corrected, if she'd had money for such repairs. However, with so much work for a potential buyer to do, Mrs. Hunter's profit would be affected considerably.

I glanced at my watch again. *Sheesh.* I had been here over an hour already, and she still hadn't signed. Mrs. Hunter knew I had children, and I'd happily shown her pictures when she'd asked to see them. I'd smiled at the "My, how do you ever tell them apart" comment when I told her my boys were twins and accepted the tea she insisted on making while I tried to explain the more complex details of the contract.

Although Mrs. Hunter was willing to sell her home, she was fast turning into what we real estate agents deemed "a tough sale." Whenever I visited, something managed to go awry. The first time, her toilet overflowed. Since money was an issue, I'd called upon my husband, Greg, to come fix it. He wasn't happy since I'd interrupted Sunday afternoon baseball but, realizing this was possible income for me, had immediately taken care of the issue.

During my next visit, Mrs. Hunter's cat escaped when I opened the front door. I'd spent an entire hour outside yelling, "Here, Madame Puss," and gave up counting how many snickers and wise cracks I'd endured from neighbors—most of them children. When I'd finally found the temperamental kitty hiding behind some bushes and scooped her into my arms, she'd rewarded me by sinking her fang-like teeth into my thumb. Mrs. Hunter assured me that Madame Puss was up to date on all of her vaccinations. At least, she thought so. Days later, my thumb still smarted.

"Mrs. Hunter?" I called again and touched her arm, hoping she'd wake up before I missed my open house and maybe the rest of the day as well.

Her eyelids flickered, then widened with fear as she reached inside the deep pocket of her flowered housecoat. "Who are you, and what are you doing in my home?"

Good grief. I'd heard from neighbors that she was in the early stages of dementia and hoped she wasn't packing a Smith & Wesson. "I'm Cindy York from Hospitable Homes. You asked me to sell your house for you."

Recognition slowly replaced the dazed look on her face. She took her glasses out of her pocket, put them on, and peered at me. "Oh, Cindy, dear." She yawned. "I'm so sorry, I must have dozed off. Never fear. I'm back now."

"That's all right." I handed her a pen and placed the contract on the table in front of her. "Now that you're ready, I'll need you to sign and initial on page one. When you're done with that, you sign and date—"

Mrs. Hunter studied me. "Did I ask if you wanted a cup of tea, dear?"

I grinned and raised my cup in the air.

"Oh, good." She smiled and smoothed the tablecloth in front of her, apparently relieved her good manners hadn't failed her.

"Okay. I need you to sign and initial on the bottom of page one. Yes, right there." I flipped over the sheet. "Here, on the bottom of page two, I need a full signature. And on page three—"

Mrs. Hunter paused and lifted her pen away from the

papers. She observed me cautiously over the rims of her glasses. "What am I signing?"

Uh-oh. I closed my eyes and blew out a slow breath. *Maybe she's worse off than I thought.* "The contract for me to list your home, Mrs. Hunter. Remember?"

Mrs. Hunter shook her head and took off her glasses, wiping them with a tissue that sent a puff of dust into the sunlight. "Oh, my dear, I can't sign that."

Now I was confused. "I don't understand. What do you mean, you can't sign it?"

"Well, I signed another contract yesterday."

My heart skipped a beat. Okay, I must have heard her wrong. "Are you sure? Why would you sign with another agent when you were supposed to list with me?" Please let her be joking. I needed this listing. *Bad.*

"Oh dear." She blinked several times. "Well, I know I'd planned to, but the other young lady was so sweet, and she said you wouldn't mind since you both work for the same agency anyway. She even brought flowers and my favorite candy."

No, it can't be. I sucked in a sharp breath. "Would her name happen to be Tiffany Roberts?"

"Why, yes, it was." Mrs. Hunter nodded. "Oh, good, so you *are* friends. Isn't it nice how this all worked out?"

I bit my lip hard, afraid I might cry that second. "Tiffany and I both work for the same agency, but that doesn't mean anything. She's the one who will be selling your house now, not me."

Mrs. Hunter frowned. "But you two could work together and split the money you earn. Isn't that the way it works?"

"No, not if you've already signed the contract and only her name is on it." I shook my head in disbelief. "Mrs. Hunter, Tiffany will be stopping by to see you. She's going to void that contract. I'll be back tomorrow with a new one for you to sign."

"Well, all right, dear. That is, as long as Tiffany doesn't mind." She folded her glasses and tucked them back into her pocket.

A huge knot formed in the pit of my stomach. "I'll see to it personally that she doesn't mind." My heart softened as the old lady stared at me, obviously disoriented. It wasn't her fault that she'd been duped by the most dishonest agent alive.

I clutched my briefcase tightly and stood. "I have to go now. I'm meeting some—some friends for lunch."

"Well, now isn't that lovely." Mrs. Hunter smiled. "Please be sure and say hello to that lovely Tiffany for me."

Oh, I'd say something all right.

A well-fed, black cat with a large spot of white on her enormous chest was stationed by the front door, blocking my escape. Madame Puss had six toes on each paw and bore more than a slight resemblance to Bigfoot.

The last time I'd called to say I was coming over, Mrs. Hunter asked if I wouldn't mind stopping at the grocery store to pick up some canned salmon for her precious kitty. Madame Puss ate a can of it every day, and apparently, the cupboard was bare. When I'd dared to suggest Madame Puss should eat dry food like my cat, Mrs. Hunter gasped so loudly on the other end of the phone that I was afraid she'd been in acute pain.

Madame Puss observed me eagerly, probably hoping to sneak out at my expense again. I tried to open the door around her, but she refused to budge. Already late and angered by Tiffany's audacity, I glowered at the robust cat. "Move."

Madame Puss continued to sit there, staring at me as if I was the stupidest human on the face of the earth. She brought her paw to her mouth and started to clean it carefully, daring me to interrupt her.

I scooped up the cat with both hands, fearing for my other nine fingers and ignoring her meows of protest. Once I handed Madame Puss to Mrs. Hunter, she continued to glare at me from her owner's arms.

"I'll have Tiffany call you tonight after we sort things out." I straightened my blazer and brushed tiny, black Madame Puss hairs off of it.

Mrs. Hunter nodded. "That would be nice, dear. Why don't both of you stop by for tea tomorrow? I could use a ride to the grocery store too."

I opened my mouth to say something, thought better of it, and nodded. "I'll see what I can do." I managed a quick smile for Mrs. Hunter, disregarded the hiss Madame Puss directed at me, and quickly closed the front door.

Why me? Why can't I ever have one sale go off without a hitch?

Tears of frustration started to fall as I backed my car out of Mrs. Hunter's driveway. My contact lenses clouded over, and before I reached the end of the street, I started sobbing, almost hitting a large orange cat that looked like it could have been Garfield's brother.

I took a left at the end of the street and then an immediate right to get on the highway, heading toward my open house. My face burned as I grabbed a tissue from my purse to blow my nose and wipe my eyes. Good old Tiffany had tried to put one over on me again. *Damn her. How could she do this to me?*

Yet I knew very well how.

Tiffany Roberts was arguably one of the most successful real estate agents in New York State. A gorgeous blonde with a perfect size-four figure, she was commonly referred to as a "dirty agent" by her fellow colleagues, which meant she lied to potential buyers about the homes they were going to purchase. If the buyer called six months later, crying because water was leaking into their basement, she'd claim she knew nothing about it and blame the inspector, other agent, or anyone else easy for her to manipulate. Somehow she always managed to win, charming client after client while she let them think their happiness was her first priority. What a crock.

If another agent had already secured a listing on a home, that didn't stop Tiffany from trying to pry it away from them. Although the practice was deemed unethical, she'd find a way to worm her way into the house or conveniently run into the sellers at the supermarket or just happen to stop by while they were having a garage sale and convince them to tell their current agent they'd had a sudden change of heart. A couple of weeks later, the previous agent would see their former listing reappear under the sales category in the MLS (Multiple Listing Service) with Tiffany's name as the broker.

I'd been the victim of Tiffany's underhanded dealings before. I'd thought about taking her to court but couldn't prove anything. A client had called me one day and claimed he'd changed his mind about selling, so I'd released him from the contract. A week later, Tiffany happened to be going door to door in the neighborhood and re-convinced him to sell. At least, that was her explanation. Considering it was a very rural neighborhood and the middle of winter, it made perfect sense that she'd be taking a stroll through the countryside on a day that hit minus fifteen degrees. But the seller stuck to his story, and I had been the one left out in the cold.

She's not going to get away with it this time. I blew out a sharp breath, pushed aside my long, dark hair, and inserted the Bluetooth into my right ear. When I reached a red light, I searched my contacts section and angrily clicked on Tiffany's number.

After one ring, it went directly to her voice mail. "Hi, this is Tiffany Roberts with Hospitable Homes. I'm sorry I can't take your call right now as I'm in the middle of a real estate transaction. Please leave your name and number at the tone, and I'll call you back as soon as I can. Remember, make it a great day."

There was a huge lump in my throat, and I choked back tears, my voice hoarse and tight, barely above a whisper. "Tiffany, it's Cindy. I'd like to talk to you about Six Partridge

Lane. You know, the Hunter house. Call me back soon. Unless you want to die young."

With that, I disconnected, never dreaming that my message would come back to haunt me later.

CHAPTER TWO

*A*s it turned out, ironically enough, the open house I'd agreed to host was for one of Tiffany's listings. When she'd discovered she had a closing scheduled at the same time, she'd asked me—ever so sweetly—if I could fill in for her. In return, she'd promised to give me any leads that might develop. So here I was, setting myself up for disappointment again. *What the heck is wrong with me?*

Astor Lane was one of the area's nicer suburbs. The house I parked in front of was a pristine, white Colonial with an immaculately landscaped yard, even at this time of year. I sighed. My lawn was still soft with mud from the rain showers yesterday. There was also a huge hole in my backyard where Stevie and Seth, my 8-year-old, energetic twins, had recently decided to dig to China—or perhaps the nearest GameStop.

The house was in excellent condition and probably wouldn't take long to sell, even in this year's dismal market. Unlike me, Tiffany didn't get leftovers. As Greg affectionately once put it to me, "No one can sell a dump like you can, Cin."

By the time I reached the driveway, the catering truck had

already pulled in ahead of me. To my dismay, another car sat parked across the street with four or five people sitting inside. The open house didn't start for another fifteen minutes. I was guessing these weren't prospective buyers. More than likely this was a family who had seen the advertisement in the paper and were looking for a free lunch.

I grabbed my eKEY from the glove compartment. Real estate agents only had to punch their pin numbers into this handy device and then sync it with the electronic lockbox located on the front door. I gathered together Tiffany's flyers, an *Open House* sign, and the gift card to Macy's that she was giving away as a door prize. I hurried to unlock the door for the caterer, who had his hands full with a plate of tempting-looking sandwiches.

Tiffany could well afford to pay for the luncheon herself, but the meal had been donated by one of the mortgage brokers she worked with. They were only too happy to provide food as long as Tiffany kept recommending their services to potential buyers. Sadly enough, tar paper shacks didn't qualify for catered affairs, otherwise they probably would have been delighted to donate a lunch to my listings too.

In addition to the sandwiches, there was also an assortment of single-serving potato chip bags, bottled water and soda, plus another platter that held a delectable array of sugar and choco-late chip cookies for dessert. This must have cost the company at least a couple of hundred dollars. Yes, anything for Tiffany.

After two trips, the caterer and I had everything inside. I thanked him, signed the receipt, and walked down the driveway to attach the *Open House* sign to the mailbox. As soon as I did, the freebie party slowly disengaged themselves from their vehi-cle. I turned away, rolled my eyes toward the sky, and walked back into the house to wait for their arrival.

Within one minute, someone gave a slight tap on the door.

Before I could cross the room, the door was pushed open by one of my potential new friends. I smiled and fought to find a silver lining to the day. "Good afternoon. How are you today?"

They nodded in return and accepted the flyer I handed them. I asked them to sign in and while they did, took a minute to look them over. The two kids, both teenage boys, wore Old Navy jeans and shirts. I prided myself on my knowledge of teen attire, thanks in part to my fifteen-year-old daughter, Darcy, who knew what was in fashion and what was considered detrimental to your popularity status.

The parents appeared to be in their fifties and wore similarly styled imitation polo shirts with Levis. They were both heavyset and had the same light-brown hair and eye color. It was almost eerie how they resembled each other. Perhaps in a few more years Greg and I would start looking identical. That was a scary thought. I studied the names on the clipboard. Joe and Debbie Waters, 22 Robin Road. Robin Road was located in a middle class neighborhood less than 10 minutes away.

I led them into the kitchen where I invited them to have a sandwich, which they eagerly did, along with chips, water, and several cookies. As they munched away, I described the home. The roof was only two years old, the in-ground pool had a new liner, and wall-to-wall carpeting had recently been installed. They smiled and acted like they were interested, but I knew better.

As they reached for another sandwich, I winced. This was the part I hated. "I'm so sorry, but the sandwiches are limited to one apiece. I do have to save some for the other guests."

Mrs. Waters shook her head as if she'd heard something disturbing. The kids lowered their eyes to the floor, and Mr. Waters said simply, "Wow."

Why did I feel as if I'd slapped them in the face?

At this awkward moment, my cell phone rang, and I gladly

excused myself. I hurried into the family room for privacy and studied the number on my screen. *Ugh.* My manager from hell, Donna Cushman. How lovely. "Hello?"

"Well, now isn't that a professional greeting?" said the chilly voice on the other end.

Donna Cushman had been the manager at Hospitable Homes for about eight years. Six feet tall and willowy, her hair had turned prematurely gray years ago and still didn't quite suit her forty-something age bracket. My co-worker and best friend, Jacques Forte, had once confided in me that he longed to become a hairdresser, if only to have a chance to cut away at the dreadful mop of unkempt hair that fell over Donna's shoulders. She wasn't exactly the easiest person to get along with either. Lately, I had an uncanny knack for finding new ways to annoy her without even trying.

"Yes, Donna, how can I help you?" I struggled to keep the irritation out of my voice.

"Cindy, I need you to do me a favor."

Donna *always* needed me to do her a favor. If she knew I was coming into the office, she'd call my cell and ask me to pick up coffee for her, then conveniently forget to pay me back. She'd even asked me to grab lunch for her a few times. Unlike mine, Donna's salary was at least six figures. She might be the manager, but I certainly didn't owe her anything. And contrary to her belief, I was not her personal secretary.

Okay, be nice. You need this job. "I'm in the middle of an open house now, remember?"

"Oh, that's right, Tiffany's. Well, I didn't mean this minute. The day after tomorrow I need you to show my new husband some houses. He's looking around for his mother, who will be relocating here shortly. I have an all-day sales meeting, other-wise I'd do it myself."

I moved the phone away from my ear to stare at it. Husband?

I didn't even know she'd been dating anyone. "Uh, congratulations. When did you get married?"

Donna giggled like a school girl on the other end. "Almost two weeks ago. And wait till you see him. Ken is gorgeous. Best looking guy in town. Maybe the entire state."

I rolled my eyes at the ceiling. This was going to be fun. "Can't Jacques show them to him?"

"Jacques has an inspection scheduled. No one else is available, which is the only reason I thought of you."

How flattering. "Donna, I'm still waiting to hear about my closing. For all I know it could be scheduled for that same day."

She snickered. "You wish. By the way, your redneck client called the office this morning. Apparently, he still doesn't have enough cash to close yet. He would have called you directly but couldn't remember your name or cell phone number. You sure know how to find them." With that, she burst out into cackling laughter, which added more fuel to my fire.

"It doesn't matter. He's still a paying client." *Well, maybe.* I already knew about the shortage of funds since the bank representative had called me with the good news yesterday. My client was currently trying to get a loan from his parents. Several other agents in my office had million-dollar deal prospects going while I had issues with a house selling for a mere fraction of that.

I was tired of Donna walking all over me. "Okay, I'll show him the houses on two conditions."

I heard her suck in some air. "And who do you think you are to offer me an ultimatum?"

"Oops, it's getting crowded in here. I'll speak to you later, Donna."

"Wait!" she shrieked. "What do you want?"

"First off, if he finds something he likes, I get 25 percent of the deal. And I want an email from you stating that beforehand."

Donna had pulled something similar when I first started with her office, and I'd be damned if she did it to me again.

She clucked her tongue against the roof of her mouth for a few seconds, further annoying me. "Fine. And what's the other condition?"

"You talk to Tiffany, and tell her to give me back the listing she stole from me."

"What are you talking about?"

"Six Partridge Lane. Mrs. Hunter had promised to sign with me. Remember, I told you about it?" That had been my first mistake. "All of a sudden, I was informed today she's listed with Tiffany."

"That's unfortunate."

I clenched my fist and tried not to sound desperate, which of course I was. "Donna, that's *my* listing. I want you to tell Tiffany she can't have it."

"Why should I? It's all your fault anyway."

I was perplexed. "How exactly is this my fault?"

"If you'd been faster than Tiffany and gotten over there yesterday, you'd already have your listing."

Was she serious? I couldn't believe my ears. "I was at the twins' school all day yesterday. You know I manage their food drive for the community every year."

"Perhaps you should be worrying about your own children eating. Lack of recent sales tell me unemployment might be in your future." Donna yawned noisily into the phone. "Maybe Tiffany will split the deal with you."

"Forget it. The listing belongs to me."

"Well, if you don't want to split it, your only other option is to have Mrs. Hunter call and tell Tiffany she doesn't want her representation any longer."

"How about this," I said dryly. "I'll report her to the Realty Association. There are witnesses who overheard me tell you about the appointment."

Donna snorted. "I assure you that would be a mistake."

I laughed. "A mistake? It's about time Tiffany got what she deserves. She's a disgrace to the business."

"There's really no reason to speak that way about her." Donna loved pulling the righteous card on me. "Perhaps she would be willing to issue you referrals from the house as well."

I gritted my teeth and couldn't believe the gall of these people. What planet was this woman and my co-worker from? "I should get all the referrals anyway. It's my listing, not hers."

"Sorry, no can do," Donna said.

"Nice talking to you."

She practically barked into the phone. "All right. I'll call her and mention this conversation, but that's all I'm going to do."

"I'll take care of the rest, don't worry. And I'll be waiting for your email." Since I was on a roll, I decided to go for the jugular. "By the way, you owe me $26.50 for coffee in the past month and $15.00 for last week's lunch."

Her tone was so sharp I was afraid it might shatter the window I was standing next to. "Fine. I'll leave the money in your office. And Ken will call you with the list of houses he wants to see." She clicked off without another word.

I pumped my fist in the air. Yes, score one for Cindy. Greg would be so proud of me. He was sick and tired of my so-called manager manipulating me. Frankly, so was I.

I put the phone back in my blazer pocket and returned to the kitchen. The freebie family was long gone, along with more than half of my sandwiches and all the beverages. I looked around, dumbfounded. What the heck had I been thinking to leave them alone with the food? I smacked my head hard with the palm of my hand. *Stupid, stupid.* Hopefully, I wouldn't get many more visitors. I quickly rearranged the sandwiches, hoping to give the impression that there was a larger quantity than I actually had.

At that particular moment, the door opened and a middle-aged man and woman walked in. The man, dressed in a Dolce & Gabbana suit, was on the stout side and balding. The woman, who I assumed was his wife, wore a black Chanel dress and carried a Gucci pocketbook the size of my kitchen sink. She was petite and had short, dark hair that showed off large diamonds in her ears. She scanned me up and down and attempted a smile, but it felt like more of a smirk to me.

"Would you mind signing in?" The man took the pen I handed him and wrote his name with a flourish while the woman stood there and appraised me further. Her stare made me very uncomfortable.

They followed me into the kitchen, and I reached for the plate of sandwiches and offered it to them.

"I'm sorry there aren't many left. There's been quite a crowd so far. I'd be surprised if the house is still available tomorrow." Gee, now I was starting to sound like Tiffany. I thought my little speech sounded convincing, but the man remained expressionless. The woman wrinkled her nose and shook her head.

They had written down Mr. and Mrs. Lawrence Benson on the clipboard. I found myself wondering if they were related to the Bensons who owned the various car lots in the area. They sold new cars, used cars, leased cars, and would take any vehicle in for a trade. I stared at the man again, trying to picture the obnoxious guy on television always waving his arms around, telling you to come on in for the deal of a lifetime. Yes, it could be him, except the man in the commercials had more hair. Maybe he wore a toupee.

I led them on a tour of the home and pointed out various things I thought might be of interest—the pool, hot tub, etc. We climbed the plush carpeted stairs so that I could show them the bedrooms. "Have you been looking for long?"

Mrs. Benson laughed. "The house isn't for us." She acted as if I'd offended her by suggesting such a thing. "It's for our daughter. She has very particular taste though. I don't think this would quite meet her standards."

"That's unfortunate." I certainly wouldn't have minded living here. The house was 2,500 square feet with a gorgeous California kitchen and a walk-in closet upstairs larger than my entire bedroom.

When the front door opened, I took a step backward. "Please excuse me for a moment?"

They nodded, and I took off downstairs. I knew I didn't have to worry about them taking anything. It was obvious nothing here was good enough for them.

As I came down the last few steps, I noticed two elderly women in the foyer writing their names on the clipboard. Between them stood a robust, brown-and-white bulldog on a bright-red leash.

The dog looked up and growled at me.

"Be still, Sherlock." The smaller woman had white hair and weighed about a hundred pounds soaking wet. She extended her hand. "Hello, I'm Gloria Danson. This is my sister, Lila."

"Cindy York with Hospitable Homes." I shook their hands. While their facial features were very similar, Gloria's hands were cold and frail to the touch and her sister's warm and moist.

I glanced down at the dog. "I'm very sorry, but we don't allow animals in here. He'll have to wait in the car."

"His name is Sherlock." Lila, the same height as Gloria, but much heavier, glared at me.

I was taken aback by her tone. "Well, Sherlock will have to wait in the car until you're done."

"He doesn't like to be by himself," Gloria whined. "He gets lonely. Can't he stay? He'll be good."

Were these people for real? "Miss Danson, please don't ask me to go against my orders. I can't let you keep him in the house. The owners don't want pets in here."

"Don't they like them?" Gloria drew her eyebrows together in confusion.

I blinked. "It really doesn't matter if they like them or not. We don't allow animals of any kind during the showings."

Lila pursed her lips. "Well, you don't have to be so rude."

"I apologize. I'm not trying to be rude. But I do have to follow my instructions, and the dog can't be inside the house." I gestured toward the door. "Please take him outside now, or I'll have to ask you to leave."

With that remark, Sherlock growled at me again, exposing large, snarling teeth this time. I backed up a little. *Okay, maybe not.*

"You won't touch him," Lila said.

She was probably right. I had no desire to experience another animal sinking their teeth into my fingers. "He either stays outside while you tour the house, or you all have to leave. It's your choice."

Lila motioned to Gloria. "Let's go. You don't want this rat-infested dump anyway. Come on, Sherlock."

As they moved toward the door, Sherlock refused to budge. Lila tugged at the leash, but Sherlock sat back on his haunches and wouldn't move. I guess he liked it here.

I grabbed a sandwich off a plate and walked toward the door, holding it out to the dog. "Come on, Sherlock," I crooned. "Here, boy."

"Don't you dare give him that—he has allergies!" Lila shrieked.

At that moment, Sherlock got off his haunches, walked toward me, and peed on the Pergo floor. He missed my shoe by a mere inch.

"Oh, Sherlock, that was very naughty." Gloria shook her head at me. "He never does that. See how upset you've made him?"

I shut my eyes and started to count to ten, but perhaps ten million would have been a better number. Something tugged on my hand, and I opened my eyes to see Sherlock grabbing the sandwich I held. While I watched, he swallowed it in one gulp. "Please take him outside. Now."

Lila pointed a finger in my face. "You'd better hope he doesn't have a reaction, or we'll sue!" She picked Sherlock up around his thick middle and carried him out the door, with Gloria following close behind. The dog looked back in my direction, and I swear he winked.

Maybe I need a career change. I searched around in the kitchen cabinets and quickly located some Formula 409 spray. Thank goodness Sherlock's puddle hadn't hit the wall. I grabbed some paper towels and got down on my hands and knees to clean up the mess.

A step sounded from behind. The Bensons stood there, silently watching me. Perfect timing. I scrambled to my feet. "We—uh, had a little accident here."

Mrs. Benson smiled. "Why, honey, aren't you a little old for that?"

I bristled inwardly but chose to ignore her comment.

"We're done here but do have one question for you," Mrs. Benson said. "Are the owners interested in selling any of the contents of the house?"

I hadn't been expecting this. "I'm not really sure. This isn't my listing. I'd be glad to find out for you though."

"Not your listing?" Mr. Benson seemed confused.

"I'm hosting the open house for the listing agent. She had a conflict, so I'm filling in."

Mrs. Benson spoke sweetly. "Of course you are."

"What is it you're interested in? The living room set?" It was a handsome brown leather sectional with a loveseat to match. It would have been nice to have something like that in my own house, but between the twins and our puppy, it wouldn't last a day.

Mrs. Benson laughed. "Oh, no. I'm wondering how much they want for that ruby necklace."

Now *I* was confused. "You want to know if the jewelry is for sale? Did the owner leave it out somewhere?" Instantly, I panicked. I'd meant to do a quick scan through the house when I first got there but hadn't had time. I hated when people left things of value right out in the open, such as a ring on the fireplace or a bracelet in the bathroom. If something went missing, it would be my fault, and I might be fired. Tiffany wouldn't have a problem making that happen.

"Why no." Mrs. Benson gave me a look as if I was some type of idiot. "It was in the owner's jewelry box."

I couldn't have heard her right. "Excuse me?"

"I saw it in her jewelry box." She slowly pronounced each syllable, as if this might somehow help me to understand.

My mouth dropped open. "You went through her jewelry box?"

"We didn't take anything," Mr. Benson volunteered.

Mrs. Benson tossed her head. "I didn't do anything wrong. This is an open house, right? That means you come in and look around, which is exactly what I did."

"Well, yes, but you—you can't do that."

She giggled. "Too late, darling. I already did."

I clearly wasn't getting through to these people. "I think it would be better if you left now."

Mr. Benson took a step closer and thrust his finger into my face. "Don't you know who I am?"

I crossed my arms over my stomach. "No, I don't know who you are, but that's really not the point here. You need to leave. Please."

Mrs. Benson tugged at her husband's arm. "Come on, darling. I have better things to do than be insulted by a tawdry salesperson."

I clamped my lips together tightly, not trusting myself to

open my mouth because I knew something insulting was going to fly out of it.

Mr. Benson started to speak, but apparently, he thought better of it as well. He turned toward the door, his wife at his heels. "We'll see what our attorney has to say about this." He glared in my direction and then walked outside.

Mrs. Benson gave a lingering look at my JCPenney blazer, smirked, and then followed her husband. I closed the door behind them and then rapped my head against the fake wood grain several times until my forehead started to hurt.

Mercifully, the rest of the open house went off without a hitch. Three additional couples stopped in. One was from next door, so I assumed it was more of a curiosity factor than anything else. A newlywed couple expressed a great interest in the home. They acted normal, asked a few intelligent questions, and were very attentive to my responses. Unfortunately, they were already working with someone else. If I'd been more like Tiffany, I would have done everything a real estate agent shouldn't—wined and dined them and then convinced them to sign with me instead. Too bad I had morals.

I sighed heavily as I packed up the remainder of the lunch. There were still a few sandwiches and several bags of chips left. I wrapped the sandwiches in Saran wrap and tossed the chips into my duffel bag. *What the heck. I can use these in the kids' lunches.* Except for the free food, the entire ordeal had been a complete waste of my day. Next time, Tiffany could find someone else.

It was obvious Tiffany had chosen to avoid my earlier message. I was certain she'd phone during the open house to see how everything was going and to make sure I hadn't screwed up anything. She probably didn't want to deal with me. Well, too bad for her.

I picked up the house phone and dialed her number. If Tiffany happened to recognize the number, I knew she'd answer, thinking it was her client calling to report a disaster. If not, she might think it was a potential lead. Either way, I couldn't lose.

"Good afternoon, this is Tiffany Roberts."

I was right on the money. "Well, good afternoon, Tiffany. It's Cindy York, fellow real estate agent. You know, the one you cheated out of Agnes Hunter's listing?"

There was a momentary pause. "Cindy, honey. I've been meaning to call and ask how the open house went. Did a lot of people show?"

I avoided her question. "You stole my listing, and I want it back."

She laughed. "Was that your listing? I had no idea."

I gritted my teeth. "Please don't insult my intelligence. You overheard me telling Donna I had an appointment to list the house today. I suggest you get right over to Mrs. Hunter's and void that contract unless you want me to report you."

Tiffany purred into the phone. "I'm so sorry you feel that way. Unfortunately, I'm busy for the rest of the afternoon. Perhaps we can work out some sort of deal, like a sixty-forty split with sixty going to me."

Where did this woman get her nerve? "Forget it."

"Why don't you come over to the office tonight, and we'll discuss it."

My shoulders tensed right up to my ears. "There's nothing to discuss."

"You should come over anyway. I have some wonderful ideas for marketing the Hunter home. I know it will go quickly—if we work together." The smooth tone of Tiffany's voice set me even further on edge.

Damn her. I could probably get her to split the commission with me, but why should I? I knew she wasn't lying when she said she could sell it quickly. Like King Midas, everything Tiffany touched turned to gold. Even in this dismal market, she'd listed a home last week and already had a pending sale. Lord knows I needed the money, and I suspected Tiffany knew that too.

I caved. "Fine. We'll talk. What time?"

She laughed. "How about after you get done feeding the kiddies? Is seven all right?"

I pinched the bridge of my nose between my thumb and forefinger. "All right. We can meet at the office."

"Wonderful." Tiffany sounded pleased with herself. "So how did the open house go today? Any potential buyers?"

"Only one couple you might actually be hearing from. Nancy Townsend's their agent. She may be calling you."

She cooed into the phone, and I held the receiver away from my ear in disgust. "I just adore Nancy." Her phoniness was so apparent. "What about the lunch? Did everyone enjoy it?"

And how. "Oh, yes. They definitely enjoyed it."

"Terrific. Who won the Macy's gift card?"

Oh, crap. With everything else going on, I'd forgotten to register people for the darn card. I didn't even know where it was. I lifted my purse off the countertop, and sure enough, there was the envelope.

"Um, a little old lady," I lied. "Her name was Lila. She said she was going to buy a bed for her dog."

Tiffany was silent for a few seconds. "Well, I guess if you must have pets, you should buy them the best. Funny, I didn't even know they had a pet department at Macy's. I'm usually over in shoes myself. Well, darling, I have to run. I have a check to deliver to the office for my latest closing. I'll let Donna know what's going on with Mrs. Hunter's home when I stop by. You know, that we'll be splitting the deal. The house I sold today—"

Here we go again. "I never said for sure I was splitting it with you. I thought we were going to discuss—"

My words fell upon deaf ears as she rambled on. "Yes, it was just shy of half a million. Looks like it's going to be a slow week. See you tonight. Bye now." With that, she disconnected.

I shook my head in disgust. Agents like Tiffany shouldn't be allowed to screw other people over. Maybe she'd pay for her lies someday. My mother, rest her soul, used to love saying what goes around, comes around. I threw the Macy's card into my handbag, gathered up my belongings, and prayed Mom was right.

CHAPTER THREE

"One for me, and one for you." Seth hand-fed pieces of steak to Rusty, our cocker spaniel puppy, under the table. His brother Stevie giggled and joined in the banter.

"Stop it, you'll make him sick." Greg scowled and then gazed across the table at me, his blue eyes warm and soft. We'd been married for seventeen years, and I still didn't know where he got his patience from. After days like this, I wasn't sure I had any left. "Baby, you haven't even touched your dinner."

I watched the clock with apprehension. "I'm too nervous to eat. I have to meet Tiffany in half an hour."

"Don't worry. Everything will be fine."

My husband knew how much I was dreading this meeting. Like Donna, Tiffany was a force to be reckoned with. My stomach twisted into a giant pretzel knot.

Greg leaned over and helped himself to another serving of potato salad. "How'd the open house go today? Did you get any leads?"

I shook my head. "Not really. It was actually the open house from hell."

Stevie's blue eyes were large and round. "Are you going there?"

"No, dummy, but you will someday." Seth laughed.

I narrowed my eyes at him. "That's enough."

"Mother dear." Darcy's huge, dark eyes were fixed on me expectantly. "Can I get my hair and nails done for the dance on Saturday?"

I exchanged glances with Greg. "I'm sorry, honey. We don't have the extra money right now." I felt awful when I saw her face fall. My heart ached to refuse her, but I didn't have a choice.

Darcy tossed back her long, black hair. "That's okay. No big deal."

"I can do your hair and your nails. Do you want a French twist or a braid? There are lots of different things—"

She sniffed. "No, never mind."

"But I love doing it. We'll have a great time. You'll see."

Darcy observed me in amazement. "You don't have a clue as to what styles are in now. You'll just make me look like a geek."

"You already are a geek." Stevie flicked a green bean across the table at his sister while Seth giggled.

"Guys, stop." Greg put down his fork and stared at Darcy. "You apologize to your mother. She went and bought you that expensive dress, and this is the thanks she gets? Maybe she should return it to the store tomorrow."

"It's all right, Greg."

Lately, Darcy liked to blame me for everything that was wrong with her life. I suspected it was some type of phase she was going through. I sure hoped she'd finish fast.

"No, it's not all right." Greg glared at Darcy. "Apologize. *Now.*"

Everyone at the table was silent, waiting for Darcy.

She frowned and got to her feet, looking in my direction. "I'm sorry. I think I'll go over to Heather's now."

I shook my head. "You have dishes to do first."

Darcy slammed her chair into the table. "How come I get

stuck doing the dishes every night?" She pointed at the twins. "Can't you teach those little dorks how to do them?"

"Of course. Someday when I know they won't break them all into tiny pieces first."

Darcy gave me a dirty look as she put her plate into the sink. "This sucks."

That was enough for Greg who got to his feet, knocking his chair over in the process, and walked over to Darcy. "I want you to go upstairs and cool off for a little while. Afterward, you'll come back down to finish your chores. You will not be going anywhere tonight, except to bed afterward."

"Darcy's in trouble," Stevie and Seth sang out in unison, while I tried in vain to silence them.

Darcy shot the twins a menacing stare and then turned to glare at me. "Why did I have to be born into such a dysfunctional family?" She ran out of the eat-in kitchen and into the adjoining living room, where she loudly thumped her way up the staircase to her bedroom.

Stevie raised his eyebrows. "What's dysfunctional mean?"

"If it's about you, it must be dumb," Seth said.

I sighed at Greg. "Every day it's something else with her."

"Girls." Seth stuck his tongue out. "They're too much drama. That's why I hate them." Stevie nodded in agreement.

Greg and I both managed to hide our smiles.

"You'll feel different someday." Greg put his plate in the sink.

Seth shook his head. "No way."

"Not happening." Stevie offered Rusty a green bean. He whined and walked away.

I got to my feet and started clearing the table. "I have to get going. It's time to get this settled once and for all."

"What did you decide to do?" Greg asked.

I placed some glasses on the light-blue Formica countertop. "I don't know. If she offers a deal, I may have to take it."

"Don't let her intimidate you. We don't need the money that badly."

"Of course we do." I looked toward the table uneasily. Stevie and Seth were hanging on every word we said. "Did you guys finish your homework?"

Seth gave me a thumbs up. "All done, Mom."

Stevie nodded in agreement as if he was Seth's little clone. They both continued to sit there, watching Greg and me.

Greg cleared his throat. "Why don't you guys go watch some television?"

"Nah, there's nothing good on right now." Stevie reached over to poke his brother in the arm.

"Ouch! Yeah, only some dumb cartoons." Seth pinched Stevie in return.

Greg lifted his thumb in the air and made a jerking motion toward downstairs. "Move. Now."

"Boy, everyone in this house is really weird," Seth said to Stevie.

"Yeah, except for Rusty."

They grabbed the puppy and trudged downstairs to the family room. Greg shut the door quickly behind them.

He walked over to me and put his hands on my shoulders. "You don't have to take any deal Tiffany offers. I don't want that greedy witch taking advantage of you."

I buried my face into his massive chest. "I wish I could get more sales. Perhaps it's time for me to find a different type of job."

Greg kissed my hair. "We'll worry about that later. I'm due for a promotion this summer, remember? Things will get better soon."

I smiled and tried to remain optimistic. The trouble was that every time we moved one step forward, something unexpected would happen, and we'd fall two back. The cost of living continued to skyrocket while our salaries stayed dormant.

I put my arms around his neck. "I know Tiffany's dishonest, but still, I wouldn't mind coming by a few of the deals she's gotten."

"They'll come. You don't want to stoop to her level. The market will turn around soon, and then there will be plenty. You'll see."

"I hope you're right."

Greg kissed me lightly on the lips. "Of course I am. Don't worry about Tiffany. One day soon, she'll get what's coming to her."

"Wouldn't that be great?" I gazed at the clock, which read 6:45. "Shoot, I'm going to be late."

"Let her sweat it out for a few minutes. Don't let her think you're too eager to make a deal."

I ran into the bathroom to wash my hands and check my hair. There were fine lines under my eyes from lack of sleep. I grabbed some concealer out of the medicine cabinet and applied it quickly. Tiffany was always so picture perfect, similar to the houses she sold. My face resembled my listings too— sorely in need of improvement. I ran back into the den to grab my briefcase and jacket.

Greg walked me to the front door. "Are you sure you don't want me to go with you?"

"No, I'll be okay. You're right. I'm not going to let Tiffany get the best of me this time." My watch read 6:30. "That can't be right. The battery must be dead. What time is it?"

Greg smiled over my head in the direction of the wall clock. "Uh-oh, it says 6:55. Do you need to call the cheat, and tell her you're running late? Or better yet, call her and cancel. She probably hasn't even left her house yet." He pulled me back into his arms.

I gently wriggled from his grasp. "No, she's already been there for a few hours. Tiffany always stays late on Tuesdays. First, she answers calls from three to five and then paws through the MLS, trying to figure out who she'll steal from next. Plus, Tiffany's made it perfectly clear to everyone that she considers Tuesday *her* office night, and we all need to stay away."

"I bet she's not really working. Hey, maybe she's having an affair with a married man—on the conference room table?" He grinned. "Nah, that can't be it. No guy is that desperate, is he?"

I hugged him. "I love you."

"If you loved me, you wouldn't leave me alone with these kids." Greg tried to grab me, and at that moment, a crash sounded from downstairs. "Uh-oh. The demons are at it again. Drive safely, baby." He raced down the stairs.

As I was shutting the door, I heard him holler, "Who the heck put the dog on the table?"

I jumped into my car and turned the heat on full blast. The temperature was hovering around 40 degrees, chilly for the middle of spring. Weather was often unpredictable in New York State. The following week might be a scorching 90 degrees. One never knew quite what to expect. This was true of my career lately, too.

During the drive to the office, I played over and over in my head what I would say. "This is my listing, Tiffany. You need to give it back, or I'll make things difficult for you. I'm sure you don't want to lose your license." Gee, I liked the way that sounded. Maybe other people would grovel at Tiffany's Manolo Blahniks, but not me. I was done being treated like a doormat.

I pulled into the lot, and sure enough, Tiffany's car was there. I parked my battered ten-year-old Honda Civic next to her shiny, new silver Jaguar. The real estate world had been very good to Tiffany. Too bad she didn't care about her clients. I loved being a real estate agent. To me, nothing was more satisfying than helping a person locate their dream home, usually their most expensive purchase in a lifetime. I enjoyed the process from start to finish. It was unfortunate that agents like Tiffany ruined the business for the rest of us.

I walked to the entrance and searched for the office key on my keychain. Since the sun had started to set and the porch light dim, it took me a few seconds to locate the key. Then I noticed, to my surprise, that the front door was slightly ajar. Donna would have a fit if she knew. She was always afraid someone might walk in and steal something. It wasn't like we kept any cash here, but regardless, Donna had gone into a tirade a few weeks ago and threatened to fire an agent who'd forgotten to lock the door upon departure.

"Hello?" I pushed the door open and surveyed the area. There was no sign of anyone, and an eerie silence enveloped the darkened room.

"Tiffany?" Still no response. I groped the wall for the light switch and breathed a sigh of relief when it came on. I walked slowly past the receptionist's desk and copy machine, toward the small stairway which led to the second floor. Most of the agents had offices up there. Jacques and I both had offices on the first floor, mine located next to Donna's. Tiffany, who came to the agency after me, had recently started hinting about how much she liked mine. I guessed that would be the next thing I'd end up losing.

Had someone broken in? And what if they were still here? Fearful, I searched for a weapon or something I could arm myself with. I walked over to the reception desk and located a sharp-pointed letter opener sitting in a cup filled with pens and pencils. Better than nothing. I ascended the stairs slowly, counting each step as I went. *One, two, three, four.* My heart knocked against the wall of my chest.

The faint sound of music was coming from Tiffany's office, and her light was on. Perhaps she'd fallen asleep with her iPod on. Or maybe she'd gone out with a client and left her car here.

There might be a note on her desk for me. I rounded the corner to her office and peeked inside.

That's when I saw her. My hands flew to my mouth in horror.

Tiffany lay motionless on the floor in front of her black leather, swivel chair. Her once beige Ann Taylor suit was now a maroon color. Blood had pooled around her and soaked into the powder-blue shag rug she lay on. Her beautiful emerald eyes, which I'd always envied, were wide open and vacant.

My vision blurred, and suddenly I wasn't staring at Tiffany anymore. My friend Paul's body lay motionless before me, curled up in a fetal position on his bed. Even after all these years, the memory of finding him with a gun in his hand was still vivid in my mind. I tried to block out the image as I had many times in the past, pretending it had never happened. Everything came flooding back now, and there was no escape for me.

The letter opener fell from my hand to the floor. I reached numbly into my purse for my cell phone. As I moved closer to Tiffany's lifeless body, the blood roared in my ears, and I covered them in an attempt to block out the noise. Piercing screams filled the room. Then I realized that they were coming from me.

At that moment, I fainted.

CHAPTER FOUR

"*S*weetheart?"
My lids were heavy, but I managed to force my
eyes open.

"Are you all right?" Greg was bending over me, holding an
ice pack to the side of my head. His face was pale, and I could
tell he'd been busy running his fingers worriedly through his
curly, light-brown hair. It was more unkempt than usual.

"I—I think so. What happened?" I glanced around in confusion and then realized I was lying on the loveseat in my office. A
cluster of flashing lights reflected on my window from the
parking lot outside. Suddenly, I remembered and struggled to
sit up. "Tiffany. Where is she?"

Greg eased me back down. "They're upstairs photographing
the crime scene." A murmur of distant voices was barely audible
through the ceiling.

"Then she's—" I couldn't bring myself to say the word.

Greg's expression was grim. "She's gone." He stroked my
cheek gently. "She was shot several times."

"Mrs. York?" For the first time, I noticed the stocky

policeman standing next to my husband. "I'm Officer Simon. Can you tell me what happened?"

I shook my head and winced from the pain. "Not really. I was supposed to meet Tiffany at seven o'clock. I was a little late arriving." I reached my hand up to my temple and rubbed my throbbing head, wincing when I touched the bump. "When I got here, the front door was open, and the lights were out. Then I came upstairs and found her—" The words stuck in my throat.

"When was the last time you saw her alive?" Officer Simon asked.

I shivered. "I think I fainted. My head hurts, and I'm so cold."

Greg reached for an afghan on the back of the couch and covered me. "You must have hit your head on her desk when you passed out. There's a huge egg above your ear. I want you to get checked out at the hospital."

I studied the concern on his face. "Who called you?"

Before Greg could answer, a pitiful wailing sound came from the adjoining office. I bolted upright and clutched his hand. "What's that?"

Greg put his arm around me. "It's Donna. She's the one who found you and Tiffany. She was so hysterical on the phone, I didn't even know what had happened. I thought you'd been killed." His eyes were dark as he held me close to him.

I couldn't bring myself to speak. Instead, I clutched his hand tightly, trying to imagine what had been going through his mind as he sped over here.

At that moment, Donna entered the room sobbing uncontrollably. She was supported by a policeman who introduced himself to us as Officer Lennon.

"Miss Cushman, we're done with you for now. We may want to question you again tomorrow though." Officer Simon made some notes on a pad.

Donna nodded and wiped her eyes. Her weeping continued as she clutched Officer Lennon's arm tighter.

"Is there someone who can take you home? You shouldn't be driving in your condition," Officer Lennon said.

"My husband's out of town until tomorrow, but I'll be all right. I only live a few blocks away." Donna blew her nose. Despite her apparent misery, she managed to give Officer Lennon a flirty smile.

Greg whispered in my ear. "She's *married?*"

I caught the note of surprise in his voice. "I'll fill you in later." I thought suddenly of the recent comment Jacques had said about our man hungry boss. "If she keeps throwing herself at every warm-blooded male, she's never going to land one. Hell, even I got one before her!"

Donna's gaze came to rest on Greg. "You got here so quickly, even before the police. I'm very grateful to you."

Good grief. Donna had set her sights on my husband the day she met him. The first time Greg came into the office, Donna had boldly invited him to her house for a home-cooked meal right in front of me. She was acutely embarrassed when I'd introduced him as my husband. Sometimes I think that's why she can't stand me.

Greg was silent for a few moments while he glared at Donna. "You weren't exactly coherent on the phone. I thought my wife had been killed. The drive here was the worst ten minutes of my life."

Donna turned her steely blue eyes on me. "I hope you're happy."

My mouth opened in astonishment. "Look, Donna, I'm sorry about Tiffany—"

"You're not sorry. Why would you be sorry when you're the one who killed her?" She grabbed Officer Lennon's arm with one hand and pointed at me with the other. "Arrest her. Now!"

There was total silence in the room as Greg removed his arm from my shoulders and rose to his feet. He glowered at

Donna as he approached. "Cindy never laid a finger on her. Tiffany was dead before she even arrived."

Donna sneered. "Of course you'd say that. You'll do anything to protect your precious wife."

Greg's face turned crimson, and his voice became a low, angry growl. "You know nothing about my wife, except how to cheat her out of the listings she works her butt off for. Besides, Cindy hates guns. She's afraid to even go near one. Do you know why?"

"Greg," I protested.

"No, your so-called boss needs to hear this."

"Mr. York, where is this going?" Officer Simon wanted to know.

Greg ignored him as he kept his eyes fixed on Donna, who started to squirm under his gaze. "When Cindy was in high school, a friend of hers committed suicide. He shot himself with a gun. Cindy's the one who found him."

I closed my eyes and shuddered as the image of Paul's body entered my mind again. God, how I hated reliving that moment. There had been no warnings or signs that Paul would take his own life. If we'd only known what had been running through his head that day.

Greg sensed my agitation and sat back down, gathering me in his arms. "I'm sorry, baby. I know how much that upsets you."

"It's all right." A tear rolled down my cheek.

Donna laughed in disbelief. "Yeah, right. Nice try, Mr. and Mrs. York. What a touching story. I'm not buying it though."

Officer Simon spoke in an irritated tone. "Miss Cushman, you're upset. You don't know what you're saying."

"Don't you get it, officer? All she cares about is her precious listing. She called me earlier today and complained Tiffany had stolen one from her. And she said she'd stop at nothing to get it back." Donna shot me a venomous look, then started weeping again.

Officer Simon made a face. "Ma'am, I *insist* you go home. You need to rest."

Yeah, and take a Valium too.

Donna covered her face with her hands as she sobbed. "I can't believe it. My dear friend is gone."

"More like your cash cow." Greg muttered under his breath as Officer Simon shot him an inquisitive look.

Officer Lennon led Donna from the room. She turned around to glance at me hatefully. "If you did this, I'll make sure you pay. And that's a promise you can take to the bank."

I was too stunned for words. Donna carried a lot of clout in this town. She was definitely going to make trouble for me. Perhaps it was time I started looking for gainful employment elsewhere.

Officer Simon interrupted my thoughts. "Mrs. York, when was the last time you saw Miss Roberts alive?"

"I think it was today. No, wait, it was yesterday. She was at the office when I came to pick up an *Open House* sign." My head throbbed with pain.

"Do you know anyone that might have wanted to hurt Miss Roberts?" Officer Simon asked.

I answered as truthfully as I could. "Well, frankly, yes. There are a lot of people who didn't like her, including myself. She was mean, talked behind other people's backs, and was a dishonest real estate agent."

I glanced at Greg. His eyes were blazing. *Uh-oh. Maybe I should have kept my mouth shut?*

Officer Simon grunted. "Is that why you left her a threatening message earlier today?"

My voice faltered. "I—I did what?"

He cleared his throat. "We found Miss Roberts' cell phone on her desk. We just finished listening to her messages. There was one from you, asking her to please call you back right away, unless she wanted to die young."

"Oh, no." Greg rolled his eyes at me.

Officer Simon glared at him and then turned back to me. "Mrs. York, would you care to explain yourself?"

The lump in my throat was growing larger by the minute. I didn't want to speak because I ultimately knew what was going to happen. "She stole my listing. I told her to give it back. I'd never do anything to hurt her though. Honest." My eyes filled with unshed tears.

"Baby, you should rest." Greg shot me an irritated look and then addressed the policeman. "Officer, I'd like to get her to the hospital. Can we finish this tomorrow?"

What did I do now? "What'll happen to my babies if they put me in jail?"

"An ambulance is on the way." Officer Simon's cell phone rang, and he turned away from us to answer it.

Greg took the opportunity to whisper in my ear. "You need to stop talking before you make things worse for yourself. Now lie still. I think I hear the ambulance coming."

"I don't want to go to jail."

"Baby, you're not going to jail. You're going to the hospital to have your head examined."

So the day everyone feared had finally happened for me. "With the men in white coats?" I managed to squeak out.

Greg looked at me like I had corn growing out of my ears. "What in God's name are you talking about?"

I started giggling hysterically and couldn't bring myself to stop, even when tears gushed from my eyes and over my cheeks. The sound reminded me of a hyena. "I'm glad you're not angry with me, honey."

Officer Simon finished his call and looked over at me with a strange expression. "Is she having some type of seizure?"

Greg managed a painful smile. "I think she's in shock and a little confused. But she'll be okay. Right, hon?"

I heard Greg's voice clearly and did my best to nod before I slipped into unconsciousness again.

When I awoke, I found myself in a dimly lit hospital room. Greg sat in a chair next to me, watching the news, his large hand massaging mine.

"Hey," I croaked. My throat burned.

Greg gave a slow nod, then turned the volume down. He leaned over and kissed me softly, his eyes full of concern. "Well, at least there's nothing on here about the murder yet. How do you feel, princess?"

"Did I faint again?"

"You came to in the ambulance for a few minutes, but went out like a light again." Greg smiled. "I told them you're a chronic fainter when you get stressed."

I winced. "Like when I found out we were having twins."

"Exactly. And on our wedding day, remember?"

"God, don't remind me. It was *so* embarrassing." I licked my parched lips. "I need a drink."

Greg reached over to the tray at my bedside and poured water out of a plastic, blue pitcher. He held the cup to my lips. "Slowly, sweetheart."

I drank gratefully and laid my head back against the pillows. "Who's watching the kids?"

"My mom's there."

I tried to stifle a groan. Greg's mother couldn't stand me. If she knew what happened, she'd be licking her chops in anticipation of taking over my home when I went to prison. She was also my kids' only surviving grandparent and thought the sun rose and set on them.

I wanted to protect my children from this incident but wasn't sure that would be possible. "Did you tell her what happened?"

"I had to, baby. I was a little too shocked to make up a lame excuse on the spur of the moment."

I would have smacked my head against something hard, but I'd already done that once tonight. "Couldn't you find someone else to stay with them? Some random stranger on the street?"

Greg wrapped me in a bear hug as I started to cry. "Come on. You're overreacting—as usual."

"What's going to happen to me?"

"Nothing's going to happen." He kissed my forehead. "The doctor wants to keep you overnight for observation. You hit your head pretty hard. In the morning, the police will probably be back to ask you a few more questions."

I blinked away tears. "I'm not being arrested?"

"They can't prove you did anything. It's all circumstantial at this point."

"Oh, thank God." I let out a huge sigh. "But who could have killed her?"

Greg shrugged. "Who didn't want to kill her? That seems to be the real mystery. You're not the only one who got burned by her." He examined my face. "You're whiter than the sheet in your hands."

"They heard my phone call. I threatened her, and that makes me a suspect."

"Look at me."

I blinked the tears away from my eyes as Greg laced his fingers through mine. His gaze was solemn, but direct. "You trust me, right?"

I nodded.

"Don't worry. I won't let anything happen to you. Ever."

CHAPTER FIVE

I awakened the next morning to find my husband sitting on the edge of my hospital bed. His bright-blue eyes were bleary, and the unruly hair I loved was a complete disaster. His handsome face desperately needed a shave. Yet he was still utterly adorable. I managed a smile. "Hello, sexy."

"Good morning, sunshine." He grinned as he handed me a cup of coffee. "How do you feel today?"

"Like I have a hangover. How do *you* feel? If I look like you, I'm really in trouble."

Greg chuckled. "You're beautiful as always. I would've slept better if they hadn't been in here every lousy hour to take your blood pressure. Whenever I started to drift off, someone else trotted in."

"I don't remember. I must have been out like a light."

He stroked my hair tenderly. "You thrashed around a lot last night. Bad dreams about Tiffany?"

I nodded. "And your mother."

"What about her?"

"I dreamed we went home, and she was gone. She took the

kids and left the country. Someone spotted them in South America."

Greg burst out laughing. "I talked to her a little while ago. Everything's fine. The kids left for school right on time. Mom was going to tidy up a little bit and be on her way."

I smiled wanly at my husband, who clearly had no idea what "tidy up" meant to his mama. If she had her way, she'd take my house apart and put it back together again. My clothes would all be packed and waiting for me on the front porch when I got home.

I ran my fingers over the unshaven stubble on his chin. "Can we go home now?"

"Yeah, the nurse brought your discharge papers. You'll need to sign them when she comes back. But first, you need to eat breakfast." He lifted the plastic lid off the tray next to my bed to reveal a generous portion of French toast and bacon. I shook my head vigorously.

"Baby, you've got to keep your strength up."

"You eat it. I'll have the yogurt."

Greg handed me the container and a spoon while he dug into the bacon. "Hmm. This isn't half bad. Not nearly as good as yours, though."

"Flatterer."

He stood, stretched, and yawned. "You had company this morning."

"Why didn't you wake me?"

"Believe me, it was better I didn't," Greg said. "It was your buddy, Simon. You know, Police Officer of the Year."

"Oh no. What did he want?"

"He had a couple more questions. I was praying you wouldn't wake up." He grinned. "You were mumbling and moving around in your sleep like crazy. I think it scared him."

"What'd he want to know—if I threw the gun in the river?"

Greg offered me a glass of orange juice, and I shook my
head. He looked like he needed the vitamin C more than I did.

He gulped it down in one long drink, then smacked his lips.
"He asked how long you'd known Tiffany and if you knew
anything about her personal life."

"And you said..."

"I said you'd been with the agency for nearly three years, and
Tiffany had joined about two years ago. I told him you weren't
friends outside the office, and you knew nothing about her
personal life. They were going over to her house to see if they
could find anything relevant. He asked me if I knew the address
offhand." Greg snorted. "Some policeman."

I shook my head. "I've no idea where she lived. Probably a
palace filled with a zillion designer shoes though."

"She didn't have kids, right?"

"I don't think so. She was in her early twenties, and I never saw
any pictures or heard her make references to children. She probably didn't even own a goldfish. Jacques said she partied a lot."

Greg sounded surprised. "He was friendly with her?"

I shrugged. "Jacques is friendly with everyone."

"Oh, right." At this, Greg took his phone out and started
checking for messages.

Any mention of Jacques tended to make Greg uncomfortable. Jacques is my dearest friend in the world. We've worked
together for the past three years, and he's been very helpful in
guiding my career. He's second only to Tiffany in sales, but at
least he comes by them honestly.

It isn't that Greg begrudges me having a male friend. The
problem is he's not receptive to Jacques' lifestyle. Last year,
Jacques married his longtime love, Ed Kapinski. I attended the
wedding alone since Greg came down with a mysterious case of
the flu at the last minute.

Greg had a very tight upbringing with a judgmental mother

who doesn't exactly see eye to eye with me. Most days I'm convinced he was adopted as a baby. While I suspect Jacques knows of Greg's feelings, it's never been a topic of conversation between us.

"By the way, he called earlier."

"Jacques? What'd he say?" I pressed him.

Greg kept staring at his phone. "He wanted to make sure you were okay and was going to stop by. I told him we were leaving for home soon. He said he'd come by the house later, if that was all right. I told him it was fine. He can stay with you while I make a quick stop to see a client." He put his phone away and stood.

"Greg—"

He silenced me with a kiss on the lips and handed me my clothes. "No more talking. Let's get you out of here, babe."

We arrived home minutes before noon. A feeling of dread hit me like a brick wall when I noticed my mother-in-law's car still in our driveway.

"Oh, I figured Mom would have left already." It sounded more like an apology from my husband than an actual statement.

I shut my eyes tightly. *Ugh. I can't deal with her right now.*

Greg sensed my agitation. "I'm sure she won't stay long, Cin." He gently helped me out of the car and put his arm around my shoulders.

I know there's no such thing as a perfect man. If it weren't for Greg's mother, he would have come close though.

Helen York's a sophisticated, attractive woman in her late sixties or early seventies. We aren't sure of her exact age since she constantly avoids the question. Even Greg admitted he isn't positive. Once, when the twins questioned her, she said she was fifty-five. I'm pretty sure that's impossible since Greg's forty-five.

Helen had retired from the state a few years ago. She'd

worked as a secretary for the Attorney General's office for over thirty years. She gets by nicely on a decent pension, and a life insurance policy her late husband left her, but is quite possibly the cheapest woman alive.

On the rare occasions that we go out to eat with her, Helen will throw sugar packets into her purse when she thinks no one's looking. She'll ask for extra crackers and toss those in too. She told the kids she gives them to the birds in her backyard. I swear I thought I saw her pocket a spoon once. She has money but doesn't like to spend it.

Greg's a bit brainwashed when it comes to his mother.

"She only wants to help, Cin. She was really worried about you when I talked to her this morning."

Sure she was. Worried I might live.

I leaned on Greg's arm as we walked toward the house. "She's worried about you and the kids. She's never liked me. You know she didn't want you to marry me. She threatened to not come to the wedding."

He squeezed my hand. "She didn't mean it. And she was there, remember?"

"Oh, how I remember. All decked out in her best black dress."

"She just wanted to wear the same color as Dad and me."

I stared at my husband in disbelief as he unlocked the front door. Was he kidding? For such a smart man, that was a pretty dumb thing for Greg to say.

We stepped into the entranceway. I kicked my shoes off and padded through the living room in my thick, woolen socks. No sign of Helen chatting away on the phone, clucking her tongue at the disgrace I'd brought to her family. She wasn't watching the midday news on the television either, trying to discover if the world knew what a dreadful person her boy had married. The only audible sound came from the wall clock. Tick, tock, tick, tock.

"Mom?" Greg called out.

There was no answer.

I grimaced. "She's probably upstairs snooping through my things. She wants to make sure I'm not cheating on you. Then again, she'd probably like that because you'd have grounds to divorce me."

Greg chuckled. "Will you stop?" He walked into the kitchen with me following closely at his heels. "Mom?"

There was Helen on her knees, her head buried deep in my oven.

"Mom!" Greg ran to her side. "What are you doing?"

I rolled my eyes toward the ceiling. I knew exactly what she was doing.

Helen removed herself from the gas oven. She calmly put down the sponge she was holding and stood, stripping her arms of yellow, plastic gloves. She smiled with adoration at her only son. "Calm down, Gregory. What do you think I was doing?"

Greg had the decency to look embarrassed. "Um, I thought—"

She laughed. "Relax, darling. I would never do something like that. I have too much to live for. That nasty oven of yours needed a good scrubbing. It's a shame there's no one to keep things nice around here for you."

I cleared my throat loudly.

Helen barely glanced in my direction. "Oh, hello, Cindy."

I bit my lower lip hard in an effort to keep a nasty retort from falling out of my mouth. "Helen, I really appreciate your help, but I cleaned that oven last week."

My mother-in-law continued on as if she hadn't heard me and directed her next comment to Greg. "You should hire a housekeeper. I shudder at the thought of my grandchildren eating concoctions from that filthy oven."

Greg looked tired. "Mom, Cindy's right. The oven's not dirty. She does an awesome job taking care of the house and the kids."

My knight in shining armor to the rescue.

My mother-in-law sniffed. "Well, it's not like she has much else to do all day."

Count to ten. Nope, it didn't quite work. "What does that mean?"

Greg put a comforting arm around my shoulders. "I'm going to put Cindy to bed. I'll be back down in a little while. Would you like to join me for a cup of coffee before you go home?"

Helen shook her head. "No, thank you, darling. I'll have one when I get home. Would you like to come join me? *My* coffee pot is clean."

I sucked in some air.

Greg chose to ignore her last remark. "I don't want to leave Cindy alone."

Helen's smile faded. "Of course."

"So the twins and Darcy got off to school okay? They didn't give you any trouble?" Greg asked.

"Oh, no. They were perfect angels. I made them the most wonderful lunches with all their favorite foods. And don't worry, I made sure they were nutritious. I brought some food over from my house since I wasn't sure I'd find anything edible here."

I clenched my fists at my sides. *Ignore her, just ignore her.*

"That's great, Mom. Did they eat breakfast for you?"

Helen untied the spotless, white apron from around her waist. "Of course they ate breakfast. I made the twins pancakes and sausages, while Darcy and I had lovely fruit plates. They were all so grateful not to have cold cereal for once."

That was the last straw. "Helen, my children do *not* have cold cereal every morning. If they do, it's by their choice."

"Why certainly, dear." Helen feigned a cough. "Of course, Stevie told me he didn't have any breakfast yesterday—the poor baby. And he's so thin."

I pursed my lips. "Did Stevie happen to tell you the reason he didn't have breakfast? He decided to play with the puppy, against my orders, until the bus was outside honking for him. I really don't think—"

Greg ran a hand through his hair. "Hey, Mom, it was really nice of you to come over on such short notice."

"Oh, anytime. I love babysitting my grandchildren." Helen reached inside her purse and handed Greg an envelope. "For you, sweetheart."

"What's this?"

"I'm so sorry I missed your birthday last week. I didn't want you to think I'd forgotten about it."

Greg ripped open the envelope. "I wasn't worried about it. And you did call me, remember?"

"Yes, darling, but if I hadn't been out of town, I could have made you a birthday cake. I know how much you love chocolate cake." She gave his cheek an affectionate pat while I looked away, embarrassed for my husband.

"Cindy made me a chocolate cake. It was delicious."

Helen narrowed her eyes at me. "Yes, I'll bet it was."

Greg opened the ninety-nine cent American Greetings card, smiled at the caption, and removed twenty-five dollars from the inside pocket. He gave Helen a quick peck on the cheek. "I don't need anything, Mom. You should keep this for yourself."

Helen waved him away. "Nothing's too good for my baby."

Twenty-five dollars was indeed a generous gift from Mrs. Cheap-o. Don't get me wrong. Helen's very good to the kids when it comes to birthdays and Christmas, and that's what really counts. I'm the outcast. Last year she gave me a bottle of perfume for Christmas. It wouldn't have been so bad, except for the fact it was re-gifted. The reason I knew it was re-gifted is because I gave her the *same* bottle for her birthday about ten years ago. I will say she does do a lovely job with gift wrapping though.

Greg handed the cash back to his mother. "I don't like taking your money."

"Don't be silly. You're the one who needs it." Helen refused to look at me as she hunted for her car keys in her mammoth-sized purse. I briefly wondered if my grandmother's silverware might be in there. "When Cindy gets a real job, you won't need to work so hard."

Ouch. I winced.

Greg caught my reaction and winked reassuringly at me. "Thanks again, Mom. We really appreciate it."

"Remember, I'm only a phone call away. You know how much I love spending time with those little darlings. Oh, wait, I almost forgot." Helen walked into the living room, and we followed, mystified, as she picked up a sheet of paper by the phone.

"What is it?" I asked.

She handed the paper to me and managed to avoid making eye contact. "A reporter from the local paper called. They'd like to ask you a few questions about your coworker. Before you get hauled off to jail, that is."

Greg's face turned red. "Mom! You know Cindy had nothing to do with the murder."

"Oh, of course not."

I'd finally had enough. I struggled to keep my voice polite but firm. "Thank you for taking care of our children. Next time I'll be calling a babysitter."

Helen whirled around to give me the evil eye. "Well, that's gratitude! What's going to happen when they put you in prison? Will you call a babysitter then?"

Greg stepped between us. "Mom, stop it. Cindy isn't going to prison."

She tossed her head. "That's not what I heard. Your neighbor Susan was over this morning. The whole town is talking about what you did to that poor woman."

"Cindy didn't do anything. She only found the woman. Tiffany was already dead," Greg explained.

Helen's nostrils flared. "So she says! I knew you shouldn't have married her! I tried to warn you—"

I gently pushed Greg aside so that I could put my face next to Helen's. "If I did happen to go to prison, I wouldn't want you taking care of my children. I can imagine the stories you'd tell them about me."

She spread her hands wide. "Maybe they're not stories. I hope they lock you up and throw away the key! My son could have done so much better—"

Greg's mouth tightened into a fine line. "Mom, you are way out of line. Please leave. *Now*."

Helen and I stared at him in amazement. Greg had never ordered his mother out of our house before. I immediately stepped away from both of them. Helen's lower lip started to tremble, and her eyes filled with unshed tears. She darted between us to the front door and threw it open, sobbing as she ran to her car.

Greg went outside and called after her in vain. The tires squealed on the pavement, and her vehicle roared off. I hadn't thought the woman could move so fast.

Greg sighed and shut the door noiselessly.

I sank down on the couch, not quite sure what to expect. Had I forced my husband into this? I'd finally snapped after putting up with Helen's snide remarks for seventeen years. I still couldn't forget how she'd gone around to the guests at our wedding—telling everyone I must be knocked up because why else would Greg marry me?

Greg sat down at my side. He stared at the floor, not saying anything.

I couldn't bear the silence any longer. "Greg, I'm sorry. I should have just gone upstairs to bed." I always tried to avoid confrontations with my mother-in-law, but today I had failed miserably.

He didn't answer.

"Will you please say something?"

Greg forced a smile. "She had it coming. I'm the one who's sorry. Mom was wrong to say those things to you, and I should have set her straight years ago. She's been so lonesome since Dad died. Sometimes she doesn't think before she speaks. I'll call her later to make sure she's okay."

My heart ached as I examined my husband's somber face. I didn't even bother to mention the fact that his mother had been saying those things long before Greg's father had passed away. Suddenly it seemed unimportant. "Maybe I should call her and apologize, too."

He placed a hand on my knee. "No, you were right. She can't go around talking to you like that. You're my wife and the mother of her grandchildren. She has to respect you when she comes into our house. I'm going to tell her that too." He shook his head with regret.

"Are you sure? I don't mind—"

Greg silenced me with a kiss and gently lifted me to my feet. "Come on, sweetheart. You need to get some rest."

CHAPTER SIX

*B*eing a lady of leisure for an afternoon turned out to be exactly what I needed. As I lay in bed, sipping my herbal tea and watching *The Young and the Restless*, I wondered how long it had been since I'd had a day to relax like this. It must have been over a year since I'd last seen the show, while being laid up with the flu, yet I could still follow the storyline. Ah, the beauty of soap operas. One day might drag on for months in their fiction-filled land. It was the total opposite of my life, which seemed to be changing at a dramatic rate.

The pounding in my head had finally subsided. I stretched and yawned, relieved not to have to think about anything important for a while. Sweetie, our cat, lay next to me, purring away contentedly. As I reached down to pet her silky, white coat, I thought about how loyal animals were in comparison to people. They asked for nothing but love.

There was a knock on my door. Greg stuck his head in, and Sweetie leaped off our bed and ran into the hallway. So much for that theory.

"You have company." Greg ushered Jacques in, nodded to

him, and blew me a kiss. "I'll be back in less than an hour, before the twins get home." He quickly shut the door.

"That husband of yours isn't very personable." Jacques, an attractive man in his early forties with a muscular build, shook his head. He walked over to my nightstand and placed a dozen red roses in a pink, plastic vase on the top. "I brought these for you, my dear. I thought for sure Gregory would have filled your room with flowers after all you've been through."

"Oh, they're beautiful. How sweet." I threw my arms around his neck and hugged him.

He returned my embrace and tucked the blanket back around me. "You could have done better, Cin."

Jacques wasn't often wrong, but this was one of those times. He's that rare type of friend who'll do anything for you and won't sugarcoat a situation. He always tells me the truth, no matter how hard it is to hear. Once I asked him if I looked fat in a certain pair of designer jeans. Jacques assured me no, the jeans didn't make me look fat, but I did look as if I'd put on five pounds recently. I went home and weighed myself. As usual, he was right.

"No, I could never do any better. Greg is amazing." It was the truth. "You don't know him well enough." I cleared my throat. "It was nice of you to come by."

"Yes, it was." Jacques grinned. His large, green eyes were warm under the designer Prada bifocals he wore. He's blind as a bat without them and can't wear contacts because of an allergic reaction. I always tell him he looks sexier with glasses, and he never tires of hearing it. "How's the head?"

"Still attached."

"Thankfully." He kissed my forehead. "Ed sends his love. He's sorry he couldn't get away, but the restaurant's been swamped lately. The flowers are from both of us."

I sniffed at them in rapture. "Please thank him for me. I haven't seen him in ages."

Jacques pulled a chair up to my bedside. "Yeah, join the club. We're both workaholics these days. I can't remember when I saw him last either." He peered closely at me. "Are you okay, love? I've been worried about you. I can't believe you found her —like that."

I shuddered, remembering. "It was awful."

He reached for my hand. "It must have brought back some terrible memories for you."

Jacques knew about Paul. I stared at the grave look on his face, and my lower lip started to tremble.

He spread his arms open wide. "It's okay, honey. You don't have to be so brave all the time. Go ahead. Let it out."

As if waiting for the permission, I instantly dissolved into tears before him. Jacques wrapped me in his strong arms and patted my back while I sobbed.

"I'm sorry." I wept into his shoulder. "You'd think after twenty some years I'd be over it."

He squeezed my hand. "You're never going to get over it. That's just a fact of life." He handed me his handkerchief, and I leaned back against the pillows, suddenly exhausted.

"What would I do without you?"

"I *am* pretty awesome," Jacques admitted. "Hey, I was wondering—"

"What?"

He hesitated. "I hate to upset you any further, but I was curious if there were any signs that Tiffany might have struggled with her killer?"

"I don't know. She was covered in blood, and she'd been shot —several times. How would I know if she'd struggled? Please, I don't want to think about it anymore."

"Yeah, gross." Jacques sounded so much like one of the twins, I fought a sudden impulse to laugh. "Did it look like a forced entry?"

I observed him suspiciously. "What's with all the questions? Are you a wannabe policeman now?"

"Well, really! I'm only trying to help you, dear." A tone of injury filled his voice.

I sighed heavily. "I know you are, and I appreciate it. Sorry. This has been a rough day, and it's barely half over yet. For starters, I've already had a fight with my mother-in-law."

Jacques sucked in a sharp breath. "You? What happened? Did you break her broomstick?"

I grinned but continued on. "Also, the police came to my room this morning to finish questioning me. Greg talked to them, but I have a feeling they'll be back. And they have the message I left on Tiffany's phone, more or less threatening to kill her. To top it all off, a reporter had the nerve to call for an interview this morning. I don't know how much more of this I can take."

He raised his eyebrows. "Whoa, back up a second. You threatened Tiffany?"

I nodded, then stopped. "I guess. Well, not really. No. I didn't mean it the way it sounded."

Jacques scratched his thick, blond hair thoughtfully. "Exactly *how* did it sound?"

"Remember the listing appointment I had yesterday?"

"Oh sure. The little old lady who lived on—wait, was it Sparrow Drive?" Jacques asked.

I reached for my cup of tea on the nightstand. "Close. Partridge Lane. Mrs. Agnes Hunter."

"That's right. Damn birds. Yeah, I was there when you told Donna."

I took a long sip of my drink. "Which was a huge mistake. She must have told Tiffany because when I got over to the house yesterday, Mrs. Hunter had already signed with her."

Jacques wrinkled his nose. "I know you shouldn't speak ill of the dead, but that chick had no morals at all. A complete disgrace to the business."

"Anyhow, I was angry and left a message for her saying she'd better call me back unless she wanted to die—die young." I watched Jacques intently for his reaction.

"I see. Great timing on your part." His voice dripped with sarcasm. "Well, it all makes sense now."

I stared at him, confused. "What makes sense?"

Jacques hesitated. "Maybe I shouldn't tell you."

I grabbed his arm. "Oh, for crying out loud. Now you *have* to tell me."

His face was pained. "A police officer came to the agency this morning. He questioned everybody there, but Donna spent the most time with him. Alone in her office."

I sucked in a breath. "Oh no. She told him I killed Tiffany, didn't she?"

"Cin, it really doesn't matter what Donna says. She didn't see you pull the actual trigger. She made a very good point though."

"What'd she say? And how do you know all of this?"

Jacques laughed. "You forget, darling, that I am the world's greatest eavesdropper. What the eyes miss, the ears make up for. I could hear a pin drop a mile away."

I forced myself to relax and sit back. "Okay, go on."

"Well, you told the cop that the front door was open when you got there. Donna said Tiffany would never have left the door unlocked if she was there alone."

"She knew I was coming. Or maybe she had a client stop by. They might have left the door unlocked when they left."

"Well, where's the client then? There was nothing on the sign-in sheet to indicate anyone came by. Plus, you have a key. So why leave the door open for you?"

I rubbed my forehead wearily. "My brain's starting to hurt. What's the point here?"

Jacques crossed one leg over the other. "Donna seems to

believe—and now the police as well—that whoever shot Tiffany had a key to the office."

My blood ran cold. This was not good news for me to hear. "There's another reason for them to suspect me." My voice shook slightly. "I left a threatening message on her phone, plus I was the one to find her. Donna already hates my guts and basically accused me of the murder in front of the cops last night. Of course—"

"No way! She did what?" Jacques breathed.

My shoulders sagged. "Last night she told me I'd pay for this. I said I was sorry Tiffany was dead, and she said why, since I was the one who killed her."

"Dang, this is so not looking good for you." Jacques stared at me, his face full of sympathy.

"Great. Exactly what I needed to hear."

"Hey, don't worry. Since they're questioning everyone in the office, it'll be days before they even try to arrest you."

I punched my pillow in frustration while he waved his hands in front of him. "Perhaps that came out wrong," he said.

"Did you talk to the police as well?"

"They asked me a few questions about Tiffany. I told them what I knew."

I leaned forward in anticipation. "Which was?"

"She was selfish and dishonest. I told them I didn't believe she had any living relatives except for a half-sister somewhere but no idea how they'd go about finding her."

"Interesting. Why is it you always know everything about everyone?" I asked.

"People enjoy talking to me. I have a very honest-looking face."

I tried to hold back a laugh. "Oh, please."

"Well, the police must have thought so." Jacques stared down at the floor. "I didn't want to, but I had to tell them about Pete." There was a note of regret in his voice.

"Pete Saxon, the newbie? What's he got to do with it?"

Jacques nodded and hesitated before answering. "I overheard him threaten Tiffany yesterday."

My jaw dropped. "Get out. What happened?"

He sighed. "Well, the poor guy's a little green. Don't forget, he's only been with the agency a couple of months. Since he's totally new to the business, Tiffany offered to help him out. They were working as co-brokers on a house he'd found and agreed to a sixty-forty split."

"With Tiffany getting the sixty, I'm sure."

"Of course. But since she would show him the ropes, it didn't sound like such a bad deal for him. Well, the house pended sale quickly, inspections passed, and everything rolled along as smooth as can be. In fact, Tiffany went to the closing yesterday. She told Pete one agent was required to be on hand, so he shouldn't bother. He was grateful since his kids had fevers, and his wife didn't have any more sick time left."

My stomach filled with dread. "Tiffany offered to help another agent? Sounds fishy to me. Wait a second. That's the closing she must have been at while I was busy entertaining weirdos at her open house."

Jacques laughed. "You get all the good ones. Anyhow, when he asked Donna for his check yesterday, she didn't know anything about it. She said the house was Tiffany's listing. Pete hadn't bothered to look online since the listing pended. Originally, both their names were on the listing, but Tiffany removed his name weeks ago."

"No way. What about the contract?"

Jacques took his glasses off, polished them with a fresh handkerchief he produced from his pants pocket, and put them back on. "She informed Pete only one agent's name needed to be there, so he let Tiffany sign."

My mouth dropped open. "Didn't he make a copy of the

original listing agreement for his records? Who entered the information for the listing online?"

"He said they both entered the information. That's how he knew his name was originally there, but it doesn't sound like he saved a paper copy."

"I can't believe he'd be so trusting."

Jacques shook his head. "Stupid is the word that comes to my mind. And yes, believe it. The guy was new and apparently didn't know about her reputation." Jacques shook his head. "For Tiffany, it was like taking candy from a baby. I should have kept an eye out for him. I knew what she was capable of."

"It's not your fault. Donna's the one who should've kept an eye on things. She is the manager, for cripes' sake. Wait a second." I clutched Jacques' arm. "Did Donna mention this to the police too?"

"Not that I'm aware of. I only overheard her talking about you, and when they came out of her office, I went ahead and told the cop about Pete screaming at Tiffany yesterday. He said she was evil, and he was going to get her for crossing him. I couldn't very well lie when Pete made such a threat right in front of me."

Donna clearly had it in for me, so why would she bother trying to implicate someone else? I shivered and pulled the blanket tighter around me. "I bet she didn't tell them about Pete's threat because she wants to see *me* arrested."

"She doesn't hate you that much." He patted my hand.

"Oh yes she does. You should've seen her after I found Tiffany's body. She'd like nothing better than for me to land behind bars."

"What she'd like isn't important. Take a couple of days off and then come into the office like nothing happened. If you stay away too long, it'll look bad. Do you have anything planned for tomorrow?"

"I think I'm going to stay in bed for the next month or two.

And what's the point of coming into the office? No one will want to sign with me now. Donna's going to fire me."

"No worries. I've got plans for you."

"Am I supposed to know what that means?"

"We'll get into that later. But you'd better make sure you don't miss the weekly office meeting on Friday. If you don't show, it's like an admission of guilt." Jacques glanced at his watch and stood. "I'm late picking up my clients. They're here in town for the day. We've got nine houses to view before our seven o'clock reservation for dinner."

"I wish I could afford to take my clients out to dinner."

"It's a tax write off, you know," Jacques said.

"Yes, but it's nice if you have money up front to actually pay the bill. Clients are always a big help too."

"You've got a closing coming up soon, don't you? Mr. Redneck, right?"

I nodded. "The attorney's office called a little while ago. It's on Friday. I didn't expect it so soon. His parents must be loaning him the money. This is a good thing, since I may be unemployed soon."

Jacques gave me a perfunctory kiss on the cheek. "Get some rest, and call me if you need anything."

"Thanks. Perhaps a good criminal attorney?"

"Stop talking like that. I do happen to know the best though. I sold him a house last—"

At that moment, my door flew open. The twins leaped onto my bed, hugged me, and managed to drop cookie crumbs everywhere during the process. They were followed by Rusty, who sat on the edge of the bed, barking incessantly.

"Are you okay, Mommy?" Stevie asked. "We got scared when Dad left last night. Seth started crying."

Seth pushed him. "I did not!"

"Okay, enough." I held each boy at arm's length. "I hit my

head, but I'm fine now." I gestured toward Jacques. "Where are your manners?"

"Hi, Uncle Jacques. Did you bring me anything?" Seth asked as Stevie leaped into Jacques' arms to give him a bear hug.

"How are my two favorite rug rats?"

Stevie peeked inside Jacques' shirt pocket, prompting a laugh from him.

"Hang on, hang on. I was worried about your mom, so I forgot to stop for candy. Here you go." He reached into his wallet and produced a five dollar bill for each boy.

"Wow, thanks." Stevie hugged him.

I shook my head. "That's too much. You don't need to give them something every time you come by."

"Don't listen to her, Uncle Jacques," Stevie said. "She hit her head and doesn't know what she's saying. Grandma said so."

"Ten would be better," Seth chimed in. "Five won't buy anything good."

I stared at my mouthy child in shock. "That's a rude thing to say."

"Okay, okay. Thanks, Uncle Jacques." Seth grinned.

"You're most welcome. Now where's that beautiful sister of yours?"

Stevie let out a yawn. "Cheerleading practice."

"Well, you be sure to give her my best. Okay, kiddos, I've got to run. There are some people waiting for me. Take good care of your mom, and try not to drive her crazy."

Seth held the five-dollar bill above his head, trying to get the puppy to jump for it. "But she likes it when we drive her crazy."

Jacques was laughing as he closed the door. "I'll call you later, dear. Bye, guys."

Once he was gone, the boys turned their attention back to me.

"Are you sure you're okay, Mommy?" Seth drew his

eyebrows together and looked so much like his father at that moment.

"Of course I'm fine, don't worry. The doctor wants me to rest today. That's all." The thought of leaving my precious boys for a life behind bars was too awful to even imagine. I pulled them both into my arms and fought the sudden impulse to weep.

"Did you have a concussion like Jimmy Parker?" Stevie asked.

I nodded. "Who's Jimmy Parker?"

"He was in our class last year, remember?" Seth bounced on my bed. "He's the one who kept getting zeroes on all the math tests. He fell off his bike last week and hit his head. He got to stay out of school for two whole days."

I laughed. "Wow. Lucky kid."

"I know, right?" Stevie helped himself to another cookie and gave Rusty one before I could protest. "So when he came back to school, Mrs. Bailey asked what happened, and he told her he hit his head. Then she said to him, 'I hope you didn't knock any more of your brains out.'"

My jaw dropped. "That's a terrible thing to say."

Seth nodded, his mouth full. "That's what Jimmy's mom and dad said too. They called the principal and everything."

"What happened to Mrs. Bailey?"

"She's still teaching," Seth said. "They moved Jimmy to our class now. I heard Mrs. White tell the lunch lady that if they moved one more kid into our room she might jump off a bridge. Why'd she say that?"

I thought this was a good time to change the subject. "Did you have fun with Grandma last night?"

Stevie nodded. "Oh yeah. Grandma's always fun. We had ice cream, and she played Hangman with us."

"Who won?"

"Grandma," Seth replied. "She kept calling the hangman Cindy. Why did she call it by your name?"

Granny strikes again. I smiled at the twins but said nothing.

Seth stretched out on the pillow next to me. "Grandma said you should give us some kale for breakfast."

"Yeah, I told her we never had it before, and she looked really scared, like the time she found my pet snake, remember?" Stevie munched on another cookie.

I glanced up and winked at Greg, who stood in the doorway with a fresh cup of tea for me. "Too bad you still don't have that snake. You could have let it sleep with Grandma."

Seth agreed. "He was a really nice snake."

Greg placed my tea on the nightstand and folded his arms across his chest, grinning down at me.

Seth observed his father. "Uh-oh. When you look at Mom like that, it means you want to kiss her."

"What a great idea." Greg sat down on the edge of the bed and covered my mouth with his.

"Ew, gross," Stevie squealed. The twins picked up the cookies and made a beeline for the door. The puppy followed closely at their heels, barking up a storm. Greg and I laughed.

"You looked like you needed a break."

I kissed my husband again. "Very perceptive of you, my dear."

CHAPTER SEVEN

Greg fixed dinner with Darcy's reluctant assistance. He came upstairs to get me when everything was ready and insisted I lean on his arm for support while we descended the staircase.

"Really, I'm fine, honey." It was a surprise when he didn't actually try to carry me the entire way.

Greg pulled my chair out and kissed the top of my head. "No, you're not. A concussion can be serious business." He glanced over at the twins. "I bet you guys can't guess what we're having for dinner?"

"Gee, Dad, maybe spaghetti?" Seth asked.

"How'd you know that?"

Seth grabbed the Parmesan cheese out of the fridge. "Because it's the only thing you know how to make."

Greg's smile vanished. "Well, hey, I know it's your favorite."

Stevie looked up from his Nintendo DS. "Dad can cook. He makes hamburgers on the grill."

"It's not the same, dork," Darcy said. "Anyone can cook on a grill."

"Don't call your brother a dork," I admonished her.

"Did you make meatballs?" Stevie asked.

Greg shook his head. "No, but we've got some delicious meat sauce."

Stevie threw the game on the table and kicked his chair. "If I can't have meatballs, I don't want any."

Greg leaned down by Stevie's chair and whispered in his ear. "If you don't eat all of your dinner, that game system is going on eBay tomorrow."

Stevie raised his arms in the air. "Yay, meat sauce."

The meal progressed with its usual banter. Greg ate with the evening paper propped up between his plate and a glass of milk. Stevie shoveled his food in without looking at it. Seth would take a bite of garlic bread and then give the dog a piece when he thought I wasn't looking. Darcy pushed the meat sauce around her plate with a fork and concentrated more on the salad.

I folded my arms on the table as I watched my daughter. "Are you a vegetarian now?"

Darcy shrugged. "I might be. We eat too much red meat."

"You seemed to enjoy the steak Daddy grilled for you the other day."

She tossed her hair back defiantly. "I don't remember that."

"Hey, Mom," Stevie mumbled with his mouth full of spaghetti. "Don't forget that tomorrow is Career Day at school."

I exhaled sharply. "Oh, Stevie, this isn't a good time. Can't Daddy go?"

"Dad went last year," Seth said. "The kids don't want to hear about brake pads again."

Greg was an auto parts salesman. "Hey, we just got new ones. They have organic material in them now. I could bring some samples with me."

Stevie ignored him. "Please, Mom? We've never had a real estate agent come in before."

I sighed. "Well, my morning is free so far."

Darcy wrinkled her nose. "I'm sure your afternoon will be too."

I caught the note of sarcasm in her voice. "What's that supposed to mean?"

Darcy avoided my gaze. "Oh, nothing."

"Maybe you should bring some business cards to the class." Seth reached for his glass of milk and accidentally knocked it on to the floor. Fortunately, it was almost empty.

I rose to grab some paper towels and spray. "Oh, right. I'm sure I'd sell a lot of houses that way." *Hmm...wait a second.* "You know, that's not a bad idea. I could fill little baggies with candy and attach cards to each one. They could take them home and show their parents."

Greg winked at me. "Go get 'em, tiger."

Gee, if Tiffany were here, she would have been so proud of my attempt to solicit to eight-year-olds.

"Wow, that's so lame." Darcy got to her feet. "Can I go over to Heather's house?"

"Is it to study or talk about boys?" Greg teased.

Darcy gave him her best saccharin smile. "Oh, Daddy, you're precious. We have to study for a math test tomorrow."

Greg was putty in her hands most of the time, and they both knew it. She kissed him on the cheek and started for the front door.

"Be back in an hour to do the dishes," I called out. She tossed a frown over her shoulder in my direction, then quickly exited the room.

"Mom?" Stevie asked. "When will Darcy stop calling me a dork?"

Seth kicked him under the table. "Maybe when you stop being one?"

"Okay, guys, enough. Who wants to shower first?" I asked.

Stevie put his plate on the counter. "Seth does. He smells bad."

"You're the one who needs some deodorant." Seth threw a piece of garlic bread at his brother's head.

Within seconds, they were rolling around on the floor with Rusty barking and bouncing between the two of them.

"Do not!"

"You do too!"

Without a word, Greg calmly put the paper down and lifted each boy off the floor and into his arms. He half dragged, half carried them toward the bathroom. Both kids kicked and shrieked with laughter while Rusty trotted up the stairs behind them all.

I got up to clear the table, relieved to leave the dishes for Darcy. My head ached again, and I wanted to lie down for a few minutes. As I stacked dishes in the sink, my cell phone buzzed. I studied the screen, but didn't recognize the number. I cringed inwardly. What if it was another reporter? I could always hang up. Then again, it might be a lead. Boy, did I need one of those right now. "Hello?"

"Good evening, is this Cindy?" a deep male voice asked.

"Yes, speaking."

"Hi there. Ken Sorenson here."

I was drawing a blank. Maybe I was like Jimmy Parker, and the concussion had knocked my brains out. "Hi, Mr. Sorenson, how can I help you?"

"It's Ken." He breathed low into the phone. "Donna—my wife, said you would be willing to show me some houses tomorrow?"

"Oh!" I'd totally forgotten about him. "Of course."

"Donna mentioned what happened. I'm so sorry about your injury and hope I'm not imposing. I just got back into town today, and tomorrow is the only day I'm available. Are you sure you're feeling up to it?"

I took the phone away from my ear to stare at it. This was certainly not the way I expected anyone married to Donna to act. He sounded kind and genuinely concerned. Not to mention sexy as all get out.

"No, Mr. Sorenson, err—Ken, it's perfectly fine. What time would you like to get together?"

"How about noon? We could see a house or two, go to lunch, and then view the rest."

I hesitated. It wasn't that I minded the lunch part, but it was a little out of the ordinary for me in my income bracket. I was already racking my brain wondering what I could afford. I hoped he liked Big Macs. "Um—"

"My treat, of course."

Well, that was a new one. Agents always paid, not the clients. "I can't let you do that. It wouldn't be right."

"I insist. It will give us more of a chance to talk anyhow."

The hairs stood up on the back of my neck. My gut instinct told me to say no to the entire arrangement, but I thought of Donna and our deal, so I gave in. "Okay, that sounds—nice. Thank you. Do you know what houses you'd like to see? These are for your mother, right?"

"Correct." His voice was smooth and sensual. "I have a list of addresses. I viewed the pictures online already, Let me know when you're ready."

I grabbed a notepad and pen off the kitchen counter. Out of the corner of my eye, I noticed Greg watching me from the living room. I mouthed "client" at him. He nodded, then turned back to the television. "Go ahead."

"There's 65 Princely Lane, 55 Riverview Drive, and 4 Lincoln Place."

I jotted the information down. "Got it. I'll call and arrange the showings right away."

"Appreciate it. You can text me at this number to let me know it's a done deal or if you run into any problems. Where shall we meet tomorrow?"

"How about at the first house? I'll let you know which one when I text you."

"Sounds great." I listened to him again and couldn't help wondering what his profession was. The silk-like voice could be deceiving. Was he a disc jockey, perhaps? In that case, it might be a letdown when I met him. Heck, there was a reason why many of them were heard and not seen.

"Thanks again, Cindy." He paused for a few seconds. "I'm looking forward to meeting you. I have a feeling we're going to be very good friends."

He clicked off.

A chill went down my spine. Something seemed totally off about this guy.

I went into the den and sat down in front of my computer, pulling up my Multiple Listing Service software program. One by one, I punched in the addresses of the houses and proceeded to quickly scan the listings. My mouth went dry at the asking prices. They were all near the million dollar range. It sounded like Donna had married well. Money goes to money, my mother used to say.

My modest three-bedroom ranch looked like a dump compared to these homes. I usually tried not to get ahead of myself, but it was difficult to contain my excitement. If I could sell Ken's mother one of these houses, our money problems would be over for quite some time.

After printing the listings, I was able to set up the showings directly online without having to phone customer service. One requested twenty-four hour notice, but the other two were confirmed with no problem. I sent Ken a quick text, simply saying, *4 Lincoln Place not available, but the other two houses are good to go. Meet you at 65 Princely at noon?*

My phone pinged within seconds. I glanced down at a message that made me shiver inwardly. *Sounds great. Saw your picture on the company's website. Very nice. See you tomorrow.*

Yikes. I'd heard the horror stories about agents who were robbed or murdered while on listing appointments. He seemed a bit overly friendly, but maybe I was reading too much into it. After all, he was Donna's husband, so I really didn't think he would try anything.

"Someone's deep in thought." Greg stood in the doorway, watching me.

I never even heard him come into the study and must have jumped about ten feet in the air. I deleted the message off my phone. "Oh, hey, honey. I'm showing some houses tomorrow. I needed to check them out on the MLS, and they're both pretty pricey. They're in the ritzier area of town."

"That's great, baby. Who's the client?"

"Donna's new husband. She has an all-day sales meeting and asked if I could show him some places. They're for his mother."

He drew his eyebrows together in confusion and then came to stand behind me, gently massaging my shoulders. "I still can't believe she's married. She ran after every guy she saw."

"Especially you."

He laughed and then was silent for a minute. "This seems kind of weird. I mean, why can't she show them to him some other time? I don't think you should go."

My stomach filled with dread at his words, but I didn't want to pass up the possible chance of a sale. "I'll be okay, sweetheart."

"Are you sure you're feeling up to it? The trip to the boys' school in the morning might tire you out. Will you be able to handle everything?"

I hesitated for a moment and then exhaled a long breath before I stood and pecked his lips. "Of course. I told you I'm fine. This will be a piece of cake. Trust me."

CHAPTER EIGHT

*T*he next morning after Greg left for work and the kids departed for school, I flew upstairs to take a quick shower. I wanted to hit the grocery store before heading over to the boys' school. I was due there at 10:30.

I tried to force any doubts from my mind as I carefully selected my best suit from the closet. It was black silk and lower cut in the front than most things I wore, but my other two suits weren't back from the cleaners yet. And I loved how the gathered bodice made my waist appear smaller. As a general rule, I never wore much makeup, so I applied lipstick and a coat of mascara. I flipped the curling iron around my hair, reminding myself again that everything was going to be fine.

I grabbed my keys and purse and opened the front door. A young woman stood there expectantly. I shrieked and took a step back. "Oh, wow."

She flashed a gleaming smile. "I'm sorry if I startled you."

I laughed. "No problem. I wasn't expecting to find anyone standing here. Can I help you?"

"Hi, I'm Stephanie Winters." The definitive air with which

she spoke suggested that that should explain everything. She held out her hand to me.

Having no choice, I shook it, which gave me time to survey her more closely. Stephanie wore a brown leather jacket and beige slacks. She appeared to be in her early twenties, with jet black hair held back in a long braid down her back. A pair of Coach sunglasses covered a large portion of her alabaster face. She seemed harmless enough.

"Hi, Stephanie." I tried to prod her on for further information. "Do I know you?"

Her lips parted, and she acted insulted. "I'm from the *Hourly Times*. Do you have a few minutes so that we could talk?"

Oh, great. Another reporter. Or maybe the same one who had called yesterday. "I'm afraid I don't. I was on my way out and have a very full day ahead of me. What's this regarding anyhow?"

Stephanie opened her mouth wide and proceeded to laugh so hard that I was afraid she might hurt herself. "Oh, Mrs. York, you're so funny."

"Thanks, but I wasn't trying to be."

"I think you know why I'm here." Stephanie's voice took on a singsong quality.

I folded my arms and leaned against the door. "You'll have to explain."

"Mrs. York—um, may I call you Cindy?"

I shrugged.

"I'd like to do a feature article on you for the paper. A real and powerful in-depth story about how it feels to be accused of murder."

My mouth opened in amazement. This had to be some type of joke. I smiled at the girl politely. "I haven't been accused of anything."

"Cindy, please understand. I'm on your side. After everyone

reads the article, they'll be able to relate to you better. Now do you know when the trial is scheduled for?"

If anything, I had to admire the girl's audacity. "There is no trial. Like I said, I haven't been accused of anything. There's no proof I was even involved." I wanted to bite my tongue as she proceeded to scribble down every word I rattled off in her steno pad. "If you want a story, you need to go ask the police department for one."

"I heard they found your fingerprints in Miss Roberts' office."

I laughed. "Yes, of course they did. They found many fingerprints in her office. Tiffany had clients and other agents in there all the time. Remember, she was a very successful real estate agent."

Stephanie jotted down more notes. "And you resented that, right?"

I sucked in some air. "I think it would be best if you left now, Stephanie. I really need to get going."

She acted surprised. "Oh, right. How about I come back this afternoon?"

"How about you come back—oh, I don't know, maybe never?" This girl clearly wasn't getting it. I checked my watch.

Stephanie's lips curved into a smirk. "You don't mean that."

I stared directly into her green, cat-like eyes. "Yes, I do. You need to leave now. Your behavior constitutes harassment."

My comments brought out the hyena laugh again. "Oh, that's rich coming from a murder suspect."

"Good-bye, Stephanie." I shut and locked the door, hoping she'd get the message. If I didn't leave now, I might be late getting to the school and would never hear the end of it from the twins. I narrowed my eyes at the girl and walked past her toward my vehicle.

Stephanie's eyes widened in alarm as she stepped away from me. She turned around and flounced off the porch. Maybe she was afraid she'd be my next victim. In Stephanie's haste, her high-heeled shoe slipped along the edge. She screamed as she tumbled into the nearby lilac bush.

"Are you okay?" I ran to help her up and hoped Greg had remembered to pay the homeowner's insurance premium.

With the exception of some dirt and a small tree branch in her hair, Stephanie seemed fine. "You pushed me."

My jaw dropped as I let go of her arm. "I didn't lay a finger on you."

Stephanie brushed herself off and then glanced around, probably seeking a witness. Since no one was in sight, she leaned toward me. "If you let me do the article, I won't tell anyone you hit me."

Furious, I pointed to her car. "Good-bye, Stephanie."

"You really did kill Tiffany Roberts. I knew it." Stephanie burst into tears and fled for her vehicle. Within seconds, she peeled out of my driveway.

This was going to come back to haunt me. I was sure of it. My hands trembled as I got into my vehicle. I took several deep breaths to steady myself, then took off for the market, hoping I'd seen the last of the roving reporter.

My phone buzzed as I stopped for a red light. I adjusted my Bluetooth and saw Jacques' name pop up on the screen. "Thank God it's you."

"Wow, not even nine o'clock and already a bad day?"

"You've no idea," I sighed.

"Got time for a cup of coffee? My treat."

I was sorely tempted. "Not sure. I'm headed to the market and then over to the boys' school."

"Lucky you. Come on, what store are you headed to? I've got gossip," Jacques pleaded.

He was impossible to resist. "Groceries Galore. The one over on Grady Avenue. But I don't have much time."

"Perfect. Starbucks is right next door. I'll meet you there in twenty minutes," Jacques said. "Trust me, you're going to want to hear this. Don't I always have the best gossip? You said so yourself. You once told me—"

I pulled into a parking space near the store's entrance. "All right. I'm headed inside now. Order me a caramel macchiato with lots of whipped cream, please."

"God, that's *so* fattening. You definitely are having a bad day."

I groaned. "No lectures, please. I really need a sugar rush right now."

"All right, all right, don't get all PMS on me. Consider it done. See you soon." He clicked off.

I didn't need much at the market. I loaded milk, bread, cereal, cookies, apples, and juice into the cart. I added a dozen eggs and headed for the checkout line.

"Hey, Mrs. York." Todd Simpson waved from behind the meat counter. A nice young man in his early twenties, he held up a finger, signaling for me to wait while he weighed some pork chops for an elderly couple.

"Hello, Todd. Sorry, but I'm in a hurry today." I started to move on until he called out to me again. Exasperated, I turned around.

Todd gave the couple their package and scurried over. "Listen, I'm real sorry to hear about all the trouble you've been having."

I stared. "This is nuts. Was my entire life featured in the *National Enquirer* this morning or something?"

Todd grinned. "You know how small towns are. Everyone likes to gossip."

That was an understatement. I thought of Jacques and nodded wearily.

Todd leaned closer and lowered his voice. "You can level with me, Mrs. York. I know what it's like."

I took a step back. "You know what what's like?"

"Come on. When someone promises you something and

they lie to you. I was supposed to get a raise this month. My manager promised. I asked him about it yesterday, and you know what he said? 'I never promised you anything, Todd. You're not right in the head.' Nice, huh? Well, I'll fix him." Todd produced a meat cleaver from his apron pocket. He laughed when he noticed my expression. "Relax, I'm not going to kill him. Not today anyway."

I started to steer my cart forward. "That's always a good thing."

"I know, right? But, hey, it doesn't mean I don't think about it. Like you. I know you didn't kill that lady. So don't feel bad if you ever thought about doing her in."

Yikes. I forced a smile to my lips. "Thanks for the advice, Todd."

"Hey, anytime, Mrs. York. Have yourself a blessed day."

All I could think about was how badly I needed my macchiato with that thick layer of whipped cream. A towering inferno of whipped cream. Maybe I should buy a can of Reddi-wip to tote along with me for emergencies. The way this day was shaping up, I felt sure I was going to need some type of crutch.

My neighbor, Susan Farrell, stood in the line opposite mine. When I waved and smiled, she let out a loud shriek, whirled her cart right around, and headed for the back of the store.

I definitely didn't have many fans today.

I put the bags in the back of my car and spotted Jacques' convertible nearby. As I pushed through Starbucks' entrance, the aroma of coffee beans and cinnamon greeted me. Jacques was already seated at a table near the door, sipping his nonfat latte with one hand while scrolling his smartphone with the other.

I slid into the seat across from him where my macchiato waited with its avalanche of whipped cream. Somehow I managed to refrain from sticking my face in it. "You're an absolute doll."

Jacques glanced at me and let out a low whistle. "Damn. Looking hot today, girl. Someone has a busy day ahead. Obviously, you're feeling better."

"Well, I was until I got approached by a reporter this morning." I took a long sip of my drink. "She was waiting for me right on my porch."

He shook his head. "You've got to love the press. They're like real estate agents—ruthless."

"Gosh, you're right. I never thought we were that bad though." Placated by caffeine and sugar, I folded my arms. "So what's the gossip?"

"First things first. Pete Saxon left the agency yesterday."

"Get out! Why?"

Jacques always looked pleased when he knew something I didn't. "He told Donna he had a better opportunity with another agency elsewhere."

"Do you think that's true?"

Jacques stared at me in disbelief. "How hard did you hit that head anyway? The guy made one sale in two months, and Tiffany took it away from him. Does that sound like someone you'd want to hire?"

I sipped my cappuccino. "This is kind of an awkward time for him to leave."

"Exactly my point." He leaned forward and lowered his voice. "It's as good as an admission of guilt."

"Did the police question him?"

"They questioned everybody, and they'll probably be back, so prepare yourself."

I groaned. "I don't know how much more of this I can take. Everyone's treating me like a leper."

Jacques squeezed my hand. "Don't worry, doll. We'll figure out who did this."

I grinned. "Oh, so now we're a team? Like Holmes and Watson?"

"I prefer Poirot and Hastings from Agatha Christie."

"Well, since you happen to be a quarter Belgian, I guess that'll be okay," I teased.

Jacques sniffed the air as if I'd offended him. "Not a quarter, I'm one third. Get it right, girl. And I want to find the killer as much as you do. The problem is, too many people had motives. Look at Bill Prescott."

"Bill? Did Tiffany steal a listing from him, too?"

Jacques shook his head. "Nope. But he did ask her out on a date a few weeks ago."

"Get out."

"I really hate that expression, you know."

I spooned some whipped cream into my mouth. "Yeah, I know. What'd she do—laugh in his face?"

"Pretty much. She told him if he was the only man left on the face of the earth, she wouldn't break a sweat if he hap-happened to fall off."

"She made fun of his stuttering? Wow, that's cold, even for her." I moaned as I took another long sip of my drink. "Mmm, so good."

"Careful, Cin. Keep it clean now, there are small children in here." Jacques folded his arms on the table. "Okay, I saved the best gossip for last."

"This I can't wait to hear. Come on, spill it. I know you're dying to."

He grinned like the Cheshire cat. "You will never, in a million years, guess who got married recently."

Oh boy. I almost hated to burst his bubble, he loved gossiping so much. "Um, gee, let me think. Maybe Donna?"

I watched the smile on Jacques' face disappear, and his mouth twist into a pout. "How the heck did you know?"

"Donna told me the day before yesterday. I'm sorry, with

everything else going on, I forgot to mention it. I'm actually showing her husband some houses today. They're for his mother."

He drew his finely arched eyebrows together. "No offense, Cin, but why in the name of God would Donna ask *you* to show houses to her new husband? By the way, I saw a picture of her new boy toy. The man is hot. I mean, he's to-die-for hot. I almost drooled on myself. And why would someone who looks like him marry someone who looks like her? Bet it's for her money. She's having a mighty good year. Have you seen the new Corvette she just bought?"

I laughed. "Listen to you. That's pretty harsh. It's not always about people's looks, you know."

"The heck it isn't. What a waste of a fine-looking man."

"Okay, stop this. You're a married man too, remember?"

He snorted. "Listen, honey, I love Ed to the moon and back, but I still stop and take a look around once in a while."

I shook my head at him. "You're hopeless."

"Yeah, a hopeless romantic." Jacques drained his cup. "You still didn't answer my question. Why are *you* showing him houses?"

"Donna has an all-day sales meeting, and this is the only time he's available. Plus everyone else in the office was busy today, so I assume I was her last choice. She agreed to give me 25 percent of the deal if her mother-in-law buys one of the houses. I already got it in writing."

"Well, that was smart of you," Jacques conceded. "Still, I have my doubts wherever Donna is concerned. Especially since she's not your biggest fan lately. Does Greg know that this guy could be George Clooney's double?"

My face was growing warm. "No, he doesn't, and who cares anyway? That means nothing to me. Ken's a client. That's all."

"No. He's Donna's husband. What if she's trying to make trouble for you? Get you fired?"

Crap. I hadn't thought of that. "That's ridiculous." I examined my watch. "Time to get going. Thanks for the drink. I was dying for one of those."

Jacques grinned. "The whipped cream or the macchiato?"

"Both." I slid out of my seat. "I really have to run."

"I'll have to get you a steady supply of Reddi-wip. So what's the rush? Don't want to keep Ken Doll waiting?"

I narrowed my eyes at him. "Remember, I told you I've got to get to the kids' school. Today's Career Day, and they've never had a real estate agent before."

"Wow, your day keeps getting better and better." He stood and held the door open for me. As we walked toward my car together, he looped his arm through mine. "Cin, please be careful."

I tried to fight the panic starting to rise within me. "Nothing's going to happen."

"I hope not," Jacques said soberly. He gave me a quick peck on the cheek. "I've got inspections for a house out in Millbrook, but call if you need me. You know you always come first." With that he turned and got into his car.

My heart melted as he waved and zoomed off, his CD player blasting Lady Gaga's "Born This Way." I thanked my lucky stars for that man. I couldn't have asked for a better bestie.

I pulled into the driveway and rushed to unload the two bags from my trunk. As I hurried toward the porch, a piece of paper taped to the front door caught my eye. Someone had typed out a message in bold letters on a piece of printer paper. Had Stephanie come back and left me a little note?

The paper read: *Turn yourself in. I know you did it, and I'll be coming after you.*

My arms grew numb, and I let the bags slide to the cement. I ripped the piece of paper from the front door and threw it into my purse. Hands trembling, I unlocked the front door and peered inside, but no one waited to pounce on me, except Rusty in the gated kitchen area. He was eager to show me the fresh puddle he'd left in my absence. Gee whiz, why did this pup refuse to be house-trained?

I let Rusty outside into the backyard for a few minutes while I unpacked the groceries and cleaned up the puddle. I checked my watch, which read 10:20. Thank goodness the school was five minutes away. Once Rusty was back inside and I'd secured the kitchen gate, I grabbed my briefcase and purse. The note fluttered out of my purse and fell on the floor.

My stomach churned. While I knew I should report the threat, I was afraid. What if the police thought I'd made up the story? I folded the note carefully and placed it back inside my purse so that I could show it to Greg later. I locked the front door and double checked that it was secured.

As I pulled my seatbelt across me, the truth of the situation dawned on me. Someone had waited until I left the house to place the note there. That meant someone was watching me. Why? Was I in some type of danger? And what about my family? My head started spinning as I desperately tried to calm myself. *No. It's only your imagination working overtime.*

I whispered a short prayer asking for strength to help me get through this day, then drove off toward the twins' school.

CHAPTER NINE

I found myself standing in front of twenty third graders and their teacher. I had met Mrs. White several times before. A pleasant, elderly woman with thick-rimmed glasses and an outdated beehive hairdo, her thin face was tired and drawn. I suspected she had a hidden calendar that she used to count down the days to her retirement.

The children whispered amongst themselves and pointed fingers at me. I should have begged Greg to come. Brake pads *can* be interesting. I hoped they weren't wondering if I'd brought the murder weapon with me.

Mrs. White clapped her hands together, and the talking stopped abruptly. "Stevie and Seth, would you like to introduce your mother to the class?"

Stevie jumped to his feet while Seth remained sitting. "My mom's name is Cindy, but you can call her Mrs. York. She's a real estate agent."

"Can anyone tell me what a real estate agent does?" Mrs. White asked.

In the front row, a little girl with bright-red hair and freckles raised her hand. "They buy houses and make lots of money."

I laughed. "Well, we don't actually buy them. We help people —our clients—sell them to other people. And we don't always make a lot of money. Our salary, known as commission, is based upon the price of the house."

The little girl appeared nonplussed. "You mean, if it's a mansion you'll get a lot of money, but if it's a dump, you don't see much dough?"

The room was getting warm. "Well, that's one way of looking at it. But our main goal is to help people."

"Yeah, right." A chubby, blonde girl in the back row scowled at me. "My daddy says you guys are nothing but crooks."

I was startled by the sarcasm coming from an eight-year-old's mouth and forced a sweet smile in her direction. "What does your daddy do for a living, dear?"

"He sells cars."

Mrs. White stared at me as if daring me to respond. Before I could manage to say anything, another hand shot up.

Tyler, one of the twins' best friends, got to his feet. He lived in our neighborhood and had been to our home on several occasions. "My aunt just bought a house. It's on Livingston Avenue."

My smile faded. "Oh, that's nice."

I found this especially interesting since Tyler's mother, Anne, was a friend of mine. I'd shown her sister, Leslie, several houses earlier this year, but she'd told me she wanted to wait until the market got better. Was there no loyalty anymore? "Well, you be sure to give Aunt Leslie my best."

"Yeah, the lady who died sold her the place. Aunt Leslie said real estate agents will tell people anything to make a sale. Is that true?" Tyler asked.

The heat rose through my face. I hadn't been prepared to answer questions like this.

Fortunately, Mrs. White interrupted before I could muster a response. "Now, Tyler, real estate agents have to tell people the truth about the homes they sell. Remember, honesty is the best policy."

"Well, the dead lady wasn't honest with her, and the house is a big mess. Aunt Leslie said she should've stuck with Mrs. York. She told my mom she's glad that lady's dead."

A murmur ran through the classroom. Mrs. White clapped her hands again in clear frustration. "Children, please."

A knock sounded on the door, and the school secretary poked her head in. "Mrs. White, there's a phone call for you in the office."

When Mrs. White glanced at me, I gave her my best reassuring smile. "Don't worry. We'll be fine until you get back."

She grimaced but nonetheless hurried out of the classroom. I was glad for a chance to be alone with the kids. I leaned back against the desk and smiled at Tyler. "So why didn't Aunt Leslie like Miss Roberts?"

"Is that the lady who got shot?"

"Yes."

"She was a bad lady. She lied to Aunt Leslie about the house and said the fur nest was like new."

"The what?"

"You know, the heater thing," Tyler explained.

"The furnace?"

"Yeah, that's it. The first day Aunt Leslie moved in the house, she called my mom crying. The furnace was already busted. She said the agent lady knew but didn't care. She wished her dead over and over. My mom got angry too, but when we heard she got killed, my dad thought you did it."

A chill went down my spine. "Why would he think that?"

"I don't know. He said he hoped not because he thinks you're kind of cute. My mom got real mad when he said that."

"Ew, gross." Stevie made a face.

"I'm telling my dad," Seth chimed in.

"Okay, enough, guys." I focused on Tyler again. "So what did

Aunt Leslie say when she found out Miss Roberts had been killed?"

"I heard my mom tell Dad that Aunt Leslie was acting weird, and she was worried about her. She said Aunt Leslie did something really bad. She went to see Miss Roberts and—"

"Well, now how are we doing in here?" Mrs. White stood next to me, glaring.

I nearly jumped out of my skin. I hadn't even heard her come back into the room.

Tyler addressed his teacher, wide eyed. "Mrs. York was asking me about Aunt Leslie. She bought a house from the dead lady."

Mrs. White shook her head at me in such a disapproving way that I wondered if I should volunteer to go stand in the corner. "Okay, who would like to ask Mrs. York how she figures out what a house will sell for?"

Tyler raised his hand again. "Did you kill Miss Roberts?"

I gazed at him, shocked. "No, of course not. I can't believe you'd ask me such a thing."

"Well, I guess Aunt Leslie might have done it, but I think it was you. My mom said the bad lady cheated you out of a sale." Tyler wiped his runny nose with his sleeve.

Mrs. White's mouth fell open. "Tyler, that will be enough. And for goodness sake, grab a tissue."

I stared at the twins, hoping to gauge their reactions. Much to my surprise, they seemed unperturbed by their friend's accusation. They met my gaze and grinned. Perhaps it was all surreal to them.

I decided this would be a good time to hand out my little care packages. They had been fun to make last night with the boys and Rusty helping. Seth and Stevie were beaming at me now, and I smiled at the class. "If Mrs. White agrees, I have presents for each one of you to take home."

"Of course. What a lovely gesture, Mrs. York."

I reached into my briefcase and brought out the packages of candy with my real estate card attached. I began to hand them out to the children.

Tyler observed his package with care. "My mom and dad aren't buying another house, Mrs. York."

This kid was priceless. "Yes, I'm aware of that. Why don't you tell them to hang on to the card, okay? They might know someone who wants to buy a house later on."

"Well, there was only Aunt Leslie, and I don't think she likes real estate agents anymore."

I chose to ignore his last comment and kept distributing the packages while glancing at the classroom clock. *It's almost over, hang in there.*

"I can't take this." A little girl with solemn, brown eyes and matching braids that hung over her shoulders waved her hand at me.

I raised my eyebrows. "Is there something wrong with the candy?"

"No, it's not that. My mother doesn't allow me to take candy from strangers—or killers."

"Elizabeth!" Mrs. White gasped. "You apologize to Mrs. York right now."

Elizabeth wore a pained expression on her face. "I'm really sorry you're a killer, Mrs. York."

Mrs. White groaned. "That isn't what I meant."

Lisa frowned at her package. "How come there's no good candy in here? I don't like the cheap stuff."

Mrs. White watched me with hesitation. I nodded to let her know I was okay. I could handle anything now or so I thought.

"Why do they call jail cells a slammer?" Elizabeth wanted to know. "Is that because people get slammed around a lot? Do they beat you up in there?"

"I'm not sure. I've never been in prison."

"Not yet," Elizabeth reminded me.

I wiped at my perspiring forehead and glanced hopefully at the clock—again. It was 11:15. Thank goodness—time to go.

Another hand shot through the air, and the chubby blonde met my gaze. "Mrs. York, you should watch out. My mom said people can catch all kinds of diseases from those jail cells."

I had never been so relieved to leave the twins' classroom before. I'd finally been paroled but nonetheless, managed a wide grin for the children. "Time for me to go now, kids. I have an appointment to show someone a few houses this afternoon."

"If they won't buy, will you threaten them with a gun?" Tyler nearly bounced out of his seat with excitement.

"That will be quite enough." Mrs. White mopped at her forehead with a handkerchief. She'd probably have to go on stress leave for a week after my visit.

Elizabeth raised her hand but didn't wait for either Mrs. White or me to acknowledge her. "Why do people still want you to show them houses? I mean, aren't you going to be locked up soon?"

"My mom's not going to prison," Seth insisted. "She never hurt anyone."

Stevie nodded. "Yeah. And even if she does go to jail, the guards will let her come home at night to make dinner for us."

My headache was back. I picked up my purse and briefcase and started for the door. "Well, guys, thanks. This was, um, interesting."

Mrs. White smiled, obviously relieved to be rid of me. "Let's all say thank you to Mrs. York for coming in today."

I received a chorus of "thank you" and "I want to go to your house" as I nodded good-bye to Stevie and Seth, who both gave me thumbs up.

"Good luck in prison," Elizabeth said. "Maybe we can come visit you."

I sighed. "I'm not going to prison, Elizabeth."

"Will you get your picture on TV and in the paper?" Lisa asked.

"Maybe they'll put you in one of those reality shows," the chubby blonde volunteered.

"Miss Roberts wasn't a nice lady," Tyler said thoughtfully, "but my dad told me she was smoking. Does that mean she liked cigarettes?"

"If you say one more word, you're going down to see the principal," Mrs. White threatened.

He looked at her, puzzled. "But if she was bad, maybe it's okay someone killed her?"

"Killing someone is *never* okay."

"Somebody took out the trash." Seth exclaimed in an exaggerated Italian accent.

Some of the kids giggled while the color drained from Mrs. White's face. I stood there clutching the doorknob, speechless. Last month, while I was out showing a house one Saturday afternoon, Greg had discovered the twins watching a rerun of *The Sopranos*. Apparently, it hadn't been the first time either. He'd changed the station immediately, but it appeared the damage had already been done.

Mrs. White hurried over and took my hand in both of hers. "You were great to put up with all of this. Thanks, and good luck to you."

I chuckled. "Good luck to you too. You've certainly got your hands full with this bunch."

"Only 398 calendar days until I'm out of my prison for good," Mrs. White said wearily. "But who's counting?"

I knew it.

CHAPTER TEN

The clock in my car alerted me to the fact that the
noon hour had officially arrived. By some miracle, I'd
been early to meet Ken. I arrived at the house first and took a
little time to go through my emails until a man zoomed up next
to me in a bright-red BMW. He got out of the car, and my jaw
dropped.

Ken Sorenson did bear a striking resemblance to George
Clooney—square jaw, rugged handsome face, and exuding an
air of confidence. He had thick, dark hair, which showed no
signs of receding, and was tanned and powerfully built in a
dark-blue, Calvin Klein suit and matching silk tie. His enormous, dark eyes focused on my face as he approached my car. I
remained frozen in the seat, still staring.

His perfect white teeth gleamed in a grin, and he opened my
car door before I had a chance to react. He extended his hand to
help me out of my seat. "Hi, Cindy. I'd recognize you anywhere.
It's great to meet you."

"Likewise," I said.

His eyes scanned me up and down and lingered on my chest
a bit too long. "You look terrific in that suit."

"Shall we see the house?" I asked, ignoring his compliment. Despite his good looks, something about the man and the way he looked at me made me uneasy. I walked toward the front door, and Ken followed. Holy cow. Dowdy Donna, as Jacques called her, had hit the jackpot with this guy. So if he was such a catch, why was being around him making me nauseous?

I presented Ken with a copy of the listing, and he leaned against the railing while I took my eKEY out of my purse, entered the code, and slid the electronic lockbox open. I inserted the key into the door and stepped back to let Ken enter first.

Ken did a quick circle around the kitchen, stopped to look at the bathrooms, and peeked into the family room. He then took the stairs two at a time to inspect the bedrooms and other rooms. I followed behind at a respectable distance.

"Nice, but the rooms are too small for my mother's elaborate taste." He walked out the front door without a backward glance. I followed, after leaving my business card on the table in the foyer. We'd barely been inside for five minutes.

I marveled at how sure Ken was of himself and seemed to know exactly what he wanted. I still couldn't believe he was Donna's husband, but what did I know? Maybe he really loved her. Something about their whole whirlwind relationship and sudden marriage bothered me, but hey, it wasn't any of my business.

With any luck, the second showing would go better. As I secured the lockbox, Ken put his arm around me. "Come on, let's go grab some lunch. I made us a reservation at a great French restaurant nearby. Want to leave your car here, and we'll grab it later?" He gave me a slow wink that made my stomach turn.

"Ah, no thanks," I said, removing his arm. "I'll follow you."

He shrugged and opened my car door, gave me one last appraising look, then turned and got into his vehicle. Was it his cocky attitude that irritated me? No, more the fact that he stared at me like he wished to devour me. Okay, maybe I was overreacting. I had to give him a chance. If he said something negative to Donna about this showing experience, I was done for.

Ken had reserved a corner booth for us and joined me on the same side, so we could both view the lake, he explained. *Uh-huh.* He continued to drape his arm across my shoulders, and I kept removing it. Finally, he apologized.

"I'm sorry. It's a bad habit of mine. I always do it whenever I'm out to lunch with clients."

"I'm sure that goes over well," I said dryly. "What kind of business are you in?"

"I own a pawn shop," Ken explained. "I sell coins and jewelry. I also buy gold and silver, along with other fine metals." He gave my arm a playful nudge, and it almost landed in my soup. "Donna said you were kind of hard up right now, so if you want to sell some jewelry, let me know. I'll give you top dollar."

I flinched at the words. "Thanks, but that's really none of Donna's concern. And I'm not hard up. Sales might be a little slow for me right now, but my husband has a very good job."

"Yes, Donna told me." Ken refilled my wine glass before I could stop him. "It must be tough for George—selling mufflers and all."

I bit into my lower lip, hoping to temper my reply. "His name is Greg."

Ken shrugged. "Oh, right. Whatever. So is there any news on your coworker's murder?"

I shook my head. "Nothing yet."

"That must be rough on you. How are you handling things?"

I sighed. "About as well as I can. Since I'm the one who found her, people automatically think I'm guilty. You know how people around here like to gossip."

Ken nodded. "The police don't have any leads?"

"If they do, they certainly aren't sharing them with me." *Ugh.* As soon as I said the words, I wanted to bite my tongue off. The darn wine was already getting to me. I remembered what Greg always said, "Give Cindy a drink, and the world will know her life story." I didn't want to divulge any more information to Ken. I doubted he could be trusted, and anything I told him he would be sure to blab to Donna. She already hated me, so why give her any more ammunition?

Ken laid his hand on my knee, and I tensed. "Please stop."

He removed his hand and smiled at me as a cat would his prey. "You have the most gorgeous hazel eyes I've ever seen."

Heat warmed my face. Whether it was from the wine or the compliment, I wasn't quite sure. Probably both. "Thank you."

His hand went back on my knee. "That George is one lucky man."

A small trickle of sweat traveled down my back as I removed his hand—yet again. "Thank you. And it's Greg."

"Greg, George, they both start with *G*, so what's the difference?"

What an arrogant jerk. I stared at my watch. "Perhaps we'd better get the check. I have to get home before my kids return from school."

"Ah, I'm sure they'll be fine alone for a while. Donna mentioned you have like half a dozen?"

"Not quite. Twin boys and a girl. Gee, you and Donna must have spent an awful lot of time talking about me."

He roared with laughter as his eyes focused on my chest again. "Well, there's quite a lot to talk about."

I was slowly suffocating with discomfort. "Um, I'd appreciate it if you'd stop touching me, or I won't be able to show you the other house."

The smile faded from his face. "I'm sorry, Cindy. I guess I get a tad crazy whenever I see a beautiful woman. You see, my wife is a bit homely in that department."

Was this guy for real? "That's a terrible thing to say about Donna. You got married—what, last week?"

"Almost two weeks ago." Ken finished his crème brûlée and signaled for the check.

My mouth fell open in amazement. "So if looks are so important to you, why did you marry her?"

Ken shrugged, and his mouth twitched slightly as he reached inside his wallet for money. My eyes popped when I saw the thick roll of bills he carried. "She has some endearing qualities about her. She's intelligent, faithful, and a good companion."

Good grief. He'd just described a Saint Bernard. I was silent for a few seconds, thinking how best to respond. Finally, I gave up. "Thank you for lunch. Shall we go now?"

His eyes lingered on my chest again as he got to his feet. "By all means. Lead the way to the next house, my dear."

This guy was trouble—I was sure of it. As we drove toward the house, his car following closely at my bumper, I found myself wondering what I would later say to Donna and wishing I hadn't forgotten my can of mace. Did I have enough nerve to tell her about the stunts her new husband was pulling, or should I clam up and leave well enough alone?

I pulled up in the driveway with Ken's car right behind me. It was a beautiful Tudor style home situated on ten acres. As I walked toward the porch, I gazed at the listing printout. It had only been on the market since last week. Then, for the first time, I spotted the listing agent's name. Tiffany Roberts. Ugh. Why hadn't I noticed that before?

"What's wrong?"

"This listing belonged to my murdered coworker. I can't seem to get away from her memory today for some reason." *Yeah, Cin, you know the reason. Because everyone thinks you're guilty.*

"Well, if you sell it to my mother, that'll fix everything, right?"

I gasped. "That's a horrible thing to say."

Ken grinned and held the screen door ajar while I punched my code in and produced the key, which I then stuck into the heavy oak door, turning the knob slowly.

Without warning, Ken grabbed my hand and gently pushed me through the doorway. "Pretty ladies first."

He was really starting to get on my nerves. Somehow I managed a slight smile and entered the home with Ken at my heels.

This was the type of house I'd always dreamed about. A large crystal chandelier hung from the high vaulted ceiling in the foyer. To the right was a formal dining room, adorned with another glittering chandelier. The eight-piece, cherry wood dining room set was accentuated by a buffet table and china cabinet. To the left of the foyer stood a winding oak staircase, which I assumed led to the bedrooms.

Beyond the staircase was a large family room with two fire-places, one opposite a handsome built-in, oak bookcase. The other was accompanied by a sectional, loveseat, and flat-screen television about 70 inches in size, which almost took up the entire wall. It was revolting, yet stunning.

French doors led to the patio and an in-ground pool with an adjacent pool house. A sunken hot tub was situated on a large wood-grain deck that ran the entire length of the back of the house. Now this was paradise.

Ken put his arm around me and led me to the right. "Let's go see the kitchen."

It was a splendid affair with stainless steel appliances, double wall ovens, a huge island in the center of the room, and pristine granite countertops. I was able to see my reflection in the polished, hardwood floors throughout the house. Persian rugs were tastefully scattered about. Everything was immaculate. As I placed my business card on the counter, I felt as if I'd cluttered the place.

We went back to the foyer and up the stairs. I thought it odd not to see any photos strewn about. They could be found everywhere in my home. Four large bedrooms occupied the second floor, each with its own connecting bathroom. The baths were completely done in marble—floor, counters, and walls. Each was a different color, ranging from pink to black, dark blue, and powder blue.

Although the baths, like the rest of the house, were elegant, the overall effect of so much marble struck me as cold and sterile. In fact, the entire house was so picture-perfect I was starting to wonder if the owner still occupied it. This hadn't been noted on the listing.

As we entered the largest master bedroom, I was unable to place the familiar scent that suddenly filled my nostrils. A light, airy smell that reminded me of lilacs. Where had I encountered that fragrance before? I wasn't surprised to find yet another fireplace. The owner seemed to be addicted to them. A king size bed was covered with a pink organza spread. The built-in California closet was full of clothes and more designer shoes than I'd ever seen in one place, except for *Sex and the City* re-runs. A white baby grand piano took up a large portion of the room.

"Kind of an odd place for a piano, isn't it?" Ken mused, leading me away from the closet where I longed to examine the lovely clothes.

"I guess so." I stopped briefly to admire an exquisite black-and-white porcelain vase, which sat on top of the piano. I gently turned it around. "How beautiful. This must be worth some serious money."

I took a step back as Ken reached out his hand for the vase. He lifted it up doubtfully, looked at the bottom, and placed it back down with a shake of his head. "This is worthless. It's nothing but a cheap imitation. Nice try though." He headed for the doorway and turned around to wink at me. "Let's see the other bedrooms."

As we walked down the sterile hallway with my high heels clicking on the travertine, I could feel the wine and two glasses of water from lunch catching up with me. "Excuse me for a second. I need to use the bathroom."

"Of course, doll. I'll have a quick peek around, if that's all right."

"Fine." It was a relief to be rid of him for a few minutes. He was creepy, and considering the come-ons, I actually felt sorry for Donna—a sentiment I never thought I'd experience.

And then there was this house. Something about it was bothering me, almost like a déjà vu affect. As I washed my hands in the sink, the front door slammed. *Maybe he's going to look at the swimming pool.* That would be good. I could meet him outside, exchange good-byes, and hopefully never have to lay eyes on the slime again.

As I exited the bathroom, Ken was ascending the long, winding oak staircase two steps at a time. Darn. No such luck.

"I thought I heard the front door shut. Are you ready to go?"

"Oh, I was examining the rose bushes," Ken said casually. "My mother's crazy about flowers, and it looks like they're going to bloom well this year. I think she'll love this house."

"Really?" My previous thoughts about the man were momentarily forgotten. "Do you want to schedule another showing?"

I tried to contain my enthusiasm and remember Real Estate 101—nothing was a sure thing until you got to the closing table. I was already calculating in my mind what kind of commission I could make on this deal. Even if Ken came in with a lowball offer, my payout would still be over ten grand. I was giddy with excitement at the thought as it meant our money problems would be over for a while. And I could always bring Jacques back with me for the next showing. Or maybe Donna would want to show it to her mother-in-law personally. I didn't want to be anywhere around this man again.

"Let me call her tonight." Ken put his arm around me and led me toward another master bedroom, done in a neutral, black-and-white color scheme. "She'll be in town next week, so I think it's a good chance. She always does exactly what her boy tells her."

I made an attempt at a half-hearted laugh while I removed his hand from my shoulder for the umpteenth time today. He let me enter the bedroom first. It was a similar setup to the other one. Huge gas fireplace with two comfortable easy chairs in front of it, a similar walk-in closet, although this one was empty, and a king size bed with a black-and-white organza spread.

"It's such a gorgeous house." I felt his hand on my backside and whirled around angrily. "You need to keep your hands to yourself."

"Come on, baby. You know you want it."

What a conceited pig. "This showing is now over." Furious, I headed for the doorway, but he grabbed me and pulled me into his arms.

I struggled to free myself. "I said that's enough."

He practically whined in my ear. "Aw, hot stuff, give me a break. Donna's boring. And ugly. I'm betting George is too."

"No, *Greg's* not. Do Donna a favor and grant her an annulment. Even she deserves better than *you.*"

I hoped this would cause him to let go, but he only tightened his grip and managed to capture my mouth with his. My insides filled with dread, and I thought I was going to be sick to my stomach. Why hadn't I trusted my gut instinct with this man?

I managed to get one hand free and push his face away. "Don't ever do that again. You need to leave. Now."

"Don't fight it, doll. Relax and enjoy." He pushed me backward up against the wall and pinned me there, clamping his hands over my arms. He kissed me again while the panic inside me rose at lightning speed.

Ken chuckled and leaned back for a second to study my face. "I love a feisty woman."

At that moment, I lifted my right leg and thrust my knee as hard as I could into his crotch. I watched the color drain from Ken's face as he released his hold on me and collapsed to the floor with a groan. Shaken, I reached inside my purse and searched inside for a weapon. Anything. The best I could come up with was my car key, which I pointed at him as I grabbed my phone with the other. Heck, it was better than nothing.

Ken grabbed the bed for support as he slowly rose to his feet. Dark eyes shot daggers at me, and his voice became a low, angry growl. "You bitch."

My breath came out in quick, short gasps. "Get out of this house before I—I call the police. And Donna too."

Ken staggered toward the bedroom doorway and turned to give me one last menacing look. "No wonder you can't get any sales. You haven't learned what it means to give and take in this business. So long, loser."

I stood there, feet frozen to the floor, listening to him thump his way down the stairs, until the front door slammed, and his BMW roared off. I rushed down the stairs, locked the front door, and ran for the safety of my car. I couldn't get away from here fast enough. The chill that I got from standing in that picture-perfect house was almost as bad as the episode I'd just experienced with Mr. Frisky Fingers.

After traveling about a mile down the main road, I pulled into a department store parking lot and reached for my phone, hands still shaking. I could barely manage to press the number in my contacts section.

He answered on the first ring. "How's it going, love?"

The tears I'd been holding back finally streamed down my face as my shoulders convulsed with sobs. "Can you come and meet me? I really need you."

CHAPTER ELEVEN

*J*acques rubbed my back in a comforting manner until I managed to pull myself together. "Do you want another drink?"

We had met in the parking lot of Starbucks, the same one we'd been to earlier in the day, but I refused to go inside. I was a hot mess, and it had taken me almost half an hour to finally stop shaking. "No, thanks. I'm okay now."

He pushed the hair back from my face. "You're not okay, love. Tell me where to find that scumbag, and I'll kill him myself."

I shook my head vigorously. "I just want to forget about it."

Jacque's jaw dropped. "Are you crazy? The guy accosted you. If you hadn't gotten away he might have—" His eyes darkened.

I put my hands to my ears. "Please don't say the word."

"You *have* to tell Donna. Maybe you should go to the police too."

I rubbed my temples in agitation. "No. She'll fire me. And Ken will find a way to deny everything. I know his type."

"Cin—"

"I need this job, Jacques."

"Listen, who cares what Donna does? And it's not the end of the world if you lose this job. I have something else in mind for you anyway."

I gave him my best pleading look. "Please. Let me think about what to do for a day or two. I have to wait until after my closing, or she might try to cheat me out of the money. And for God's sake, don't tell Greg."

He frowned. "Sweetie, your hubby barely says boo to me, so that won't be a problem. But I don't like this. Greg has to know, and I think Donna should too. I realize she's the Wicked Witch of the West's twin, but even Donna deserves to know she married a sleazeball."

He was right. "Okay, I'll tell her. But *after* the closing. Right now, I just want to go home."

Jacque's face was somber as he stared at me. I could have sworn I saw a tear behind the designer eyewear. "Cin, you're like my own sister. I don't ever want to see anyone hurt you."

A lump in my throat kept me from speaking for a full minute. I gave him a kiss on the cheek, grabbed my purse, and opened the passenger side door of his car. "If I leave now, I'll just make it before the twins get home."

"Promise me you'll think about what I said? And you'll call later?"

"I will. And thanks—for being a lifesaver. I love you."

He gazed at me soberly. "I love you too, dear."

I arrived home as the school bus pulled up in front of the house. I waved to Barb, their bus driver, who greeted me with a slicing motion across her throat. Great. Everyone was a comedian these days.

The twins waited at the front door impatiently while I locked my car and grabbed the mail.

Seth stared at me. "You don't look so good, Mom. Your face is like the color of Mrs. White's hair."

"Did you throw up your lunch?" Stevie asked.

"I'm fine, guys. How was school?"

"You were the best part of the day," Stevie said. "Everybody was talking about you at lunch. Elizabeth asked if we could go on a field trip to visit you when you land in the slammer."

Something to look forward to. "How nice."

"Mrs. White left right after you did. Mrs. Lewis came in to teach the class for the rest of the day." Seth headed for the snack cabinet in the kitchen.

I reached inside the fridge and grabbed him an apple instead. "What was wrong with Mrs. White?"

Stevie shrugged. "She said she didn't feel well. I heard her tell Mrs. Lewis, 'one more year and I'm out of this hellhole.' Why'd she say that?"

I chose to ignore his question. "Hey, who wants cookies to take downstairs if they do their homework?"

"Is this a bribe?" Seth asked.

"Only a little one."

After the twins headed downstairs, I went to my room and changed into jeans and a sweatshirt. What a horrible day. The bed looked so inviting that I decided to lie down for a few minutes. I found myself thinking about Ken again, and the bile started to rise in the back of my throat. I knew I had to do something to keep my mind occupied, so I got up and folded some laundry sitting in a nearby basket.

Downstairs, the twins shrieked with laughter. There was a repeated thud, with something loud hitting the wall. I guessed they were throwing Rusty's ball across the hardwood floor and laughing as he'd slide across to get it, banging his head into the wall in the process. He was cute but not the brightest of pups.

I got up and went down to the kitchen to start dinner. Tomorrow morning was our weekly office meeting. How I was dreading it. I thought about not going this time but feared it would make me look worse if I didn't show. And how the heck was I supposed to face Donna after what happened with her husband today?

I'd been playing phone tag with Sylvia Banks for the last couple of days but had finally managed to reach her last night. I knew she was looking for another agent and now had an appointment to interview with her agency, No Place Like Home Realty, tomorrow morning. If she was aware of Tiffany's death, she hadn't mentioned it. I was starting to wonder how the current circumstances would affect my being received at other prospective offices.

I flipped through the mail I'd brought in with me. A couple of bills, a flyer, and an envelope addressed to me. My name and address were typed neatly, all in capital letters. I turned it over. No return address. I remembered the note from this morning, and a sick sensation swept over me. I tore the envelope open with shaking fingers.

Inside was a picture of Tiffany, lying on the floor of her office. My heart stuttered in my chest, and my breathing became so rapid that I was afraid it might suffocate me. A sheet of white copy paper accompanied the picture with a two-line message, also typed in all capital letters. It read, *I know you did it, and I can prove it with this picture.*

The picture lay on the floor, face up, where I'd dropped it. Tiffany's face blurred, and I saw Paul again. He was lying motion-less with a gun in his hand. I became light-headed and sat down on the couch, shuddering violently. The urge to scream or cry was great, but I didn't want to frighten the boys. The walls began to close in as they always did when I became panicked. Lunch and the wine I'd consumed weren't helping, either. With my head between my knees, I focused on my breathing as I gave myself a mental pep talk. *You are not going to faint. Don't worry. You did nothing wrong.*

I reached for my phone and dialed Jacques' number.

He answered on the first ring. "Cin, are you okay?"

A tear rolled down my cheek before I could stop it. "I don't think so."

"Did you tell Greg about Ken the Groper?"

"No, it's not that. I—I got a picture in the mail. It's her—Tiffany. Someone's threatening me." I gulped.

"You're not making any sense."

I took a couple of deep breaths. "It's a picture of her—when she was murdered. It must have been taken right after she was killed."

"Oh my God."

"They said they have proof I did it."

"You've got to take it to the police."

"No way. Don't you know what this means? The police might think I took it when I killed her."

Jacques snorted into the phone. "I guess you don't understand what this really means. Whoever took the picture *is* the one who killed her."

"Why should they believe me? I'm scared, Jacques."

"Okay, okay. What does Greg say?"

"I haven't told him yet. He's been at a conference all day, so I'll show him tonight. But I'm *not* going to the police."

Jacques clucked his tongue in disdain. "Honey, you have to go. Not only for the note but because of old frisky fingers, too. What happens when his mother calls next week and wants to see one of the houses again? By the way, which ones did you show him today?"

A car door slammed, and I looked out the window. "Shoot, I've got to go. Greg's home early, and I haven't even started dinner yet."

"All right, call me later. And don't be late for the office meeting tomorrow," Jacques reminded me.

"I don't even want to think about it. How can I face Donna after everything that happened today?"

"I'll be there to protect you, don't worry. I won't let you down."

My heart overflowed. "You never do." I disconnected and ran into the kitchen to turn the oven on.

"You're quiet tonight, babe."

Greg was sitting at the kitchen table, reading the newspaper. He seemed to be concentrating unusually hard as he'd been reading the same page for over twenty minutes now.

Stevie and Seth were out back on the trampoline, and Darcy was upstairs, talking on her cell phone. She said she was doing homework, but I knew better.

"Just tired, I guess." I glanced up from the stove, where I was making meatloaf and mashed potatoes.

"So, anything interesting happen today?" he asked.

I shivered. That was a loaded question. I didn't want to tell Greg what had happened because I knew he would track Ken down like a rabid dog and probably kill him. Or, at the very least, maim him for life. Like most married couples, Greg and I often knew what the other one was thinking. We even finished each other's sentences. I was afraid he'd figure it out before I told him.

The smart thing would be to get it over with and somehow try to make light of it, but I couldn't bring myself to do it. Instead, I gave him a blow-by-blow account of my day. "Well, a reporter came to the house and wanted to do a story on me. You know, the killer-of-the-year feature. Then I went to the school, and the twins' classmates basically accused me of murder. After that, I showed a couple of houses to a client, and we stopped for lunch. I told you about it last night, remember?"

Greg put down the paper. His eyes burned into mine as he

spoke in a low, angry tone. "Yes, I remember. Donna's new husband, right? Ken, wasn't it?"

I started to feel sick at the mention of his name. "Yes."

He studied the paper again. "I heard you looked quite cozy together at lunch."

Please let this day be a bad dream. My heart skipped a beat. "What are you talking about?"

Greg slammed the paper down. "Tom Shipley was having lunch right next to you and said he heard you guys laughing and carrying on. And who the hell is that scumbag to put his arm around my wife?"

Wonderful, a full report. "Who's Tom Shipley?"

"He's the warehouse manager. You met him and his wife at the Christmas party. You were a bit snookered then, too, so perhaps you don't recall him. He remembered you though. Described my wife perfectly, and the jerk who couldn't keep his hands off her." His voice became acid-like. "Who does he think he is to touch my property?"

"Your *property*?" I managed to squeak out. What was this, the Middle Ages? I flung the dishcloth down on the counter and squared my shoulders against him. In the past twelve hours I'd been threatened by a reporter, interrogated by a class of eight-year-olds, groped and nearly attacked by my boss's husband, delivered two menacing notes, and now my husband thinks I may be cheating on him?

I fought to control the anger rising inside me. "I don't believe this. What do you really think, Greg? That I went to meet my manager's husband at some sleazy hotel?"

A muscle ticked in his jaw. "No. I know you'd never do something like that."

"Then what's the problem?"

"What's the *problem*?" Greg echoed, in full-blown screaming mode now. "Tom said the guy looked like George Clooney, and he was all over you. And you're asking me what the problem is?"

This would have been a good time to tell him the truth, but my pride wouldn't let me. At that moment I was more concerned with the fact that my husband didn't trust me, so I said nothing.

"Don't you have anything to say for yourself?"

I sighed wearily as I turned off the stove and headed for the front door. "Tell the kids dinner is ready."

He jumped out of his chair and followed me. "Where are you going?"

"For a walk. I need to clear my head."

Greg scoffed. "Well, that figures. Whenever things get rough you rush right out the door."

I turned on him, exasperated. "I'm leaving because I can't talk any sense into you when you act like this. For the last time, nothing happened. Not what you think anyway."

"And what exactly does that mean?"

I took a deep breath. "It means I love you and would never do anything to hurt you. But I can't keep defending myself to you or anyone else. This is all getting—" My voice broke as tears filled my eyes, making it difficult to see.

"Cin." Greg put a hand on my shoulder, but I angrily shook him off and reached for the doorknob. At that moment, the twins came running in from the backyard.

"Is dinner ready?" Stevie wanted to know. "Where are you going, Mom?"

"I need to get some air." I didn't want the boys to know we'd been arguing, so I kept my tearstained face turned in the other direction.

"Are you going to the police station to turn yourself in?" Seth asked excitedly.

I shut the door behind me so that they wouldn't see me cry, then took off at a run down the driveway. I ran from Tiffany, Ken, and Donna—all the people causing havoc in my life. I made it to the next street in our development and quickly slowed to a walk, gasping for air, with my chest about to explode. I'd never been a runner. Back in high school, it was all I could do to finish one lap in gym without falling on my face in exhaustion.

In my haste, I'd forgotten a jacket. The early evening air was brisk, although not as cold as the night I'd gone to meet Tiffany. I walked with my arms wrapped around me, head bent down against the wind.

This day was growing worse by the minute. I was on pins and needles wondering if the police might show up to arrest me. Since finding Tiffany, I couldn't stop thinking about Paul. My entire career was in the toilet. And now this whole episode with Ken. I *had* to tell Greg. I knew this, but wasn't looking forward to it. The coward in me just wanted to forget about the incident. My only hope for some relief was to find out who Tiffany's killer was.

I stopped dead in my tracks. Was this why the killer was sending me things? Were they afraid that I knew something? Could it be someone in the office? Bill, or maybe Pete? Perhaps Jacques was right. I had to be at the office meeting tomorrow. Someone might slip up, and I needed to hear what was said.

With a deep sigh, I turned back toward the house. The sun sank quickly in a vibrant sky streaked with orange and red. As I watched it disappear, I was ashamed of myself. Greg had always been there for me, and now I didn't even have the nerve to tell him the truth. I tried to put myself in his shoes. If someone tried to hurt him, I'd be upset if he didn't share it with me. Trust was the basis for our marriage. Without it, we wouldn't have one.

I thought again about the house Tiffany had listed days before her death. There was something unsettling about the place, and it was really starting to bother me. Why couldn't I get it out of my head?

I slowly turned the front doorknob and entered the house. Silence greeted me at first, interrupted by a faint sound coming from the kitchen where Greg was washing the dishes. I stood for a moment behind him, watching his powerful shoulders move back and forth. He sensed my presence and turned around.

"Where's Darcy?" I asked. "She's supposed to be doing those."

"She said she had a history test to study for, so I let her off the hook." Greg observed me carefully for a long moment. The beautiful ocean-blue eyes I adored were full of pain. He turned back around to the sink.

My heart ached. The last thing I wanted to do was hurt my husband. I started toward the den, then stopped and flung my arms around him from the back.

He switched off the water, calmly dried his hands on a towel, and turned around to gather me in his arms. "I'm sorry," he whispered into my hair. "I was way out of line."

Tears spilled over my cheeks. "You have nothing to be sorry about. It's all my fault. I should have told you what really happened when you asked."

His body tensed against mine. "What are you talking about?"

I blew out a sigh. "I never should have taken him to see those houses today."

Greg held me away from him at arm's length so that he could study my face. His mouth hardened into a thin, firm line. "He made a pass at you, didn't he?"

I lowered my eyes to the floor. Greg lifted my chin in his hand until my eyes were level with his blazing ones. "Answer the question, please."

"Yes," I whispered.

A four-letter word spilled out of Greg's mouth. He stood there for a moment, clenching and unclenching his fists at his side. "I'll kill the bastard."

"No. I think we should forget about it."

"Not likely. Tell me exactly what he did."

Not a good idea. "That's not important."

"The hell it isn't." As he continued to stare at me, a look of alarm swept over his face. He gripped me by the shoulders, his face turning white. "Did he try to—?"

I burst into tears. Again. "No. It didn't get that far. Please, Greg. I don't want to talk about him anymore." I threw my arms around his waist, burying my face into his chest. "Don't worry. He won't forget about it anytime too soon."

He lifted my face and cradled it between his hands. "What did you do to him?"

"Let's just say that my knee happened to connect with a sensitive part of his body that he seemed very fond of."

Greg's mouth twitched at the corners. "That's my girl."

I wiped my eyes with the back of my hand. "I promise to tell Donna, but I'm sure she won't believe me. Please don't do anything for now. We have to wait until after my closing tomorrow. We can't afford to lose the money."

"Cynthia Ann, think about me for a minute. How am I supposed to live with myself if I don't go to this guy's house and punch his lights out?"

"I never have to see him again. Even if he does want one of those houses, which I doubt, I'll have no part of it. "

Clearly frustrated, Greg ran a hand through his hair. "All right, baby. I'll let you handle it your way—for now. But if I happen to see him, or he comes anywhere near you again, he's going to lose a few teeth." He kissed the tip of my nose. "I'm sorry I got angry with you."

"I'm the one who's sorry. I should have told you as soon as you got home."

Greg wiped a lone tear off my cheek. "Forgive me?" His voice filled with raw emotion as he tenderly covered my mouth with his.

I sighed with contentment after we broke apart. "There's nothing to forgive. But I do have to tell you something else. And don't worry, it has nothing to do with Ken."

His face paled. "Now what?"

I grabbed my purse off the kitchen counter, then handed him the envelope with Tiffany's picture and the note that had been on our door.

Greg pursed his lips together as he examined the picture and then glanced anxiously at me. "When did you get these? And why didn't you tell me about it sooner?"

"One this morning, and the other in the afternoon mail." I folded my arms across my stomach. "I was afraid and knew you'd want to take them to the police. I'm scared. What if they think I killed her and took the picture?"

Greg was silent for a minute. "You have to tell the police, Cin. The killer took these."

That was the same thing Jacques had said. "They might think I wrote the notes myself, trying to throw them off track."

He placed his hands on my shoulders. "First off, you've done nothing wrong, so why shouldn't you report it? Second, if you give these to the police, it might help them catch the real killer."

I hadn't thought of that. I'd been too busy panicking and worrying about what the police would do to me. "You're right. Okay, I'll go down there in the morning, after my office meeting."

"That's my girl." He hugged me. "What time does your meeting wrap up?"

I tucked both envelopes back into my purse. "Around eleven or so. And my closing is scheduled for 1:30, so that doesn't leave me a lot of time."

"Call me when your meeting is over. I'll come to the police station with you. I don't want you to go alone."

I threw my arms around his neck. "Thank you."

He stroked my cheek gently with his fingers as he gazed into my eyes. "There's no need to thank me. I happen to love you and our kids more than anything in this world."

"What would I ever do without you?" I said softly.

Greg smiled as he brushed his lips lightly across mine. "You'll always have me. We're in this together, babe."

As I hugged my wonderful husband, I felt a twinge of sympathy for Donna. She thought she'd won the lottery with her new, snake-in-the-grass husband. The truth was that I had hit the jackpot long before her. Seventeen years ago, to be exact. Something told me her marriage was not destined for such a long term.

"This might sound crazy with everything else going on, but right now, I feel like the luckiest woman alive."

Greg didn't say anything. His only response was to wrap his arms tighter around me while I rested my head against his broad chest. We stayed like that for several minutes, listening to the boys' roughhousing with the puppy downstairs and Darcy's lilting voice coming through the ceiling above. *So much for that history test.*

I clung to my husband gratefully, hoping that our world would return to its normal chaotic state soon.

CHAPTER TWELVE

*T*he school bus honked again as I shouted in the direction of the stairs. "Darcy, the bus isn't going to wait forever."

"Mom, I'm not a moron." Darcy gave me one of her cute little pouts as she appeared in the doorway of the kitchen and grabbed her lunch from me.

"Don't forget I need you to come straight home with the boys today. I have a closing and will probably be late."

Darcy didn't even look in my direction. "Yeah, whatever. Bye, Daddy." She blew Greg a kiss and strolled nonchalantly out the door.

"She's only fifteen, Cin." Greg shook his head as he watched his daughter board the bus wearing tight designer jeans, flip flops, and a flimsy tank top. At my insistence, she carried a sweater, but I knew she wouldn't wear it. "What kind of father lets his daughter go to school dressed like a hooker?"

"She doesn't look like one of those, and please don't say that again." I turned around to see the twins at the kitchen table pouring Cheerios into bowls until they ran over onto the floor. Rusty lay at their feet, gorging himself on cereal.

I handed Greg his lunch. "What can I do? She refuses to listen to me, and all the girls wear that stuff these days."

"What's a hooker?" Stevie asked.

"Remember that episode of *The Sopranos* we saw?" Seth glanced over at his twin. "You know, when Tony meets a lady in the bar?"

My mouth dropped open, and I exchanged a glance with Greg. "You guys are forbidden to watch that show. Period. You're way too young."

"Aw, Mom," Seth said. "I'm really mature for my age."

Stevie nodded. "Yeah. Me too. I think. What's mature again?"

Greg sighed heavily. "Okay, guys, go upstairs and get dressed. Your bus will be here soon."

"Are you and Mom going to yell at each other again?" Stevie asked.

Greg's face reddened. "Now."

"Guess so," Seth mumbled as he and Stevie hopped off their chairs. They ran out of the kitchen and could be heard clattering up the stairs.

I got a broom and started to sweep up the mess from the floor, much to Rusty's chagrin.

Greg brought his briefcase in from the den. He waited until I finished sweeping and pulled me into his arms. "Are you feeling okay?"

I smiled reassuringly. "I'm fine. Thanks to you."

He pursed his lips together. "Cin, what happens if that jerk wants to buy one of those houses you showed him? How will you deal with that?"

"I doubt he's going to be calling me. Not after what I did to him."

Greg grinned and kissed me tenderly. "No one messes around with my girl. I never knew what a great hook you had."

"More like, what a great knee," I teased.

Greg laughed as he released me and picked his jacket up from the chair. "Later, baby. Call me after your meeting."

"I will. Love you."

"Love you too. Good luck today."

"Thanks. I have a feeling I'll need it."

As I PULLED into the parking lot of Hospitable Homes, I realized the last time I'd been in the building was when I'd discovered Tiffany's lifeless body. I turned off the engine and sat motionless behind the wheel. I was nervous about seeing Donna. How was I supposed to tell my boss she was married to a sleaze? It was doubtful she'd believe me, so why even put myself through the grief?

I'd just restarted the motor when a sharp tap sounded on my window. I glanced around, startled.

Jacques motioned for me to roll the window down, and I obliged. "Don't even think about it."

"Come on. I can't go in there."

"Yes, you can. Just put one foot in front of the other."

I groaned as I turned off the motor again. "What's the point? She's going to fire me no matter what."

"You still need to collect your check from the closing later." Jacques extended his hand to help me out of the vehicle. "Plus, it looks better if you're here."

"I know, I know, so you keep telling me. We don't want them to think I have anything to hide."

Jacques hooked his arm through mine. "I won't leave your side, I swear."

"Well, I need to use the bathroom, so there goes that theory. I'll meet you in the conference room."

"Hurry up, honey, your macchiato's getting cold."

I could've kissed him. Instead, I went upstairs, flashbacks of the last time I'd been here haunting me. Tiffany's office door was shut, with crime scene tape still stretched across the front. Her murder wasn't a bad dream as I'd been trying to pretend. I wondered if the blood had been cleaned up or if it was still all over the floor. My stomach rumbled, but not from hunger, and I barely made it to the bathroom in time.

I was washing my face when I heard a tap on the door. I opened it a crack, barely enough to see who was out there.

"Cindy, are you okay?" Jacques looked alarmed when he saw my face. "Holy cow, did you get sick?"

I nodded, too weak to say anything.

Jacques put his arm around me and led me down the stairs. "Cripes. For someone who's given birth to three kids, you've got the weakest stomach of anybody I know. You must have spent your entire pregnancies in the bathroom."

"You have no idea."

"Try to hold it together, girl. This is important. And for God's sake, don't faint when you see Donna."

"I'll do my best, but I can't promise anything."

"Yeah, I know your track record."

Everyone else had already gathered in the large conference room downstairs. It was a comfortable room, with wood-grain paneling and plush, beige carpeting, which we used primarily for the weekly office go-around and private client meetings. Donna also brought agents in there for performance evaluations, another occasion I always dreaded. Since mine was already past due, it seemed safe to say I probably wouldn't have to endure another one.

If there was a guest for the meeting, such as a mortgage broker or motivational speaker, they would be seated at the head of the mahogany table. Today the spot was occupied by Donna. I tried to walk in inconspicuously, but everyone stopped what they were doing to gawk at me.

I purposely sank into a chair at the back of the room.

Jacques appeared a minute later with my macchiato and a can of ginger ale. He sat down next to me and handed me the soda.

"What would I do without you?" I squeezed his hand tightly.

Jacques whispered in my ear. "Something's up. She's acting like you're not even here. Do you think Mr. Libido told her what happened?"

"I doubt it. Would you tell Ed if you made a pass at someone?"

"Point well taken." He sat back in his chair.

When Donna cleared her throat, we stopped talking. She didn't mention Tiffany or the murder and immediately turned her full attention to Jacques. "Where are we with the Goldman deal?"

He stared calmly back at her. "The bank issued the approval letter yesterday. I expect to hear about a closing sometime next week."

Donna placed her hands on her hips. "Excellent. That sale was almost a million, wasn't it?"

"Yes. The sellers were anxious to relocate, and the price is still above market value. They granted a seller's concession to the buyers as well, which will save them some money, so I think it worked out well for all involved," Jacques said quietly.

I gazed at my friend in admiration. The man made the real estate game look so damned easy.

Donna smiled at the rest of us. "Well, I'm glad to hear someone is actually bringing in money. Does anyone else have news to report?"

I raised my hand. "I have a closing today on—"

"Yes, Bill?" She didn't even glance in my direction.

Jacques rolled his eyes at me. *Oh boy.* Maybe Ken did tell her. I wouldn't put anything past the woman or her slimeball of a husband. I glanced at the clock and shifted uncomfortably in my seat. *Please let this be over soon.*

"I-I have an appointment this afternoon to list an a-apartment complex over on Vista Lane," Bill replied.

Donna looked like a cat waiting to pounce on a mouse. "And what are you planning to list it for?"

Bill shrugged, clearly uneasy under her scrutiny. "Well, I, uh—"

"How many units are in the building? Is there oil heat or gas? What's the number of bedrooms?"

Bill took off his glasses and polished them nervously. In desperation, he turned to Jacques for help.

Jacques cleared his throat. "Bill asked me to take a look at the building with him. It's in pretty good shape overall. The foundation might have some cracks in it. I have a friend who's a mason, and he's willing to check it out free of charge. If all goes well, I'm guessing Bill could put it on the market for half a million or so."

Donna made a face. "That's all?"

She was obviously disappointed. *Note to self. Do not mention your insignificant, chump-change closing unless you want to be laughed at.*

"I-I'm sorry, Donna," Bill stuttered. "I'll try to do better next time."

"See that you do."

Jacques pursed his lips. "Now wait just a minute."

Everyone looked at him and then turned back toward Donna to gauge her reaction.

"What is it, Jacques?" Donna's voice took on an acid tone.

"Bill's only been here for a few months. He's doing his best. I know you want us to pick up the slack now that—well, Tiffany's gone, and we're all trying. It's not going to help to belittle anyone though."

Donna's face turned a bright shade of red. "I'd like to speak with you in private after the meeting."

Jacques didn't even flinch. "My pleasure."

"Does anyone have anything else to report?" Donna's eyes glittered as she rapped a pencil on the table. "We need sales, people. Start pounding the pavement!"

Jacques waved his hand. "Oh, I did forget to mention one thing."

Bill stood. "I really have to get going since I have a—"

"Sit." Donna spoke sharply, as if addressing a dog. Bill reluctantly obeyed. "Yes, Jacques?"

"You asked me to reach out to Mrs. Hunter, who'd signed a listing with Tiffany earlier in the week."

I gaped at him. Jacques knew that was my listing. Where was this going?

He crossed one leg over the other. "Mrs. Hunter was only too happy to void the contract and indicated she'd like to re-list the house with Cindy, who rightfully should have had it in the first place."

Everyone murmured their approval while I smiled at Jacques gratefully. He winked in return.

Donna concentrated on shuffling some papers in front of her. "Well, that's fine. Of course, the place does need a lot of work and won't fetch much money. It's really a waste for us to spend a lot of time and resources on her account. I do hope you understand that. I think I need to give this some further thought and decide whether or not it's in our best interest to pursue this listing."

I didn't know if she was speaking to me or Jacques. It was difficult to tell since she refused to make eye contact with either one of us. Not that it really mattered anyway. I wasn't surprised she would pull something like this.

Jacques tapped his pen against the side of my chair. "A sale is a sale."

Donna slammed her notebook shut. "If you think it's so easy to run this agency, perhaps you'd like to give it a try."

"Thank you very much, but I have other plans."

Her mouth fell open in surprise. She couldn't afford to lose Jacques in addition to Tiffany and certainly wasn't dumb enough to engage him in a heated public argument. "Let's talk about this later. I'm sure we can work something out."

"Of course." He gave a slight nod.

I was intrigued. Jacques had his broker's license and had dreamed of opening his own agency for years, but I thought that was still a way off. This place would never survive without him. It was definitely time for me to abandon ship.

"And now, everyone, I've saved the most important part for last." Donna folded her hands together.

Here it comes.

"Please join me in praying for our dearly departed coworker, Tiffany Roberts, who suddenly left the world three days ago." She glanced around at all of us. "Bow your heads."

We all looked helplessly at one another, then stared back at Donna, puzzled.

"Now."

With no choice but to oblige, I bowed my head.

"May God protect and welcome her into His pearly-white gates," Donna breathed.

Jacques kicked me under the chair. When I dared to open my eyes and steal a glance at him, he was shaking his head in disbelief.

"We'll all miss her so." Donna's touching speech ended with a sob.

At that very moment, Linda Earl, our receptionist, started to giggle. Jacques had a smile forming at the corners of his mouth while everyone else kept their heads bowed.

Donna's nostrils flared. "Is there something funny?"

Linda stopped laughing immediately, her dark eyes wide with alarm, and had the decency to appear embarrassed. "Oh, no. I'm sorry for interrupting the prayer. I couldn't help thinking that—"

"You thought today? Well, there's a start." Donna wrinkled her nose.

My jaw dropped at the rude remark. In her mid-twenties, Linda was a very attractive brunette with enormous, brown eyes and a killer figure. She was a little slow on the uptake some days, and we all knew that Donna had only hired her to attract more business. Linda's face was also featured on the home page of the company's website. She was definitely not here for her business skills.

Linda's face turned crimson, the remark not lost on even her. "I know this sounds bad, but she wasn't exactly a nice person. No one liked her."

Bill clenched his fists. "That's true." I was surprised that he dared to speak again. "I did-did an open house for her last week, and she was supposed to g-give me all the leads. When I went to-to call people on the sign-in sheet, I couldn't find it. That lit-little witch had stolen it right off my desk."

Everyone, except Donna, clucked their tongues at this new bit of information while Jacques kept his head down so that no one but me could see him smiling. I found myself wondering if Tiffany would have done the same thing to me if I'd had any good leads at her open house. Actually, there was no doubt in my mind.

Linda tossed her hair. "I've seen her do worse. Monday night we both left the office at the same time. My car wouldn't start, so I went to ask her for a ride. I knocked on her window, but she pretended she didn't hear or see me. She almost drove right over my foot."

"Horrid," said Ariel Jones, an African-American woman a few years older than myself. She'd been with the agency about the same length of time as me. "That's what she was—horrid. I found her going through my desk last week. When I asked what she was doing, she said she needed a tissue, even though there was a box right on top of my desk. She stole my lead sheet. As far as I'm concerned, that wench got what she deserved."

"It's karma." Bill glanced around the room, as if for approval. "Wh-what goes around, comes around."

The others nodded in agreement as Donna rose to her feet, trembling with fury. She slammed her fist on the table and everyone jumped. "You should all be ashamed of yourselves. Tiffany was the bread and butter of this organization. She could outsell all of you every month."

Jacques folded his arms across his chest. "Because she stole everyone's listings. She was dishonest and despicable. I know it's wrong to speak ill of the dead, but come on, Donna. Don't act like she was a saint. Look what she did to Cindy, for cripes' sake."

Oh no. Not a good thing to say. I had a sudden impulse to crawl under the table.

As Donna finally met my gaze, a sudden gleam came into her eyes. She placed both hands on her hips and thrust her chest forward. "Speaking of Cindy, I have the question of the day for her."

I forced my eyes to meet hers. "I hate to disappoint you, Donna, but I did not kill Tiffany."

"She had every right to though." Bill nodded in approval. "How many listings and clients did sh-she steal from you, Cindy? It's probably more than she took fr-from the rest of us combined."

"Tiffany treated me like her personal secretary," Linda interrupted. "If I didn't write a detailed message of who called and when, she got really ticked off." She glanced at me. "No one would have blamed you if you'd killed her, Cindy. Heck, I thought about it myself sometimes. Especially the other night."

"Oh, honey, who didn't?" Ariel asked.

Linda grinned. "Hey, it's too bad we didn't all plan to do it together. We could have had a drink to celebrate afterward."

The others laughed until Donna gasped out loud. "That's enough!"

The room went deadly silent as Donna's unwavering gaze remained fixed on me. "Thank you for clearing that up, Mrs. York, but I wasn't referring to the murder."

"I don't understand." What was she getting at?

Her smile twisted until she reminded me of the Cheshire cat. "Why were you at Tiffany's house yesterday? Your eKEY code showed up in my email this morning."

My jaw dropped so low that I thought it must have hit the floor. "Her-her house?"

Donna looked victorious as she watched me squirm like a fly trapped in a spider web. "Yes, Cindy, you were at Tiffany's house. The address is 55 Riverview Drive. It's a Tudor style home that came on the market last week. Does it sound familiar?"

All eyes in the room turned toward me. No one was laughing now.

CHAPTER THIRTEEN

I sat in my office, arms wrapped around my knees, rocking myself back and forth like a frightened child. Jacques had gone to get me a glass of water in the hope that my shallow breathing would return to normal.

Although startled, I had tried to explain to Donna why I had been at Tiffany's house, but she'd refused to listen. She'd immediately dismissed everyone from the room and had left the building herself seconds later. I, in turn, had started to feel sick again and made a mad dash for the bathroom, but this time it was a false alarm.

Jacques shut my door so that our conversation couldn't be overheard. He held the cup of water out to me. "Drink this, dear."

My words came out a whisper. "Thank you."

"My God, love, your lips are blue." Jacques reached for the sweater on the back of my chair and draped it around my shoulders. "Do you want me to call Greg?"

I took a sip. *Greg.* "Darn it. I was supposed to call him after the meeting. He wanted to go to the police station with me about the notes I received."

Jacques arched his eyebrows. "I thought it was only a picture. They left you a note too?"

I nodded and took another sip.

His face took on a worried expression "Greg's right. You do have to go to the police."

"Not after this. How do I explain why I was in her house? What am I going to do?"

"It doesn't look good, that's true." Suddenly, he snapped his fingers. "Wait a second. What about Cool Hand Ken? Would he be willing to tell the police he's the one who wanted to see the house? And all you did was arrange the showing for him?"

I rolled my eyes. "Yeah, I'm sure he'd be more than willing to help me out after what I did to him."

Jacques flashed a wicked grin. "I'll bet he's still hurting. Did you tell Greg about it? He must have wanted to beat the guy senseless."

"Yes, but I convinced him to let me handle this on my own for now. I wanted to wait until after my closing, but maybe that was a mistake. I'm not sure what to do anymore."

He looked at me doubtfully. "You really didn't know that was Tiffany's house?"

I shook my head. "Jeez, how the heck was I supposed to know?"

Jacques shrugged. "Don't take it so personally, dear. I thought you would have done a scan on the MLS to see where your fellow coworkers lived. Personally, I'm a bit of a stalker, so I always check those things out."

"I should have been more observant." I had known from the beginning that there was something off about that house. And the smell of lilacs in the bedroom. I should have recognized Tiffany's perfume.

Jacques stared absently at the knickknacks on my wall. "How weird of a coincidence is it that Ken would even want to see that house? I mean, what are the chances?"

We both looked at each other, thinking the same thing.

He put his arm around me. "Cripes, Cin. Do you think maybe Donna wanted him to set you up?"

A chill went down my spine. "I think there's a good chance. She'd love for me to take the blame for this. Why does she hate me so much? We've got to find out who killed Tiffany so that I can clear my name."

Jacques sat down in the chair behind my desk and snatched a memo pad off the top of it. "Okay. So let's look at the suspects. Anyone here could have done it. There's you, me, Bill, Linda, Donna, Ariel, and, of course, the newly departed Pete Saxon. But it could have been a disgruntled client too."

"Wait a second." I got to my feet. "Yesterday, when I was at the school, one of the kids started to tell me something about his aunt. She closed on a house recently with Tiffany."

He shrugged. "So? Tiffany had closings nearly every day."

"Yeah, well, Tyler's aunt—the one who bought the house— was really upset because the furnace broke down the day she moved in."

Jacques snorted. "Sounds like someone didn't have a good inspector."

"I didn't ask Tyler, but she might not have had inspections done since she was short on cash. I only know this because she was my client before Tiffany even got involved."

Jacques shook his head. "Tiffany stole her too? Damn, that chick was something else. And how could she advise a home buyer not to have inspections done?"

"You know how. Because she didn't care about her clients. Anyhow, Tyler told me something else. He said Leslie was so upset that she did something to Tiffany."

He leaned forward in anticipation. "What'd she do?"

"I don't know. The teacher came back into the room, and I never got the chance to find out. I should have invited the kid over after school yesterday so that I could quiz him."

Jacques observed his watch. "Do you have time for a little road trip before your closing?"

The wheels in my head were spinning. "Where are we going? Oh, wait. You mean to see Leslie?"

"Exactly. Do you know where she works?"

"She's a stay-at-home mom. Tyler said she bought a house on Livingston Avenue. I didn't catch the number, though."

"Piece of cake." Jacques pulled up the MLS on my computer screen, typed the street name in, and several houses popped up at once. He pointed at the screen. "Here you go. Twenty-three Livingston Avenue. It sold about two weeks ago. Agent for the seller was Tiffany Roberts. There's our baby."

I studied the information on the screen. "Leslie never even wanted to look at houses in that section of town. And that was more than they could afford to pay. What on earth did Tiffany do, brainwash her?"

"Honey, now *you're* asking stupid questions." He winked. "Where's your closing?"

"At Marcia Steele's law office. It'll take me a good forty-five minutes or so to get there from Leslie's house. What about you? I thought you were meeting Ed for lunch."

"I'll reschedule for a little later. He'll understand. Is this the closing for the country hick who wanted to know if he could camp on the lawn last week?"

I looked around the desk for my client's folder, then tucked it inside my briefcase. "It's the last day of the month, so that means less interest Mr. Anderson has to pay the bank, which works out well for him. It's bad enough that the other agent and I each have to take a cut on our commissions since he didn't have enough money to cover his closing costs, but the owner agreed to pay half the closing expenses so that we could get this done and over with."

Jacques blew out an exasperated breath. "I knew the guy was going to be trouble the first time I saw him here. Weren't you guys in the conference room for, like, three hours? People were starting to talk."

I flinched at the memory. "It took me that long to explain everything to him."

"Who's the other agent?"

"Tricia Hudson from Primer Properties."

Jacques let out a low whistle. "Ooh, she must have loved that." He spun around in my swivel chair like a little kid as he tapped the screen on his phone. "She's the greediest agent alive, next to Tiffany. Oops, I mean, she really *is* the greediest agent alive."

"Jacques, that's awful."

"Not a bad little house, if I recall. I showed it a few months ago before the price dropped. Solid, with good bones. It just needed cosmetics, right?"

"Yes, some touch ups here and there. It's about all this guy could handle anyhow." I took my compact out of my purse and stole a quick look at myself in the mirror. "Speaking of cosmetics, I'm a complete mess. Look at the circles under my eyes!"

Jacques examined my face. "You need an all-day beauty treatment, hon. Facial, massage, makeover—the works. Your birthday's coming up soon. It'll be my treat."

"That does sound good."

He got to his feet and grabbed my arm. "Let's get out of here. I sent Ed a text and explained the change. You'd better tell hubby you can't meet him either. We're going to have to move fast to get you to redneck's closing on time. Follow me. And for God's sake, girl, try to keep up."

Jacques was usually a law abiding citizen. His one major flaw was that he drove like a lunatic. I was immensely grateful to follow and not have to ride shotgun with him. In the past, when I'd had this pleasure, I gripped the door handle with constant fear. His lead foot earned him several speeding tickets. Since he numbered many policemen among his clients, he usually

managed to find a way out. He was now going over fifty miles
per hour in a residential neighborhood.

I tried to lay off the gas as much as possible. The last thing I
needed was for a cop to pull me over. When I finally reached
Leslie's house, Jacques was already there, leaning against his car,
tapping his foot.

"God, you take forever."

I snorted. "And you're a maniac. Hang on one second. I have
to text Greg and let him know I'm not going to the police
station."

"Why didn't you call him on the way over?"

Because I don't want a lecture right now. "Um, I'd rather not. I've
a feeling he's going to be ticked off at me."

"Gee, where'd you get that idea?" Jacques' voice dripped with
sarcasm. "You're just like Ed. You need to start listening to your
other half. It's the basis for a good marriage."

I finished my text and started up the stairs behind him.
"Married ten months and already an authority on the subject,
eh?"

Jacques stopped me about halfway up. "I'll pretend I didn't
hear that remark. So, Miss Detective, have you thought about
what you're going to say to Leslie? Or were you planning on
going with, 'Hey, did you happen to shoot your real estate agent
the other night?'"

I gave him my best irritated look. "Of course not. I figured
I'd say I dropped by to congratulate her and let her know that
there were no hard feelings."

"She won't buy it."

I scowled. "Well, can you think of anything better? Maybe we
should tell her we're the neighborhood welcome wagon."

We stepped onto the porch, and Jacques rang the doorbell.
Within seconds, a little cherub face appeared on the other side
of the screen door, smiling at us.

I waved at the little boy. "Hi, Jackson."

"Cute kid." Jacques made funny faces at him.

The screen door opened, and Leslie Garrett peered out at us. Her brown, frizzy hair was in need of coloring and a good brushing. She was dressed in a beige bathrobe and slippers. Her thick, overgrown eyebrows arched when she recognized me.

I glanced at my watch again. Yes, it was past noon, yet it looked as if we'd awakened her.

"Well, lookie who's here. It's Miss Real Estate Agent of the Year. So sorry, but you're a little late. I've already bought a dump." She threw her arms open wide. "What do you think of my palace?"

I couldn't help but stare. This was not the well-kept, pleasant-mannered client I'd come to know a few months ago. It was as if she'd done a complete turnaround. "Leslie, this is my co-worker, Jacques Forte."

"A pleasure." Jacques extended his hand.

She shook her head at him. "You people never give up, do you?"

Jackson toddled out from behind his mother's robe and stepped onto the porch in front of me. My heart sank at the sight of the little guy. He was dressed in a yellow sleeper that had seen better days. There were green stains down the front that resembled baby food, perhaps peas or spinach. Smiling wide, he proudly handed me his empty bottle.

"Thank you, Jackson."

When he put his arms out to me, I hesitated and glanced at his mother. Leslie seemed indifferent, so I lifted him into the air. When he squealed, I wrinkled my nose as two different aromas quickly overpowered me. The most apparent one was that Jackson needed a diaper change—badly. The other odor was the scent of stale liquor emanating from his mother.

I cleared my throat loudly. "I wanted you to know that there are no hard feelings. People decide to change agents all the time."

"Oh, please." She scratched her head. "What do you really want?"

"Um, actually, I was interested in seeing your new house." I hugged Jackson tightly to me, despite the overwhelming smell. "I have a client who is looking for one similar to this."

Leslie burst into peals of laughter. "Well, how about you show them this one? Then I can unload this pile of crap to someone who was as stupid as me." She pushed the screen door open with a vengeance, allowing us entrance.

Jacques gestured for me to go in ahead, then followed close behind.

Jackson started to squirm in my arms. With reluctance, I set him down on the dirty hardwood floor. He ran to sit in front of a television tuned to *Dora the Explorer,* bottle dangling from his mouth.

The main level was L-shaped, with the only furniture in the living room being the television and a lumpy, brown couch decorated with food stains. A small dining area extended off of the living room and held a card table, two folding chairs, and a rickety-looking high chair. Beyond it, I caught a glimpse of the kitchen with both the sink and countertops stacked high with dirty dishes. A litter box in the dining area begged to be cleaned.

When I thought about Jackson crawling around on the dirty floors, I was horrified. Jacques frowned, which led me to believe he was thinking the same thing.

Leslie sensed our disdain. "Lovely, isn't it? And I owe it all to that tramp Tiffany Roberts."

My ears pricked up. *Okay, get her talking.* "What does Tiffany have to do with it?"

"Are you kidding me?" She shook her head at me in amazement. "That witch lied about the house. She said it was in excellent condition when it was really falling apart."

"What's wrong with it?" Jacques wanted to know.

Her response was to sit down on the lumpy couch and cry.

Jacques and I exchanged glances as he leaned down next to her and offered his handkerchief, which she took gratefully.

"What *isn't* wrong with it? She lied about everything. We didn't have much money. The owners wouldn't budge on the price, so she convinced us to pay more than we could afford. I didn't want to do it, but Hank insisted. He'd do anything that tramp said. She had him under some type of spell."

"Tiffany?"

Leslie scowled. "No, my freakin' Aunt Tilly. Of course Tiffany. Who else do you think I mean?"

Jacques caught my eye and put a finger to his lips.

Leslie sniffled. "We didn't have money for inspections. Tiffany told us not to worry, that the place was fine. It didn't need anything. She even had some friend of hers look at the place for free. She claimed he had a license. Yeah, right. That bimbo would do anything to make a sale. And then you know what? As soon as we moved in, the furnace went. The very first day."

She started crying again, while Jacques patted her shoulder reassuringly. "Thank God winter's over because I don't have any money to buy a new one right now. We've been getting by with the wood stove in the kitchen."

"Perhaps you could get one on credit," I offered.

She ignored me. "It's like owning a money pit. The day after that, the roof started leaking. We found someone to repair it, but I had to sell my dining room set in order to pay him." The tears started again. "I don't know how much more of this I can take."

"Did you tell Tiffany?" I asked.

She glared. "Oh, I told her. She laughed and simply said it was bad timing. How unfortunate for us. Too bad, so sad."

A muscle twitched in Jacques' jaw. "You can file a complaint, you know."

"Oh, believe me, I wanted to. But Hank said no, don't do that.

It's not her fault." Her face twisted into an angry expression. "Every time he got near that slut, it was all he could do to keep from drooling on her expensive shoes."

Jacques knelt down to squeeze Leslie's hand. He nodded to me as if to say I told you so. It wasn't the first time we'd seen this happen with Tiffany's clients.

She went on, mimicking her husband. "'You're so stupid, Leslie. How could someone as pretty and sweet as Tiffany lie to us? You're so jealous of her. It's pathetic.' So guess what? I told him to get out. I'd had enough. He finally packed his stuff yesterday and left. Want to know where he is now? At his mother's. He couldn't afford to go anywhere else."

I cleared my throat and decided to take the plunge. "So what do you think about Tiffany's murder?"

Leslie snickered. "What do *I* think? That someone did us all a huge favor. We should have a party!"

It had to be the alcohol making her act so strange. My heart went out to her, seeing the mess her life had become, but I was nervous about what I was going to say next. "You wouldn't happen to know who killed her, would you?"

She jumped to her feet in a flash and waved an angry finger in my face. "I know what you're trying to do. You think I killed her. Well, I didn't."

I held up both hands. "Leslie, no—"

"Yeah, you believe it. I can tell." She looked from me to Jacques. "That's what this is all about, isn't it? You're afraid someone might think one of you guys pulled the trigger, so you're trying to pin it on me instead."

"That's not true." Jacques tried in vain to calm her.

Leslie pointed toward the front door. "I want you two out of my house. And don't come back!"

"Fine, we'll leave." I started toward the door. When Jacques looked at me questioningly, I gave a sly wink in his direction. "We know what you did though."

Leslie gaped at me. "What the hell are you talking about?"

"I know you did something to Tiffany that you're not proud of. You even told your family about it."

Leslie took a step toward me. "Anne would never tell you anything."

A hint of confidence swept through me. "I didn't say it was Anne. Maybe someone else overheard the two of you talking about it and told me."

"Oh my God. Bob." Leslie's face fell as she said the words. "Why'd she ever marry that jerk? I can't believe he'd do this to me." She sank back down into the couch, her head in her hands.

I sat next to her, ignoring the stains on the couch. "It's okay. I've done things I'm not proud of either." None of them consisted of murdering someone in cold blood, but hey, no need to get technical right now.

She turned to face me. "I don't care what you think. I'm not sorry I did it."

My pulse quickened. "Aren't you?"

"No," she growled at me, her face ashen. Then her tone changed, and she was pleading. "Look. It wasn't that big of a deal. I only wanted to get even for what she did, okay?" She reached into her bathrobe pocket and withdrew a cigarette.

Jacques removed a pack of matches from his suit jacket and lit it for her. The man doesn't even smoke, but somehow he's always prepared.

"Thank you." She smiled. "You're such a gentleman. I wish I'd married someone like you, instead of my loser husband."

Jacques nodded, a fabricated smile on his lips as he examined the couch cushion then sat down gingerly at her other side. I bit my lower lip for fear I'd burst out laughing. *If she only knew.*

"Tell us everything, Leslie," Jacques said. "Maybe we can help."

She watched him with sad, doe-like eyes. "I was so angry. I

went grocery shopping the other night and decided to drive past Tiffany's office afterward."

"Were you alone?" he asked.

"Yeah, Hank was home with the baby." She took a long drag of her cigarette.

Jacques got up and quickly walked toward the kitchen with a self-possessed air like he owned the place. When he returned with an ashtray, Leslie flashed him an appreciative smile.

"What'd you do then?" I prompted her.

She hesitated for a few seconds. "I wanted to make her pay."

Jacques and I exchanged a look as Leslie sucked in some more nicotine, oblivious to our thoughts.

She shrugged. "I parked my car about halfway down the block and then walked over to the parking lot. It was pretty dark out, so I figured no one would see me. A car had just left the lot, and hers was the only one left. So I went over to it and—"

"And what?" I couldn't stand the suspense anymore.

"I slashed her tire. There, I said it." She let out a long breath, then threw her arms around Jacques and started sobbing. "Oh, my God, what is wrong with me? I've never done anything like that before. I've always been in control."

Jacques blew out a sigh and patted her back reassuringly. "That was Tuesday evening, right? Do you remember about what time?"

Leslie blew her nose in Jacques' handkerchief. She offered it back, but he shook his head politely. "It was right before seven o'clock."

I tried to contain the excitement in my voice. "Do you remember what the car looked like?"

Leslie seemed confused. "Tiffany has a Jag. You should know that."

I leaned forward. "I meant the car you saw leaving."

She sat there, lost in thought for a minute, a cloud of smoke swirling around her head. "It was dark colored. Maybe an SUV? I can't be sure. Does it even matter?"

Jacques came to the rescue. "Leslie, this is really important. The car could've belonged to the person who killed Tiffany."

"Liar. You think I killed her, don't you? Yeah, that's why you're here. You've come to cart me off to jail." Leslie leaped to her feet and grabbed Jackson off the floor. She stood at the bottom of the staircase, her back to us as she murmured something to the baby.

I came up behind her and spoke softly. "We didn't say that."

Jacques made a circular motion to his head with his index finger then slowly backed away to the front door. "Leslie, we're going to leave now. We won't bother you anymore."

She turned to look at me, her face startled. "Do you really have to go? I'd rather you didn't. I'm afraid to be alone right now. You-you won't tell the police what I did, will you?"

"Maybe you should go down to the station and tell them everything that happened." I volunteered, as gently as I could.

Her eyes widened in alarm. "No way! Forget it!"

"Okay, okay. But if you remember any more details about the car you saw, can you let one of us know?" Jacques handed her his business card.

She gazed at him, a bit confused. "Oh, of course." With that, she started singing and whispering in Jackson's ear.

While I was worried about Leslie, I feared for the baby even more. "Leslie, why don't you let me change Jackson and put him down for a nap. Then we'll call Anne and ask her to come over. It's a lot of work taking care of a baby. I know she'd love to help you with him for a little while."

Leslie hesitated, then nodded slowly. She handed Jackson to me and trudged upstairs while I followed with the baby in my arms.

"Yes," Leslie sighed. "A nap sounds good right about now."

CHAPTER FOURTEEN

"What do you think?" Jacques asked once we were standing on the front porch of Leslie's house, out of earshot.

I shook my head with regret. "I've never seen her in such a mess. It's so sad."

He grimaced. "I know, but what do you *think*?"

Once again, I shook my head. "No. She didn't kill Tiffany."

"Cin, she was there that night. And, God knows, she had a motive."

"You said it yourself. Lots of people had motives. It must've been someone else."

Jacques put his hands on his hips. "Oh, come on. And what's with the story about the car leaving the parking lot? She said it was a dark SUV type. Please. She had to have seen a license plate or something."

"She didn't know she was watching a murderer leave. Jeez, give the poor woman a break."

Jacques folded his arms across his chest. "Why are you defending her?"

"I just don't think she's capable of murder."

"She might have blocked it all out. Look at the state she's in now."

I reached inside my purse for my phone. "I've got to call Anne. Leslie shouldn't be by herself. And she's in no shape to take care of that baby."

Jacques examined his watch. "Um, you might want to call her from your car. It's already one o'clock."

"Oh, no!" I shrieked and ran down the steps. "I don't believe this."

He shouted after me. "Call me when you're done. We've got more work to do."

I waved my hand in acknowledgement and jumped into my car. As I put my Bluetooth on and went to dial Anne's number, I noticed Greg had sent me a text. When I stopped for a red light, I quickly scanned the message. *No joke. You need to go to the police. Call me after your closing. Love you.*

There was no way I could go to the police station now. Donna wouldn't waste any time informing them about my so-called showing at Tiffany's house. She'd probably say I'd made the whole appointment up in order to get inside the house and remove any clues that might lead to my conviction. I knew Ken wouldn't back me, plus I'd deleted his text from the other evening about scheduling the showings. How could I possibly prove my innocence now?

I left a voicemail on Anne's cell. "Hey, it's Cindy. I was over at Leslie's house, and I'm really worried about her. I don't think she should be alone. Could you go over and check on her and Jackson? Let me know when you get this, and please call if you need anything."

I glanced at the clock on my radio. It was 1:30, and I still had another ten minutes to go before I reached Marcia's office. *It's okay. No big deal if I'm late. I'm really not important to the sale at this point.*

I thought about calling Marcia to tell her I'd been detained but didn't think she'd care as long as Eli was there. The attorney situation was yet another embarrassing part of this particular deal. Eli Anderson, my client, had eagerly agreed to use the real estate attorney I always recommended to clients—Marcia Steele.

Marcia was honest, intelligent, and basically left no stone unturned when doing title searches. We worked well together, and I was proud to call her one of my closest friends in the industry. Lord knows I didn't have many these days.

Eli had originally indicated to Marcia that her six hundred dollar fee wouldn't be a problem. Last week, when Marcia told him he could write her a check at the closing, he'd seemed bewildered. "I thought you came with the house."

"This could very well be the stupidest person alive," Marcia had confided to me afterward.

Born and raised in a rural section of Upstate New York, Eli had been a hillbilly all his life. Now that he was past thirty, Eli's parents had decided it was time he left the nest and started his own family. He'd been quick to tell me he needed to find a good house and a great woman. I was more than willing to help with the house but refused to help play matchmaker.

I turned left on Lerner Street and then made a quick right into the parking lot of Marcia's office. As I was getting out of the car, I spotted her Mercedes and Tricia's Audi nearby. I locked the doors of my clunky, but reliable, Honda and frowned as I looked around. It seemed that everyone in the real estate industry had a cool car, except me. Normally, it was days like this when I enjoyed my own personal pity party. Today, there wasn't time.

The receptionist indicated the Anderson/Bovie closing was being held in Conference Room B. I started down the hall and quickly found the room. At the doorway, I peered in and spotted Mr. and Mrs. Bovie, their attorney, a bank representative, and Marcia. Eli was nowhere to be found.

Now it was time to panic.

Marcia instantly got to her feet and walked over to me. She was an attractive woman about my age with curly, auburn hair and a dusting of freckles on her petite nose. Her emerald linen suit looked spectacular with her matching eyes and great figure. She grabbed my arm.

"Don't get upset. He's on his way." Marcia hid her annoyance remarkably well.

I groaned. "What the heck happened now?"

Marcia pulled me out into the hallway so that we wouldn't be overheard. "I told the sellers he had a flat tire. How I wish it was something like that. The dimwit thought the closing was actually being held at the house itself. When he wasn't here on time, I called his cell phone. Thank goodness he answered. I told him he'd better get his butt over here in fifteen minutes, or I was charging him double."

I closed my eyes and leaned against the wall. A low-pitched squeak escaped from my mouth before I could stop it. "Only I could have a client be late to their own closing. Marcia, I am so sorry."

"Hey." She put her arm around my shoulders. "It's not your fault. Sometimes it takes a while to see people for what they really are. Dumber than a box of rocks definitely qualifies." She smiled. "I know you're going through a rough patch right now. This will all work out. Remember, the house is ten minutes away, so he should be tearing in here any second now."

As Marcia spoke, the sound of tires squealing on the pavement greeted us. I braced myself, afraid the beat-up Chevy truck Eli drove might crash through a nearby window at any second.

I sighed. "If he does anything else, I may shove him right out the window."

"That's fine, but wait until after he pays me," Marcia winked. "Oops, perhaps I should have said *if* he pays me."

We watched with fascination as Eli rushed down the hallway toward us, a huge goofy grin on a face that resembled a young Grizzly Adams. "Hey, Mrs. Style."

"Steele," Marcia corrected him politely.

As I suspected, he'd made sure to dress for the occasion with a ripped T-shirt and jeans that had both seen better days. Eli was country through and through, but his family did not live in squalor. He had access to soap and clean clothing. When he drew closer, it became evident he'd forgotten to apply deodorant as well.

"Oh, right." Eli turned to me. "Nice to see you too, Carol."

I winced inwardly. He either called me Charlotte or Carol all the time. "My name is Cindy, Eli."

Eli smacked his forehead with his hand. Hard. "Oh, sure."

"Let's not keep the sellers waiting any longer, shall we?" Marcia grabbed me by the arm. While she smiled warmly at Eli, she shook me by the shoulders and muttered, "Try to keep calm."

"I need a drink," I said.

She nodded, still smiling. "I've got a bottle of Merlot waiting in my office. We can celebrate together after we get through this mess."

We walked into the meeting room, the stark white walls in sharp contrast with the black marble conference table. Mr. and Mrs. Bovie and their lawyer were already seated. They looked up at us expectantly. The bank representative, an elderly woman with salt-and-pepper hair, smiled at Eli. "Mr. Anderson, you made it. How's the truck?"

"Uh, fine," Eli answered, confusion registering on his face.

Marcia took Eli's arm and directed him toward the other side of the table, away from the sellers. "Eli, you're the guest of honor. I need you to sit down right here and get ready for all the fun paperwork you have to sign."

"Right, that will be fun."

When Marcia looked at me and winked, I rolled my eyes back at her. This was going to be a long afternoon.

Since there wasn't enough room for me at the table, I gladly eased into a stray chair directly behind Marcia and Eli. Tricia sat behind her clients as well. She was busy texting away on her phone but looked up long enough to shoot a dagger-filled stare in my direction.

After a few minutes, Marcia leaned her head back and motioned me forward. "What's Tricia's issue with you?"

I shrugged. "It might be the loss of commission we both had to take. Or maybe it's because of Tiffany. I heard they were friends."

"I didn't think Tiffany had any friends." Marcia glanced at the paperwork in front of Eli and shook her head. "No. Not there! Sign on the line above where your name is printed."

After a few minutes, I was surprised to see Eli pull a check from his pocket and hand it to Marcia—for her fee, I assumed. Sitting right behind them, I noticed the check was signed by Eli's mother.

Eli grinned sheepishly. "My mom writes all my checks for me. I'm not real good at signing my name."

Tricia snorted loudly from the other side of the room. "Probably can't even write it in the snow."

Marcia shot Tricia a dirty look but said nothing.

Mercifully, the rest of the closing went off without a hitch. The sellers became visibly annoyed with Eli's antics, and Marcia gave up trying to explain the documents as it became obvious Eli would never understand them. She shoved page after page under his nose and simply said, "Your name right here, Eli." He complied without question.

When it was finally over, the bank employee distributed a handful of checks. She handed me mine, and I gave her the agency invoice. I scanned through it to make sure everything was correct. It was written for five thousand dollars, payable to the order of Hospitable Homes.

My watch read 3:30. The twins and Darcy should be home by now. If I hurried, I could get to the office and turn the check in to Donna before she left at four. She'd write me a personal one in return, and I could run to the bank, cash it, and be home before five. Maybe I'd order takeout tonight. Or perhaps we'd all go out to dinner as a treat. It was rare that we did that these days.

Tricia presented Eli with the house keys. "Good luck. You'll need it."

"Gee, thanks." He grinned.

Marcia noted the sarcasm in Tricia's voice. "I'll thank you to keep your opinion to yourself, Miss Hudson."

Tricia huffed and turned on her heel without even bothering to acknowledge me. She went to the Bovies, hugged each one in turn, and presented them with a congratulatory bottle of champagne. Usually, I'd give my buyers or sellers the same type of token gift. Money was tight though, and I was still smarting over the fact I'd lost five hundred dollars in commission due to Eli's idiocy. I figured he'd already gotten his bottle of champagne—about fifty times over.

I shook his hand. "Good luck, Eli."

"Thanks, Carol." His lopsided grin revealed a huge gap between his front teeth.

I was too tired to correct him again.

Marcia stood so that I could give her a hug. "Do you really have to rush off? I was hoping we could have a drink and talk about—you know, things."

"I'd love to, but can I take a rain check? I need to get home to the kids."

"No problem. We still have a couple of things to finish up here anyhow." She heaved a huge sigh. "I'm so glad today's Friday. This guy has worn me out."

"You and me both. Hey, thanks for everything. You've been great, as usual."

"Hang in there. Let me know if you need anything, and stay positive." Marcia gave my arm an affectionate squeeze. "Call me next week, and we'll do lunch. My treat for all the clients you bring me."

If I wasn't in jail by then. So much for being positive. I was free to leave, so I thanked the bank employee, congratulated the Bovies, and left the room.

On the way out, I started to check my phone for messages. I shielded my eyes from the bright sunlight and glanced across the parking lot. I was startled to see Tricia leaning against my car, arms folded across her chest. Cold, gray eyes stared directly into mine. It was obvious she'd been waiting for me.

Great. Perspiration beaded on my forehead, but I tried to maintain my calm. "Can I help you, Tricia?"

"I seriously doubt it." She ran her fingers through her stringy, blonde hair. "You could do the whole real estate industry a favor if you quietly disappeared into the night, though."

"Look, I'm sorry about my client's antics."

Her laugh came out as a high-pitched cackle that reminded me of the Wicked Witch in *The Wizard of Oz.* "Do you really think that's what I'm upset about—your Jed Clampett in there? Oh, no. I'm sick to my stomach, thinking you'll get away with murder."

My mouth dropped open in surprise. "I didn't murder anyone. And I don't cheat my clients either, like some people."

Tricia was taken aback. "How dare you make insinuations after what *you've* done? Please. I'll call the cops on you this minute. And I hope that you look good in orange because you're going to be wearing it for a long time."

"Yes, please do call the cops. I'd love to tell them how you've been harassing me."

She snorted. "It's a wonder Donna still puts up with you. If you were in my agency, I would have thrown you out on your ear already."

"Well, thank God I *don't* work there. I've had quite enough of people stealing my listings. Now I know why you and Tiffany were such good friends." I knew that had definitely struck a nerve as I watched Tricia's round, puffy face twist with rage.

She hoisted her Prada handbag over her shoulder and started to turn away, then walked back toward me. Her face was so close that I could smell this morning's coffee on her stale breath. "Let me tell you something, you little twit. If you do happen to get away with this, I'll make sure your real estate career is over in this town. Not that you really ever had one anyway."

My stomach convulsed with dread. I was so shocked by the venom in her tone that I didn't find my voice until she'd reached her car. "Go ahead. You don't scare me."

A police car drove into the lot and parked next to my vehicle. I watched, frozen, as Officer Simon stepped out of his cruiser and approached me, a grim look upon his face.

ood grief. I was in no mood for another confrontation with one of our city's finest right now.

Officer Simon didn't waste any time. "Mrs. York, I checked with your office, and they told me you were here. And I heard you were at Miss Roberts' home yesterday. I think you'd better come with me for some more questioning." He placed his hand on my arm.

What had Donna done—run to the phone right after our meeting? I shook my arm loose and glared at him. "I'm a real estate agent and was showing the home to a client named Ken Sorenson. His wife is Donna Cashman, the manager at my office. I'm pretty sure she knew about the showing. Check it out if you don't believe me."

Officer Simon said nothing as he made a note of Ken's name on a small pad that suddenly appeared from out of nowhere.

"I need to get home to my kids right away. If it's really necessary, call me, and I will come down to the station at a later time. But I can't right now."

Officer Simon gave me a long, searching look. "Oh, don't worry. We'll be calling, Mrs. York. It sounds like you've got quite a bit of explaining to do." He tipped his hat at me and nodded to Tricia, who was enjoying the show from inside her car.

I unlocked my car door and slumped down into the seat. I fought the bout of nausea whirling around in my stomach. *Don't panic. Things will get better. They have to.* I turned the key in the ignition and slowly drove out of the parking lot.

It was minutes before four o'clock when I reached the office. At first, I was afraid Donna might have already gone since most of the agents usually left early on Fridays but was relieved to see her Corvette in the parking lot. I took a deep, calming breath. The accusation was not going to be easy for me to deliver or for Donna to hear. She was a newlywed, for crying out loud, and her husband was already coming on to other women. I actually felt kind of sorry for her.

Donna sat at the reception desk, talking on her cell phone. "Why, it's no trouble at all. We'll get one of our best agents to show you the house. Tomorrow will be fine. Okay, Two Turner Boulevard at nine. We'll see you then." She disconnected.

Turner Boulevard was right around the corner from my own house, and Donna knew it. Since my chances of being chosen to show the house were pretty much slim to none, I didn't even bother to inquire.

She glowered at me, her eyes as sharp as clear-blue glass. "Well, well, what do we have here?"

I placed the check in front of her. "The Anderson/Bovie deal closed."

Donna laughed. "Why, Cindy, congratulations. You actually made a sale this month."

I opened my mouth to make a comment, then clamped my lips shut. *Don't take her bait. Keep quiet and collect your money.*

Donna reached for a key and unlocked one of the drawers in the desk. She withdrew a ledger and proceeded to fill out a check without a single word. She tore the check out and tossed it in my direction.

I studied the amount. It was for two thousand dollars. "This isn't right. The check was supposed to be for twenty-two hundred dollars."

She switched off the laptop and avoided my gaze. "Your client cost us an additional thousand dollars with his stupidity. It seems only fair you should take a hit."

Anger formed in a ball at the pit of my stomach. "But I already took a hit. I lost five hundred dollars of my commission because of his stunts, and you know that. What gives you the right to withhold more?"

Donna folded her arms in triumph. "I can do anything I want. I'm the manager, not you."

"I'm not leaving until you give me the other two hundred." My voice quivered slightly, but there was no way I would back down now. "I'll turn you into the Real Estate Association."

Annoyed, Donna threw up her hands. "Go ahead. Do you think they'd listen to you? No. You're a murderer. They don't give two figs about you. No one does, except maybe your buddy Jacques. Oh, and did I tell you he's my new golden goose? I can deal with his snarky attitude as long as he brings in the dough."

"That's all Tiffany was to you too," I said. "She actually thought you were her friend. You were always thick as thieves, going out to lunch or parties together, but you never really cared about her. My conscience is clear. At least I never pretended to like her."

A shadow crossed over Donna's face. "You need to leave."

"Wait. There is something else you need to know." I sucked in a breath. "It concerns Ken."

Her eyes bore into mine. "You're too late. He already told me."

This was a surprise. "He did?"

"Sure." Donna put the checkbook away. "Women make

passes at him all the time. No big deal. What did surprise me was that *you* would do such a thing. I always thought you were so in love with George that you'd never even look at another man."

My body froze, registering disbelief. "Excuse me? That is *not* what happened. Your husband made a pass at *me*. As a matter of fact, he kissed me and refused to back off, so I—"

Donna held up a hand to stop me. "Enough of your lies, please." She clucked her tongue at me in disdain. "I don't know how George puts up with you."

"It's *Greg*."

"Whatever."

"Look, Donna, I'm only telling you this because I would want to know if the shoe was on the other foot. And there's more."

She gave me a bored look and leaned back in her chair. "Gee, I can't wait to hear."

My heart knocked against the wall of my chest. "I think he knew that was Tiffany's house and was trying to set me up for the murder."

Her irate gaze settled on my face, and I was aware I'd gone too far. "How dare you."

I stood my ground and returned her stare. "Your husband, Keith, is a liar."

She narrowed her eyes at me. "His name is *Ken*."

I shrugged. "Whatever."

Donna's nostrils flared as she continued to glare at me. There was complete silence in the room for a good thirty seconds. Then she opened a drawer, removed a file folder, and thrust a piece of paper in my face.

"What's this?"

"It's your release from this agency. As you're aware, when you joined three years ago, we both signed a contract stating that either party could terminate the relationship at any time.

Well, I've decided to end it. Adios. Au revoir. Get the hell out. I never want to lay eyes on you again."

Beyond angry, tears threatened to sting my eyes, but I wouldn't give her the satisfaction of seeing me cry. I blinked several times and then slammed the paper back down on the desk so hard that she nearly jumped out of her seat. "Fine. Who needs this place anyhow? You're a terrible manager. I can go to any other agency and make twice as much as I do here."

"You think so?" Donna chuckled. "Everyone knows you're a murderer. No one will hire a pariah like you."

"We'll see about that."

Donna put her hand out. "I'll take the keys to the office while we're at it."

I started to reach into my purse, defeated, then stopped. "No."

"No?" Donna echoed me incredulously.

I placed my hands on my hips and stared back at her defiantly. "You'll have to change the locks or give me my other two hundred."

Her voice was as cold as a glacier. "Give me those keys *now*."

"Sorry, no can do." I hoped she couldn't notice how my knees were trembling.

Donna's face turned purple. Changing the locks on the office was expensive. There were three different doors and all had commercial locks. How she loved telling people that her office was locked up tighter than Fort Knox was now coming back to haunt her.

"Well, bye, Donna. Do take care." I started for the door.

"Wait a minute." She reached for the checkbook and scribbled off another check in record time, tossed it on the floor, and got to her feet. "I have some mail to sort in the conference room. You have exactly five minutes to clean out your office. When I come back, you'd better be gone."

After I picked up the check and read it to make sure the

amount was correct, I removed the keys from my ring and threw them on her desk. "Happy to oblige."

I clenched my teeth and ran into my office, slamming the door behind me. I wasn't going to give her the pleasure of watching me. There was an empty box sitting on top of my desk, obviously meant to be used for my hasty departure. Donna no doubt had already been planning to dump me even before our argument. I only wished I could have beaten her to the punch.

Still smarting, I threw pictures and personal folders into the box. I grabbed my sweater and the little, house-shaped plaque on the wall that Greg had given me when I began my real estate career. The caption read, *I'm sold on you.* As I held the plaque in my hands, my lower lip started to quiver. I wrapped it in the sweater and gently laid it in the box before putting the cover on. I took one last look around the room where I'd spent so much time the past three years, then switched off the light and shut the door behind me. Maybe it was for the best.

Donna was locking up the reception desk and didn't even acknowledge my presence as I shuffled past with my box. I started for the door, then stopped and turned around. "Good-bye, Donna, it's certainly been a unique experience working for you."

She dismissed me with a wave of her hand, not even bothering to look up. "Rot in hell. And if I have anything to do with it, that's exactly where you'll wind up for Tiffany's murder."

I slammed the door, hoping to convey my anger. My legs were numb as I stumbled to my car. Five minutes later, I was in the drive-thru lane of my bank. I deposited the larger check into our joint savings account and asked for the smaller one back in cash. Since our mortgage payment was due next week, this was perfect timing.

As I drove home, I reminded myself of my appointment tomorrow with Sylvia at No Place Like Home Realty. If I signed with her agency now, things might work out perfectly. Hopefully, I'd also get the listing from my friend Nancy's parents on Monday. They were moving to Florida and anxious to sell. Perhaps everything would start to turn around for me then.

I turned onto our street to see a fire truck and a police car parked in front of my house with lights flashing. Sheer panic gripped me as I drove closer. I threw the car in park and jumped out, rushing toward the house.

A policeman met me in the driveway. "Are you Mrs. York?"

My heart stuttered in my chest. "Yes! My babies. Are they—?"

"We called your husband since we couldn't reach you," the policeman explained. "He'll be here shortly. Your boys are fine. They started a small kitchen fire. You could be in trouble for leaving two young kids alone, ma'am."

A small crowd of neighbors had gathered behind me.

I drew my eyebrows together. "I didn't leave them alone. My daughter, Darcy, is fifteen. She was watching them while I was at a real estate closing."

He shook his head. "There's no one else in the house, ma'am."

As if on cue, the twins marched out the front door, each with a Popsicle in hand.

"Hi, Mom," Stevie said.

Perplexed, I stared at them. "Stevie, Seth, where's your sister?"

Seth shrugged. "I don't know. She didn't come home on the bus with us."

A voice from behind me spoke up. "I think she might have stayed for cheerleading practice."

Startled, I whirled around and tried not to groan. Tyler.

I turned back to the policeman. "She was supposed to come home with the boys. I don't know what happened."

Stevie was concentrating hard on his Popsicle. "When we didn't see her, we took the key under the mat and let ourselves

in. Seth was hungry, so we made toast. I guess he forgot it
was on."

"I didn't forget it was on, dummy, you did!" Seth cried.

I couldn't believe my ears. "How could you forget the toaster
was on? And you know you're not supposed to be using it when
no one else is home."

"Lame brain left it too close to the curtains." Seth nudged
Stevie with his elbow.

"I did not."

"You did too."

I grabbed each twin by an arm. "That's enough. I can't believe
you guys would do something like that."

"But we were hungry, Mom," Seth whined, his mouth full of
Popsicle.

Stevie proudly showed me his orange tongue. "Sorry, Mom."

The policeman stared at me intently until I released my hold
on their arms. I forced a smile to my lips. "Um, what happened
next?"

"There was a lot of smoke, then the alarm started going off,"
Seth said. He stooped to pick up Rusty.

"And then?" I asked, incredulous.

"I called 9-1-1, just like you taught us." Stevie grinned
proudly. "And I timed them. It only took the firemen five
minutes to get here."

As if on cue, a fireman walked out of the house at that
moment and nodded toward me. "It's all out, ma'am. Part of
your countertop burned and, of course, the curtains are history.
It could have been a lot worse though." He gave each of the
twins a high five. "Good job. That was quick thinking, guys."

"Thanks." Stevie and Seth chimed in unison.

I wiped at my perspiring forehead. "Thank you so much."

"No problem, ma'am." The fireman tipped his helmet as two
other firemen exited the front door. They nodded toward me
and the boys.

"You really shouldn't leave such young kids home alone," one admonished me.

"I didn't leave them alone. Well, not on purpose," I stammered.

Greg's car screeched to a stop on the side of the road. He ran up the driveway and pushed through the small crowd that had gathered around us. He grabbed the twins in his arms. "Are you guys all right?"

"We're okay, Dad," Stevie reassured him.

Greg looked at me in confusion. "Where the heck is Darcy?"

"Apparently, she stayed for cheerleading practice." My throat tightened. I couldn't believe our daughter had been so irresponsible. I was trying desperately not to turn on the waterworks in front of the policeman. "Greg, I told her to come home. She knew she had to babysit today."

"I know you did." Greg put an arm around me. "Officer, this has been a huge misunderstanding."

The policeman nodded. "It seems that way. I'm just glad these little guys weren't hurt."

"My daughter, Darcy, was supposed to be here. She'll be home shortly if you'd like to question her. She owes everyone an apology." Greg glanced at me. "That's the least she can do for all the trouble she's caused."

Darcy had never forgotten to babysit before. I had to assume there was only one reason for this stunt of hers. She was angry and had deliberately disobeyed me.

The policeman tipped his hat and shook hands with the boys, who smiled sweetly at him. They always knew when to turn on the charm. *Such* little darlings.

The fire truck pulled away with the police car following closely behind. Our neighbors seemed content that the disaster was over and dispersed to their homes.

The twins danced into the house with Greg and me

following slowly behind. Greg shut the door, and I flopped onto the couch.

"Baby, you don't look so good. Are you going to faint again?"

"No, I'll be okay. I just need to rest for a second."

The twins took the puppy and headed downstairs while Greg paced back and forth in front of me. "I've had it with her, Cin. Look at everything we've got going on around here. And we can't even count on our daughter for any help."

"Greg," I began.

His lips pursed in a thin line. "No, that's it. She's grounded. No shopping, cheerleading practice, or formal dance this weekend."

I knew he was right, but that didn't make me feel any better. Darcy had been looking forward to this dance for a month, not to mention the two hundred dollars we'd already spent on the dress. I wondered if we could still return it to the store. "It'll break her heart."

Greg snorted. "That's too bad. Maybe now she'll learn everything in this world doesn't revolve around her."

I stretched out on the couch with my hand over my eyes and exhaled deeply while he went to the kitchen to survey the damage. Angry curse words flew through the air. Greg had put those kitchen counters in last year and spent many hours doing so. I remained quiet. There was no use arguing with him when he got like this, but I'd never seen him so angry with Darcy. She was his little girl, his princess. Sadly, I also knew it didn't matter what he said to her. Darcy would find a way to redirect her anger toward me as she always did these days.

I heard a car in the driveway and lifted the curtain to look outside. Our dependable daughter was waving good-bye to Heather and her mother.

Greg walked back into the living room. "Is that her?"

I nodded as my stomach rumbled again. I was dreading the confrontation but also knew it was inevitable.

The doorknob turned slowly, and Darcy appeared before our eyes. She had already changed from her cheerleading outfit back into jeans and a tank top. She glanced at me, sitting on the couch with my head in my hands, then at Greg who stood by the door with his arms folded, glaring at her.

"Hello." She tossed her hair defiantly to the side and headed for the staircase. The move wasn't lost on me. She was definitely annoyed about something.

Greg grabbed her by the arm. "Wait a minute, young lady. You have some explaining to do."

Darcy seemed shocked by his attitude. "About what?"

"You know exactly what. You were supposed to come home to watch your brothers this afternoon."

Darcy shrugged. "I don't remember that."

"Please don't lie," I said. "I asked you yesterday and reminded you again this morning. You knew."

She avoided my gaze. "I guess I forgot."

"I am so tired of your insolence," Greg growled. "Thanks to your irresponsibility, your brothers tried to set fire to the house today."

Her face turned whiter than paste. "Are they okay?"

Greg placed his hands on his hips. "Yeah, no thanks to you. The fire department was here, and the whole kitchen countertop is burned. Your brothers could have been killed because of your selfishness."

Darcy's eyes filled, and she immediately started crying. I got to my feet and went over to comfort her.

"They're all right." I put my arm around her. "It could have been much worse."

Darcy shook my arm off. "Don't touch me."

Startled by her action, I turned to Greg, who looked as baffled as I did.

"Don't speak to your mother that way."

She ignored Greg and stared at me, eyes filled with venom.

"Do you know why I didn't come home? Because I was pissed at you. All people do is laugh at me. They whisper when I come down the hall, and they point their fingers at me. I know what they're saying. 'Her mom's a murderer.' You're ruining my life."

My jaw almost hit the floor. I stood there, not knowing what to say.

Fortunately, Greg did. He walked over to Darcy and put his face literally inches away from hers. When she tried to back away, he followed. "You're in big trouble. And don't blame your mother. She's been through enough this week without having to deal with your selfish attitude."

Darcy was silent, studying the dark-blue carpet.

"You're grounded," Greg went on. "To school and back for the next week is the only place you'll be going. That's it. No cheerleading practice, no dates, no going over to friends' houses, and especially no dance this weekend."

"You can't do that," Darcy cried in alarm.

He raised his eyebrows at her. "I can, and I just did."

Darcy whirled around to face me. "I hate you!" She grabbed her book bag and ran up the stairs. Her bedroom door slammed seconds later.

I slumped onto the couch and managed to choke out a small laugh. "*You* ground her, but she hates *me*."

Greg sat down and put his arms around me. "Don't let it bother you. She's got to learn what she did was wrong." He kissed me on the forehead. "How'd the closing go? Did the country bumpkin show up?"

"Yes, eventually." I leaned my head on his shoulder. "By some miracle of God, we now have money in the bank, too."

"That's always good to hear."

I sighed and snuggled closer to him. "I went to the office afterward to give Donna the check. We had words."

"What kind of words?" Greg asked with interest.

"Well, not very nice ones. Besides accusing me of murder,

which, by the way, I'm starting to get used to, she told me to get out. My relationship with Hospitable Homes is now over."

Relief washed over Greg's face. "Thank God for small favors."

"There's more. I tried to tell her about what Ken did to me, but she refused to listen."

"Don't worry about it. He's her problem. I'm sure they'll live a long, happy life together," Greg said dryly. "And Donna's no concern of yours anymore either. Now you can sign on with that other place tomorrow."

I stared at my husband anxiously. "What if they don't want me now? Everyone in town knows what happened."

He tweaked my nose. "Stop worrying. Jacques will have his place up and running soon, won't he?"

"Hope so." I was silent for a few seconds as I mulled things over in my mind. "Still, I need to join up with someone right away. I have that listing appointment on Monday."

Greg released me and got to his feet. "It'll work out. You worry too much. I hate to sound insensitive, but I'm starving. What's for dinner?"

"I thought I'd order takeout, if that's okay."

"Whatever you want, baby. I'll go grab the menus. What'll it be—Chinese, pizza, burgers?"

I yawned. "You and the kids decide. I really don't care."

"Okay, I'll go consult with the other men in this family." He headed downstairs, and within seconds I could hear the twins shrieking with laughter and Rusty barking.

I smiled as I listened to them carrying on, then realized I'd left my purse in the car. As I started out to retrieve it, I grabbed my phone from my blazer pocket where I had placed it after talking with Tricia. It was still on mute from the closing since I had forgotten to change it back. I had one new text message, four missed calls, and two voice mails.

The text was from Jacques, asking me to call him tonight so

that we could discuss our case further. Poirot and Hastings to the rescue.

One of the voice mails was from the police officer who had been here earlier, asking me to please come home as soon as possible.

The other message was from Stevie. "Mommy, please come home. There's smoke coming from the curtains. I don't know what to do."

After putting the phone down, I wept quietly for a moment. I had to pull myself together before things got any worse. I said a silent prayer of thanks for the boys' safety. If something had happened to them today, I never would have forgiven myself.

CHAPTER SIXTEEN

The twins and Greg decided on burgers and fries from a local restaurant, and we were all seated at the dining room table, minus Darcy. Greg had gone up once to tell her to come down to dinner, but her door was locked.

He looked at me and shrugged. "She says she's not hungry."

"That means more for us." Seth grinned.

Greg observed me with concern. "You need to eat something."

I pushed my chair back and stood. "No appetite here either, I guess. I think I'll go upstairs."

He caught my arm as I walked by. "If you want to talk to her, that's fine. But if you take away the punishment, I'm going to ground you too."

Stevie giggled. "You tell her, Dad."

I smiled at my husband. "Oh, really? Am I supposed to be afraid of you now?"

"You have no idea." Greg winked.

I put my hands on my hips. "I'd never take away her punishment without talking to you first."

He looked doubtful. "Please. I know you, remember?"

"Oh, fine. I do need to talk to her though."

Greg reached for the ketchup. "Good luck."

I trudged up the stairs and stood in front of Darcy's door for several seconds before I let out a sharp breath and knocked. "Darcy, can I please talk to you for a minute?"

There was no answer.

"I'm not leaving till you open the door."

She fumbled with the lock but didn't bother to open the door. At least we were making some progress.

My daughter was lying on her stomach in bed, staring intently out the window. There wasn't much to look at. It had started to rain and was pitch black outside.

"May I sit down?"

Darcy shrugged but kept staring out the window.

I sat next to her on the bed, not sure what to say next. What I really wanted to do was put my arms around her and tell her everything would be all right, like I had when she was a little girl and she'd fallen off her bike for the tenth time in a day. Without thinking, I reached my hand out to stroke her hair. "It's been a long time since we had a talk."

Much to my surprise, she didn't pull away.

"I'm sorry you have to deal with all this stuff," I went on. "It wasn't my plan. Just so you know, it hasn't been easy for me or your father as well. You're almost an adult, so I feel like we can talk—about everything. Your brothers don't understand the implications here. They think this is some type of game."

Darcy frowned. "You should call the hospital and see if it's too late to return them."

When I laughed, she grinned. Hopefully, we were getting somewhere.

"I know I can't understand everything you're going through right now, but it doesn't excuse what you did today. And I didn't come up here to take away your father's punishment either."

Darcy stared down at her pillow and said nothing.

I lifted her face in my hand so that she had no choice but to look at me. "I hope you know I didn't hurt that woman."

Tears came into Darcy's eyes as she nodded. "But it was so awful, hearing kids say those mean things about you. One girl asked me if you did it so that you could get the dead lady's listings. And that Laura Winters—oh, I can't stand her."

The name sounded familiar, but I wasn't sure why. "What'd she do?"

"She went around telling everyone that you beat up people who come to our house. And it's because you're guilty."

Well, this was a new one. "Where would she get an idea like that?"

"She said you hit her older sister. She's some nobody who works for one of the local papers."

I was thunderstruck. Of course, Stephanie Winters. "Oh no."

Darcy cocked her head to one side. "Did you really beat her up?"

I shook my head. "It was all a misunderstanding. She came to the house unannounced and wanted to do a story on me. I told her to leave, and she fell off the porch."

"Oh, too bad." Darcy looked crestfallen.

"Sorry to disappoint you," I grinned. "If Laura's anything like her sister, I understand why you don't like her very much."

Darcy tossed her hair. "She always talks behind my back. I beat her out for Homecoming Court last fall, and she was really mad. I mean, what's the big deal? It's just a stupid contest that I didn't even want to be in anyway. Plus, she knows that Ryan Stanford likes me and not her. He's taking me to the sophomore dance tomorrow night." Her face fell. "I mean, he was."

"I'm sorry, honey."

Darcy grabbed a tissue off her nightstand and blew her nose. "I guess I deserve it. Most days they act like little maggots, but they're still my baby brothers. If they'd been hurt, I'd have felt awful."

I put my arms around her, and she hugged me back in return. "I know. You're a good sister to them—well, most of the time. Don't worry. If Ryan liked you before this, he'll ask you to another dance."

Darcy's face lit up. "He asked me to the prom today."

I was thrilled. "Really? Is he a junior?"

"No, he's a senior. He was eighteen back in January."

Oh, great. Greg's going to love this.

"The prom's a month away, I'll need to get a dress pretty soon." Darcy hesitated. "The one I have won't work—it's too short. Um, can we afford another one?"

"Maybe we could exchange this dress and get credit for a new one. We'll have to wait until next week when you're not grounded anymore."

She gave me a fierce hug. "Thanks, Mom. I'm sorry for being such a pain."

"You need to apologize to your father too."

"I know. I'll go do it right now." She started to get up from the bed then paused. "Mom? Will they—I mean, they won't put you in jail, right?"

"I don't see how they can. I haven't done anything wrong."

"Laura said they had proof you did it."

"She was only saying that to upset you. There is no proof. Everything is going to be fine." *Yeah, keep telling yourself that.* "Before long, the police will find the real killer."

I spoke confidently since I didn't want to worry her. If only I believed the words spewing out of my mouth. Now that they knew I'd been in Tiffany's house, would that be enough proof for the police to convict me? I wasn't sure.

I tried to put this out of my head as I handed my daughter another tissue. "Come on. I don't know about you, but I'm starving. Let's go grab some food before the guys eat it all."

Darcy dabbed at her eyes. "Sounds good to me."

We went downstairs with our arms around each other.

After dinner, the boys and Greg went into the living room to watch a movie. Darcy begged off, asking if she could be allowed to go upstairs and phone Ryan to explain about the dance. I granted permission, despite Greg's sour look.

I sat down at the computer in hopes of drumming up some more sales. I found three new expired listings that I made a note to call on tomorrow since it was too late for soliciting now.

My phone pinged. Another text from Jacques. *You never called. How'd the closing go? Mr. Hillbilly show?*

My fingers flew as I typed out a reply. *All went well. Phone you later?*

His response came back immediately. *Sure. Will be up late. Two new listings to enter tonight.*

That's great, I texted back. *Talk to you later.*

I folded my hands together and stared at the expired listings I'd printed. Who would I say I represented when I called? My Hospitable Homes business cards mocked me from the black mesh holder on my desk. I picked it up and dumped all the cards in my wastebasket. Time for a new beginning.

I checked my email and was astonished to see Tiffany's name pop up in my in-box. It was an automatic response thanking me for showing her listing and asking me to leave feedback. A chill ran down my spine. These responses were linked to our eKEYs but still it was creepy—like getting an email from the dead. I clicked on the link to her house for another look. I fantasized one last time about how lovely it would have been to sell it. That wasn't going to happen for me now.

I noticed an update had been posted. *No more showings until further notice,* read the caption at the top of the page. This must have been Donna's handiwork. I was puzzled. Why not show the house anymore? The murder hadn't happened there. I wondered if the sign was still out on the lawn. I'd have to drive by tomorrow and take a look.

Someone began to knead my shoulders gently from behind, and I let my head roll forward. "Oh, that feels good."

Greg bent down to kiss my neck, then gently pulled me up out of the chair and into his arms. "I know what would feel better." He captured my mouth with his until I was breathless. "Come on. Forget about Donna and the gang. You need to relax. Watch some TV with me and the boys while I give you a massage."

"Are there any other perks included?" I teased.

Greg grinned. "Oh, do I have plans for you, baby."

THE HOUSE WAS dark and quiet as I lay in Greg's arms, listening to the comforting sound of his even breathing. I glanced at the clock on my nightstand. Almost midnight. I was both mentally and physically exhausted, but I knew sleep wasn't coming for a while—if at all. There were too many thoughts running through my head.

With a sigh, I lifted Greg's arm and got out of bed. I groped for my robe at the foot of our bed. Sweetie was perched on it, purring away. I picked her up, and she meowed in protest. I gently placed her back down, and the purring resumed. I walked out to the hallway and then into the twins' bedroom.

Seth was in the bottom bunk, covers flung off, with his legs hanging over the side of the bed. I gave him a gentle push until he rolled toward the wall. He was heavier than Stevie, plus he'd been known to sleepwalk on occasion, making the bottom bunk a safer option for him.

Ever the opposite, Stevie, on the top bunk, slept like a dead person. I covered him with his blanket and started to close the door, but something soft and furry rubbed against my leg. Sweetie ran past me and jumped onto Seth's bed.

"Well, fine, if my bed isn't good enough for you."

She glanced at me mockingly with big, green eyes and brought a dainty, white paw to her mouth for a quick bath. I wasn't surprised she'd departed right after me. Greg had never been a huge fan of cats and barely managed to tolerate Sweetie. From what I could tell, the feeling was mutual.

I stole a glance at Darcy with her long, dark hair fanned across the pillow. She looked like an angel. Her cell phone lay next to her in bed. Shaking my head, I turned it off and placed it on the nightstand beside her.

Downstairs in the kitchen, I made a cup of herbal tea and took it into the den. As I sat down in front of the computer, I glanced at my phone and noticed Jacques had sent another text about thirty minutes ago. *Where are you? Call me if you're awake. Important.*

I dialed his number, and he answered on the first ring. "Jeez, Cin, do I have to schedule an appointment to talk with you now?"

"Sorry. It's been another crazy night here. What's up?"

"I'm still not convinced Leslie's innocent."

"She only slashed a tire, Jacques. Speaking of which, did the police happen to mention that when they questioned you the other day?"

"Silly girl. Why would they tell us anything? They probably figured whoever did it was the one who killed her. I mean, think about it. The killer worries that Tiffany's not completely dead and might try to go for help in her car. He could've slashed her tire to make sure she wouldn't get away. Makes sense, doesn't it?"

It seemed a bit farfetched to me, but I decided to keep the peace. "Yes, they might think that. Dang, you're getting good, Watson."

Jacques snorted. "I told you, I get to be Poirot or nothing. Anyhow, I keep thinking about that poor baby. I'm sorely tempted to call Child Protective Service."

"Don't do that," I begged. "Anne left me a message earlier. She said they're staying at her house for a few days. She'll take care of them."

"I should have taken that child myself."

I smiled. "You're such a sucker when it comes to kids. Are you and Ed thinking about adopting?"

"Maybe. Ed wants to wait, but I don't. We fight about it all the time."

"You'd have to take some time off from work, you know."

"Once my business gets rolling, I will. Then I'll let my associates take over for a while." He gave a fake cough into the phone.

"I have an appointment tomorrow morning at No Place Like Home Realty," I said suddenly.

There was an awkward pause for a few seconds. "Why on earth are you going there?"

I blew out a breath. "Now that Donna's given me my walking papers, I need to find employment. Fast."

"Wait a sec. She did what?" Jacques sounded confused.

"Sorry, I didn't get a chance to tell you sooner. I brought the check from the closing to Donna, and she told me to get out. Then she said she hopes I rot in hell for Tiffany's murder."

Jacques clucked his tongue loudly. "Dang. Well, so what. Who cares about her and that place? Now you can come work for me."

"You don't have your business up and running yet. I need a job now."

Jacques sighed. "I'm going to look at a building tomorrow. If I like it, I'll sign the papers, and you will have yourself a job. I promise you'll be the first person I hire, besides a receptionist."

"I want nothing more than to work for you. You're honest

and want the best for your clients. Not to mention I adore you. But I have a listing appointment on Monday. If they sign on with me, I have to be working for someone by then."

"Well, go see Sylvia then. Don't get too comfy, though, because I'll be calling soon." He yawned. "So I have another idea. I think we should go visit Pete Saxon tomorrow."

I shifted in my seat. "I don't know about this."

"Do you want to find this killer or not?"

"I have to. It's my only way out of this mess."

"Well then, what time are you free?" Jacques asked.

I cupped my mug for warmth. "It has to be in the afternoon. I'm meeting with Sylvia at eleven, and I want to try to find Ken's pawn shop first."

Silence ensued. "Cin, when Greg finds out you're looking for that loser, things are going to get ugly in your house."

"Don't worry, I intend to tell him. But I need to figure out how Ken connects to everything. I have to find him."

"He's not going to cooperate. It'll be a complete waste of time and maybe even dangerous for you as well."

"I'll take a can of mace with me. It's a long shot, but I have to try."

"I don't know of any pawn shops around here," Jacques mused. "What's it called?"

"No idea. Is there any way to search in the MLS commercial section? I only pay dues for the residential part, so I don't have access."

"I'm already three steps ahead of you." I could hear Jacques swiftly typing away. "You may have to check the internet as well, but I see two in the immediate area. One on Hamilton, and the other is over on Louise Boulevard."

I wrinkled my nose. "Louise. Isn't that in the less desirable part of town?"

"You're so politically correct. You can say slums, dear. And it sounds like a perfect match for that scumbag. This one actually just sold a few days ago."

"Was it worth anything?"

"Nah, just chump change. Probably a hole in the wall. I know that area. I sold a two-family there a few years ago. Absolutely deplorable, but I found someone who wanted it."

"Of course you did. You could sell your mother a strip club. Well, it's a shot in the dark, but I think I'll stop by both of them tomorrow."

"I really don't like the idea of you going there alone. If you find that jerk, call me. I'll be there in a flash, appointment or no appointment. By the way, I'm convinced that his wanting to see Tiffany's place was no coincidence."

"Speaking of Tiffany, I noticed something interesting about her house."

Jacques groaned. "Oh, my God, you weren't in it again, were you?"

"No, mother. Pull the listing up on your computer and take a look."

"Once again, I'm way ahead of you. Let's see, you must be referring to this no more showings until further notice comment."

"That would be the one, yes." I was struggling to keep my eyes open.

"Hmm. That's odd. Why wouldn't Donna want the house shown? Do you think the police ordered it?"

"But the murder didn't happen there. So why take the house off the market? Also, how come Tiffany is still down as listing agent? Don't you think Donna would have put her own name in there?"

Jacques yawned again. "It's too late for all these questions. My brain stopped working an hour ago. As for Donna, don't worry. She's too greedy to let the house slip through her bony fingers."

"Yeah, that's true."

"Look, sweetie, I've got to get some sleep. I'll call you in the morning, and we'll figure out what time to meet up at Pete's. Night, dear."

"Okay, pleasant dreams." I sighed and switched off my computer. Something told me tomorrow was going to be a long, eventful day. One I'd never forget.

CHAPTER SEVENTEEN

"*D*arcy, your breakfast is getting cold."

"Be down in a minute, Mom."

With a sigh, I turned back to the stove and flipped more pancakes. Greg was pouring milk into glasses for the twins and trying to stop Rusty from begging at the table. The pup had stationed himself between the twins and looked at them expectantly, tail wagging, waiting for one or the other to drop something. At least it saved on cleanup time for me.

I finished the pancakes and put them in the center of the table. I glanced at the clock—almost 9:30. Saturday mornings were usually more leisurely for me than school days, but not this one. If I wanted to find Ken's pawn shop and stop at Tiffany's house before my appointment, I needed to leave now.

I gulped down the rest of my coffee and leaned over Greg, absorbed in the newspaper, for a quick kiss. "Please get her down here to eat."

"I'll take care of it. Oh, and make sure to take my car. I noticed your brakes were squealing yesterday. I'll bring yours to the shop on Monday."

"Thanks, honey."

"I thought your appointment wasn't until eleven?" Greg asked.

"I want to see if I can find Ken's pawn shop first."

There was silence for a moment as Greg's eyes bore into mine. "Why would you want to go anywhere near that bastard?"

"I think he might be involved with Tiffany's murder somehow. I mean, how convenient was it that he wanted to look at her house?"

"Do you think Donna's involved, too?"

"Maybe. I don't know. None of this makes any sense." I pointed at my gold watch that Greg had given me for Christmas. "I only want to stop by the shop on the pretense I'm selling something."

Greg grimaced. "I don't like this. Let me go with you."

I shook my head. "I promise to be careful. I can take care of myself, remember?" I patted my knee. "All ready for action."

He grinned at me. "You've proven you can take care of yourself. But you're my wife, and I'm always going to be worried about you. That guy is no good."

I put my arms around him. "Who knows if I'll even find him? But if I call you when I get to my interview, will you feel better?" I purposely used my baby talk voice, which was a huge mistake. The puppy ran over and attached himself to my leg while the twins started shrieking with laughter.

I quickly disengaged the dog from me and brushed off my slacks. "Rusty needs to be neutered and soon."

Greg waved my comments aside. "He's just going through a phase."

"Some phase! He does it to everyone who walks through the door."

Seth laughed. "He did it to Grandma the other night. She got real mad at him. It was funny."

I winked at my husband. "Hmm, maybe we *should* wait a while."

"Cin." Greg shook his finger in warning at me.

I blew him a kiss and gave the twins each a peck on the top of their heads, despite their protests.

"We're too old for kissing, Mom," Stevie cried out.

I reached down and covered his entire face with kisses. Giggling, he tried to push me away. "You're never too old for kissing, my love. Wish me luck."

"Good luck, Mom," Seth said. "Don't get arrested."

Words to live by. As the twins started laughing, Greg shook his head and picked up the paper again.

Traffic was light, and it took me under twenty minutes to arrive at Tiffany's house. The *For Sale* sign was gone. I was intrigued. Why didn't Donna want people showing the house now? I longed to go inside. My eKEY was in my purse. I turned around in the driveway and drove down to the nearest side street, parking my car within viewing distance of the driveway and a good portion of the lawn. I reached for my cell phone and dialed Jacques' number.

As usual, he answered promptly. "At your service, my dear."

"The *For Sale* sign is gone. Why are there no showings allowed? Do you think there's some type of problem with Tiffany's estate?"

"I doubt anything's happened yet," Jacques said. "Too soon. And I don't believe she has any family either, except for a half-sister somewhere. I'm not sure where she lives, but I suspect she'll surface eventually. Money has a way of doing that to people."

"True. I wonder—" I stopped in the middle of my sentence as Donna's car turned into the driveway. She got out of the car and did a quick look around, then pulled a suitcase out of her back-seat. "What the heck is she doing?"

"What are you talking about?"

"It's Donna," I whispered. "She just drove into Tiffany's driveway."

"Cynthia, where are you?"

"I'm parked around the corner from the house—on Shelby Court."

"So you're in the car?"

"Yes. Why are you asking me these questions?" I snapped back.

Jacques laughed heartily. "Well then, why are you whispering? I don't think she can hear you, darling."

"Oh, right." I raised my voice to a normal tone. "She was carrying a suitcase."

"That does seem odd," Jacques said. "Maybe she's there to check on something. Or perhaps she's smuggling out the good silver?"

A vision of my mother-in-law crossed my mind. "Do you think so?"

"I was kidding, girl." He cleared his throat. "By the way, Donna called me this morning. I was going to tell you when we met up later."

"What now? Is she going to arrest me for trying to come on to her husband?"

"She found out about my appointment and begged me to stay put. I swear, if we'd been face to face she would've kissed my feet. I told her we'd discuss it later. And speaking of her slimy husband, she told me she hadn't seen him since yesterday. He didn't come home last night. No call, nothing. She broke down in tears on the phone."

"Oh boy."

"I told you. I feel like the office therapist some days."

"You see what this means? He *must* have something to do with Tiffany's death. He's on the run now." I thought about the vase in Tiffany's bedroom. Ken had assured me it wasn't worth anything, but who knew? Perhaps there were other valuables in the house. "Do you know anything else about Tiffany's family?"

"A little. I also knew where she lived, unlike some people."

"I'm serious! This is important."

Jacques coughed into the phone. "Her mother's family was rich. When Tiffany was about ten, she and her parents were in a car accident. Her mother died from the injuries. The father was badly hurt but survived. He was never the same afterward. Tiffany said she always felt like he blamed her."

"Boy, you and Tiffany sure had some heart-to-hearts in that lunchroom."

He snorted. "You're just jealous. I have a face that people trust. Anyhow, after the accident, he and Tiffany weren't getting along, so she went to live with a maiden aunt, her mother's older sister. It was then that she found out her dad had been married years before, and she had an older half-sister. Can you believe her father never even told her?"

How odd. "I wonder why."

"Tiffany insisted he wanted to forget that part of his life. His first wife had an affair, so he divorced her. The daughter from the first marriage sided with her mother. Anyhow, Tiffany wanted to meet her sister and tracked the woman down eventually. Her dad had a heart attack and died a few months ago."

"It makes me feel sorry for her."

"A lot of bad luck there," Jacques agreed. "She said her father never got over her mother's death. When he died, everything went to Tiffany."

I tapped my finger against the steering wheel. "Well, that explains it. I know she made a lot of money, but that house has got to be worth a fortune. Why was she selling it?"

"The house belonged to her father, and no, it's not worth a fortune. He'd mortgaged it to the hilt, and she needed to unload it to pay off his bills and get out from under that mess. Apparently, he had a few antiques left from the estate, but that was about all. Tiffany thought there might be papers for the stuff, but hadn't found anything. He was a huge pack rat."

I mulled this over. "The house was pristine. I didn't see any mess. There was a distinct vase in her bedroom that I thought might be an antique. It was beautiful, but Ken said it was worthless." Something wasn't adding up here.

"Anyhow, it took her three months to get the house on the market because she was sifting through her father's stuff. Last week she mentioned to me that her new boyfriend came by to help her one night. She said most of the mess was in the basement."

"Ah, well that explains it. We didn't go down there. Does the boyfriend know about her death? Where is he now?"

"I didn't even catch his name. She said he traveled a lot. Why don't you ask Linda?"

I drew my eyebrows together, thoroughly perplexed by this suggestion. "What does Linda have to do with it?"

"She was always answering Tiffany's phone. Remember, she treated Linda like a personal secretary."

I knew something about that too, thanks to Donna.

"Maybe she talked to him at one point and remembers his name. You know what, I'll call her for you. She doesn't come in on Saturdays, but I just happen to have her cell number."

A rush of adrenaline swept over me. "Ooh. That would be awesome. I can't believe you knew so much about Tiffany."

Jacques sighed. "Everyone at the agency comes to me with their problems—business and personal. Even Donna. And it's not like anyone can talk to her."

"By the way, I need a huge favor."

"Listen darling, I'm all out of favors today. My appointment is in ten minutes. By the way, when are we going to see Pete? Will you be done with Sylvia by eleven thirty?"

"I should be."

"Okay, I'll call you then. Now what'd you want, my pest?"

"Is there any way you can let me into Tiffany's house?" I asked.

"Why? What for?"

"I can't explain it, but I know something weird is going on there. And if my code shows up in Donna's email again, I'm dead. She'll definitely call the police."

"She's going to ask questions if my code shows up too."

"Yeah, but you still work for her and could always say there's a serious buyer who desperately wanted to see the house, so you figured it would be okay."

"I'll look like a freaking idiot."

"No, you won't. Anyhow, what can she do, besides fire you?" I joked.

Jacques sighed. "All right, we'll figure something out."

"You're a doll. Is it any wonder I adore you?"

Jacques made a loud harrumphing noise, obviously not falling for my flattery this time. "Yeah, I adore you too. But sometimes you can be an enormous pain in the ass, my dear." With that, he clicked off.

I disconnected, smiling, and turned my attention back to the house. It had been about ten minutes since Donna went inside, and she hadn't reappeared yet. I wanted to stay until she came out. I was starting to enjoy playing detective. I glanced at my watch—there was still a little time to play with.

When cars passed by, I pretended to be checking my messages. I waited another ten minutes and then, with regret, started the engine. I wasn't sure how long I might be tied up at the pawn shops and needed to be on my way. I also couldn't afford to be late for my appointment with Sylvia.

I glanced up in time to see Donna shutting the front door. As she strolled toward her car, I noticed she was still carrying the suitcase. Something very strange was going on here, indeed.

When she turned down the street I was on, I managed to duck, barely in time. Relief washed over me when I realized she wouldn't recognize my car. I waited a few seconds and straightened up, tempted to follow her, but there was no time. Heaving a sigh, I headed in the opposite direction.

I hoped to find some trace of Ken this morning. Not that I actually wanted to see him again, but my head was racing with ideas about him. I found myself in front of Pawn for All on Hamilton Avenue. I exited my vehicle and went inside.

Five minutes later, I was back in the car again. What a letdown. Pawn for All was a family-owned establishment run by a husband and wife. Their only employee was their twenty-something daughter. It appeared that I'd have to head into the seedy part of town after all.

Fifteen minutes later, I pulled up in front of World of Pawn. The red brick building, with its neon sign that read *We Buy and Sell All*, looked forlorn and deserted. The flashing sign had several bulbs blown out, and the sparse, brown grass was riddled with mud. Windows were dirty and blinds tattered.

A white Chevy Cruze sat parked in front of the building, and there were no signs of a red BMW anywhere. I got out of my car, careful to lock my doors. Since this neighborhood was known for a high crime rate, I hurried toward the front door. A light glowed in the interior, and I opened the door a crack. "Hello?"

"Come on in," a man called out.

I pushed the creaking door open and did a quick look around. The front counter glass display had been polished until it shone. There was a stool behind it and a large safe about the size of one of the twins. The only thing missing was merchandise. The display counter was completely empty.

"Something I can help you with, miss?" An elderly gentleman was standing behind the counter holding a diamond necklace. His sparse hair and beard were as white as snow and his face and stomach perfectly round. He would have made an excellent Santa Claus.

"Hello. I'm Randy Malone, the owner." He extended his hand to me.

"Hi, I'm Cindy York. I'm a real estate agent for Hospit—" Oops, no, I wasn't anymore. "It's very nice to meet you."

"Agent, huh? I'm not looking to sell, honey. I just bought the place the other day." Randy chuckled as he walked over to the safe and opened the door, depositing the necklace inside. He double checked to make sure it was secure and then leaned on the counter, looking me over.

My curiosity piqued. "Did you buy it from a man named Ken, by chance?"

"Who?" Randy's face was blank.

"Ken Sorenson. He owned—I mean—he might have owned the shop." Hey, it was a shot in the dark but all I had right now.

He shrugged. "I don't know anybody named Ken. I bought some merchandise from a guy. He didn't own the building though. He was only renting the space."

My heart skipped a beat. "Was he tall, with dark hair and a muscular build? Looked a lot like George Clooney?"

Randy nodded emphatically. "Yep, that's the guy all right." He tugged at his beard. "Like I said, he was only renting the building. Said something about it went into foreclosure a couple of years ago. Seemed like kind of a conceited snob, if you'll pardon the term."

That was the understatement of the year. "No worries. And you've described him spot on."

"His name wasn't Ken either. It was Chuck. Chuck Samuels."

I chewed at my bottom lip. "Are you sure?"

"Positive." Randy reached under the counter and withdrew a folder overstuffed with papers. "I bought the building from a company called the Tori Association. Mr. Samuels owed them some money, so I made a deal with him that I'd pay off his back rent in exchange for a few pieces of jewelry he had. He was happy to comply."

The whole situation stank worse than my burned kitchen countertop. I didn't know what to think now.

"Are you okay, miss? Would you like a glass of water?"

I nodded, unable to speak. Randy disappeared and returned a minute later with a paper cup. I drank from it gratefully.

"See here, little lady." Randy was holding up another piece of paper. "This is a receipt for the jewelry I bought from him. The necklace you just saw? It was one of the pieces. He said it belonged to a girlfriend, but she didn't need it anymore."

"Didn't need it anymore?" I echoed.

He nodded. "Said she'd had it for years and was sick of it. Wanted something new."

None of this made any sense. What girlfriend? He was married. I was willing to bet Ken knew something about Tiffany's murder. One thing was for sure. Donna's new husband, or gigolo as I referred to him in my mind, was clearly all about himself.

I glanced at the paper Randy showed me. The signature indeed read Chuck Samuels. "Did he say why he was leaving?"

Randy shook his head. "It didn't sound like business was too good. He owed a lot in back rent and didn't have much left in inventory. I think that's why the owners put it up for sale. They wanted him out and knew he didn't have enough money to buy the building. I'm planning to reinvent the whole place. Got painters and carpet installers coming tomorrow. It'll be good as new before long."

"That's nice." I was barely listening. I thought of the BMW, the expensive suit, and the wallet full of cash at lunch the other day.

"I really thought he'd fallen on hard times until I saw that vase."

My ears pricked up instantly. "Excuse me? Did you say vase?"

Randy chuckled. "Sure did. The guy had himself a vase from the Ming Dynasty and offered to sell it to me. He said it was a family heirloom. He even offered to reduce the price, but there was no way I could afford the likes of it."

My heart stuttered inside my chest, and I tried to control my excitement. "Do you remember what it looked like?"

"Of course I remember. I've only seen a couple in my lifetime. Wish I could have bought it, but I don't have that much cash on hand. He said he'd sell it for a million if I wanted to buy. If he plays his cards right, Mr. Samuels will probably get closer to two million for that baby."

That would be enough to keep Ken in BMWs and crème brûlée for a long time. *No, it can't be.* "What'd the vase look like?"

"It was black-and-white porcelain and in the shape of a flask. Had an unusual design about it. I could tell it was an original though. Any fool would know the difference."

My stomach filled with dread. "Where would he go to sell something like that?"

"Unless he knows someone who's got the cash, I'm betting he'd take it to an auction house. They fetch the most money there."

"Where's the closest one?"

Randy scratched the top of his head. "That would be New York City. I doubt you'd find him there though. They'd have to schedule it for auction, and sometimes that takes weeks. He'd probably have them wire the money to his account when it's sold."

I sighed and looked down at the display case for a minute, defeated. "So he could be anywhere now."

When I raised my head, Randy was watching me intently, his face full of sympathy. "Is he your husband? Darn shame if he pulled something over on a nice-looking lady like you."

I forced a smile to my lips while shuddering inwardly at the thought. "It's nothing like that. But I do need to locate him as soon as possible."

Randy stroked his beard again. "Look, if you're sure he's got the vase and, well, is not supposed to, you could check the auction house sites online. If it's been scheduled, they'll have pictures of it there. Then you could go down to New York City when the auction takes place. I doubt he'd show up for it, but you never know."

"Did he happen to leave you an address or a phone number?"

"Oh, sure." Randy reached back in the folder and produced a business card. He reached for a pen and turned the card over to write on it. "While I'm at it, here are websites for two possible auction houses you can check out."

I glanced at the information, then flipped the card over. Chuck Samuels. I recognized the phone number as the same one Ken had called me from the other night. I pulled out my cell and dialed it, but a female voice told me the number was no longer in service.

"Not working?" Randy asked.

"I'm afraid not, but you've been a great help. If for some reason he calls or stops by, would you please let me know?" I jotted my name and phone number down on a Post-it note from my purse. I was missing my business cards already. "Please don't tell him I'm looking for him, but call me right away, and try to stall him."

Randy examined my Post-it note. "It'd be my pleasure. Look, Mrs. York. I hate to say this, but it sounds like you're fooling yourself. It's obvious Mr. Samuel's in some type of trouble. He won't be showing up here again. And I'm betting dollars to doughnuts you know this too."

He was right. Had Ken left Donna? He'd obviously gotten some money from Randy— enough to tide him over until Tiffany's vase sold. If it *was* her vase. So where had he gone now?

CHAPTER EIGHTEEN

*A*s I rode across town for my appointment with Sylvia, I wished I had time to sit back and digest everything I'd just learned. My head was starting to spin from it all.

How had Ken learned about the vase? Had he known Tiffany? Did he have something to do with her murder? And what was Donna's position in all of this? She's married to the guy for barely two weeks, and he ups and leaves her? If Donna found out that a possible theft might have occurred during a showing, she was going to freak. She wouldn't care if Ken had been the perpetrator. The police would be notified, and it would all be my fault since I was the agent in charge.

Maybe Ken had spotted the vase in one of the listing's pictures and instantly knew its value. He'd used me to let him into the house and grabbed it when I wasn't around. He must have hidden the vase in his car while I'd been in the bathroom. I tried hard to remember if the photos online showed a picture of the vase in Tiffany's bedroom. I'd have to check when I got home.

The questions kept crowding my brain. What about Tiffany's

secret boyfriend? Did he have something to do with her murder as well? And how would I go about finding him?

I really wasn't in the mood to interview with another real estate firm right now, but I didn't have a choice. Glancing at my watch, I discovered I was five minutes late—typical of me lately. I should have had the decency to call and say I wouldn't make it on time, but it'd slipped my mind. Frustrated with myself, I pulled into the tiny parking lot of the agency.

Sylvia's company was located in a small ranch house. The building was painted a bright shade of green, like the Emerald City. The business sign consisted of an enlarged picture of Dorothy, accompanied by the words *No Place Like Home Realty* coming out of her mouth in a bubble. A little cheesy for my taste, but hey, desperate times called for desperate measures.

Sylvia Banks had started the firm about ten years ago, and she'd made a respectable name for herself. I'd worked with a couple of her agents on some sales in the past and knew they were happy with her. She seemed like a fair and honest person to deal with.

I felt guilty knowing that this might turn out to be a short-term employment stunt, depending on how fast things progressed with Jacques' business. But I desperately needed a job right now and didn't have much of a choice.

I got out of the car, smoothed my slacks, and adjusted my blazer. I stepped onto the small stone porch painted the same color as the building, knocked on the front door, and then opened it slowly.

Sylvia sat at the front desk, going through some mail. An attractive, older woman with silver hair and midnight-blue eyes, she wore jeans and a white sweater. She appeared startled when she saw me.

"Hi, Sylvia. How are you?" I extended my hand. She glanced at me, smiled, and lightly brushed her fingers against mine.

"I'm sorry for being late. I had an appointment on the other side of town, and the drive took a little longer than I expected."

Sylvia's smile seemed forced. "Oh, that's fine. Won't you have a seat, Tiffany—err—I mean, Cindy?" She corrected herself and blushed simultaneously.

Oh boy. I already knew how this was going to turn out.

"Can I offer you something to drink?"

"No, thank you." I reached into my briefcase and presented her with a list of my most recent sales for the past year, as well as some client references. She observed them for about two seconds and then handed the sheet back.

Sylvia cleared her throat nervously. "Well, these certainly are impressive."

I drew my eyebrows together in confusion. "Is something wrong?"

"Well, no, not really," Sylvia said. "But I'm afraid I've wasted your time, having you come all the way out here. You see, I had another agent start yesterday. It was all very sudden."

"Oh, anyone I know?"

Sylvia frowned. "His name is Brian Summers."

It was difficult to keep from smiling. I'd spoken to Brian on the phone earlier this week. A client of mine had wanted to see one of his listings, and I'd left him two messages, along with questions. He'd finally returned my call and apologized for the delay, explaining he was on vacation in Florida until next Monday. Now I knew the truth—Sylvia didn't want me anymore. As a real estate agent, I prided myself on honesty. I would have had more respect for the woman if she'd confessed her real feelings instead of lying to my face. So I decided to play along.

"How nice for you," I said. "And you can't accommodate another agent?"

"Oh, no." She answered without hesitation. "I only had the one empty desk. There isn't room for any more."

"Well, I'd be happy to work full time out of my house. That would solve the problem." I was enjoying making her squirm.

Sylvia shifted in her seat uncomfortably. "Thanks for the offer, but I'm afraid there's more to it than that. You see, we haven't been getting many leads. I've had to increase the office rent for agents too. Mark my words, dear, it would be a bad move for you."

"The additional fees will be fine. I think your agency would be a wonderful addition to my resume."

Sylvia twisted a tissue in her hands. "It won't work, Cindy." She got to her feet. "Thanks for coming though." She extended her hand.

I decided to call her bluff. "Who do you think you're kidding? You don't want to hire me because you think I killed Tiffany."

Her jaw dropped. "That's ridiculous. I would never accuse anyone of such a crime. I think you are way out of line."

I spoke quietly. "No, Sylvia, you're way out of line. You agreed to the interview. You told me on the phone I'd be a perfect fit for your office. Now all of a sudden you don't have room for me because you hired someone yesterday? Why didn't you just tell me the truth?"

"I don't know what you're talking about." She stared down at her desk.

I sighed in exasperation. "It happens that I spoke to Brian Summers the other day. He isn't even back in town until next week."

"Well, um, he's starting then. I meant to say I called and hired him yesterday. You're trying to confuse me."

I produced my cell phone from my purse. "Fine. Would you like me to call him now so that he knows exactly what day to show up?"

Sylvia trembled and her forehead shone with sweat. "Please. Don't hurt me."

I stared at her in disbelief. "What are you talking about?"

"I think you need to go." Sylvia stood and put her hand over her heart, turning a sickly color similar to the revolting paint on her building. Her breath came out in rapid, heavy gasps.

My mouth fell open in shock. "Are you okay?"

Sylvia tried to speak, but only a gurgling sound came out. She continued to stare at me with terror in her eyes. Seconds later, she collapsed on the floor.

"Oh my God." I ran around to the other side of the desk and felt for her pulse. It was slow, but steady. Good grief. Now I was consumed with guilt. I hadn't meant to hurt the woman. I was simply tired of everyone acknowledging me as the town murderer.

I was searching for my phone in my purse to dial 9-1-1 when the front door opened. Wearing a name tag and carrying a stack of home flyers, I assumed this was one of Sylvia's agents. She glanced at me, confused, and then at Sylvia slumped on the floor.

"Oh, no. Not again." She reached for her phone and pressed a few numbers. "Yes, this is Laurie Jacobs with No Place Like Home Realty. Our manager, Sylvia, has had another seizure." She listened for a moment. "Yes, it's the third one this month. We're at 22 Cobble Road."

Laurie took Sylvia's hand and listened to her pulse. She glanced at me, an apologetic smile on her face. "Was Sylvia supposed to show you some houses today?"

A bead of sweat trickled down my back, and I didn't answer immediately.

Before I could respond, Laurie went on. "I'm so sorry for the inconvenience. I'm sure Sylvia will be in touch as soon as she's feeling better."

"Uh, sure, no problem." I stood and reached for my purse and briefcase, then hesitated. I felt awful leaving them like this. "Are you sure you don't want me to stay?"

Laurie shook her head. "Thanks, but it happens all the time. She'll be fine. No need for you to bother."

Had I really found the only person in town who didn't recognize me? "Okay. I hope she's better soon."

Laurie thanked me, and I let myself out. I walked to the car slowly, my legs wobbling like jelly and face perspiring. I drove out of the lot and had reached a stop sign at the end of the street when an ambulance screamed past me in the opposite lane. A police car followed behind, lights flashing. I wasn't positive, but the driver looked like my buddy Officer Simon. That would have been all I needed. He would have found some way to arrest me for sure. Every time I took a step forward, I sank deeper into quicksand.

I needed a caffeine fix bad and stopped at Starbuck's for a cappuccino. As I waited my turn, I checked my phone. The text from my husband was only five words long. *You said you would call.* Shoot. He'd be upset, especially once he found out what I'd been up to.

I paid for the drink and called Greg's cell when I got back into my car.

He answered right away. "Cin, are you okay?"

I took a long sip of my drink, savoring the taste while trying to calm my nerves. "I'm fine. I was running late for my appointment with Sylvia and didn't have time to call you." I relayed my meeting with Randy, but purposely omitted the details of my disastrous interview. I could get into that later.

Greg remained silent for a few seconds. "Baby, Ken is a rat. Please leave it alone. I think it's better if you don't find him. We already know what he's capable of. The police don't have anything definite on you. They'll find Tiffany's killer before long, and people will forget all about this. You'll see."

My phone beeped with another call coming in. I glanced at the number. "Look sweetie, Jacques is on the other line. I've got to go."

"When will you be home?"

"Jacques and I have a quick errand to run. I'll be back in a couple of hours." I clicked onto the other line. "Hey, you."

"Hey, yourself. I'm on my way. Are you home yet?"

"No, leaving Starbucks. The one we were at the other day."

"Stay right there. I'll pick you up, and then we'll go see Pete."

I shifted in my seat. I was betting that Pete wasn't going to be thrilled to see us. Plus, he scared me a bit. "Do we really have to do this?"

"I'm only a couple of blocks away. Look, it will be worth it if can we get something out of him, Cin."

"I guess." I sat back and took a long sip of my drink. Whoever had invented this Italian masterpiece was a genius in my book. "Hey, did you remember to call Linda?"

Jacques groaned. "What the heck is wrong with me? I used to be so perfect. Okay, I'll call her now. See you in a minute."

I took another sip of my drink. Tires squealed, and I looked up to see Jacques, parked next to me, talking into his Bluetooth. I grabbed my purse, locked the car, and got in on the passenger side. "Gee, it took you long enough."

He grimaced. "There goes that sarcastic mouth of yours again. Okay, I left a message on Linda's cell. As soon as I hear back from her, I'll let you know."

"Why don't you let me drive?" I suggested.

"Forget it," Jacques said. "I want to get there today."

I pulled my seat belt around me and made the sign of the cross on my chest. "So tell me all about it. How'd you like the building?"

"It's perfect, exactly what I've been looking for. I'm going to sign the lease on Monday, and then I'll make Donna cry."

I laughed. "Her golden goose is taking flight."

"And how'd your appointment go? Should I be calling you Dorothy instead of Cynthia now?"

"No fear of that." I relayed the story of my meeting, ending with Sylvia's near comatose state.

Jacques almost veered off the road.

"God, remind me not to tell you any more stories while you're driving. You're a maniac as it is."

Jacques snorted. "You worry too much. Seriously, be careful. Ten to one she tries to make trouble for you. I could see her telling the cops you threatened her, just to be spiteful. Sylvia's not all there."

"Exactly who in this town *is* all there?" I applied pressure to my temples in an attempt to relieve the building tension. "I'm in enough trouble already. How could it get worse?"

"Trust me, it can always be worse. Did you find Ken Doll this morning?"

I gripped the door handle as Jacques zoomed through a traffic light, which had just turned red. "For God's sake. Remember, I have three kids."

"I know, and they all adore me. So what happened—did you find him?"

"Yes and no. I found the shop, but there's a new owner named Randy who bought all of Ken's inventory yesterday. He said Ken never even owned the place. And guess what else?" I exhaled sharply. "I think he may have lifted Tiffany's vase the other day when we were at her house."

Jacques whirled to look at me and almost hit another car. "Are you serious?"

"Watch out! Yeah, he tried to sell it to the new owner. Randy described it for me. It sounded like Tiffany's."

"Oh crap." Jacques frowned. "But you said it wasn't worth anything. Why would he bother?"

"Wrong. Ken said it was worthless. According to Randy, the vase is valued at about two million dollars. It's a piece from the Ming Dynasty. Watch out for that parked car!"

Jacques swerved to the left, his mouth hanging wide open.

I'd never seen him speechless before. Finally, he found his voice. "Do you think Randy could be wrong? I mean, is there any chance Ken owned a vase like that too? Perhaps he needed money, and that's why he's selling it."

"Do you honestly believe that?"

"Well, no," he admitted.

"Me neither. But I know one thing. I've got to get into Tiffany's house to see if the vase is still there. Please." I gave him my best pleading look.

Jacques sighed in resignation. "All right. I want to know what's going on too." He pulled up in front of the duplex where Pete lived. "After we're done here, I've got some errands to run, and I'm meeting Ed for an early dinner. It'll have to be after that."

I groaned.

"Don't get your panties in a bunch. It's better if we wait until after dark. We don't want the neighbors seeing us."

"All right. I should go home for a bit anyway. Greg doesn't like me playing detective, and I do have a family to feed. I'll stop at the store, cook dinner, and then come back to meet you."

"No, I'll come and get you," Jacques offered. "Greg will feel better about you going out if he knows you're not alone. Ed's babysitting his sister's kids after dinner. I may join them later. How does seven sound?"

"That works. I owe you one."

"No, you don't. I just got myself a new employee, remember? Come on."

We stepped onto the rickety, wooden porch where Pete lived. Jacques rang the doorbell that belonged to the entrance on the left side of the house, labeled *Saxon*. After a few seconds, Pete emerged. He was barefoot and unshaven, wearing jeans and a black T-shirt. Two little girls clung to his legs.

He stared at us in amazement. "Hey, Jacques. Hi, Cindy. What're you guys doing here?"

Jacques cleared his throat. "Can we talk to you for a moment?"

Pete peered over his shoulder into the house. "Um, it's not really a good time."

"Pete, who are you talking to?" A woman spoke in an irritated tone from somewhere behind him. I wasn't able to see her, but she had a shrill voice that could easily reach the next block.

A panicked look crossed over his face, and he whirled around to address the woman. "It's nothing. Only some people from work, honey."

"Well, I just waxed the floor."

Her voice growled, similar to an animal. A very large and scary one. Jacques and I exchanged glances.

"We'll talk outside, dear." Pete gently disengaged the little girls from his legs and told them to go play for a while. He stepped onto the porch, making sure to close the door behind him. His eyes darted from me to Jacques with suspicion.

"What's this all about?"

I went first. "We were sorry to hear you'd left the agency."

Relief washed over his face. "Oh, that. Well, you know, I had another offer I couldn't refuse."

"Uh-huh." Jacques appeared doubtful. "So where are you working now?"

"Um," Pete paused. "I—I'm supposed to be working for Primer Properties."

I suspected he was lying. "You are? Funny, Tricia didn't say a thing about it to me when I saw her yesterday." Tricia would be the last person to tell me anything about her business, but Pete didn't need to know that.

"Who?" He asked, dumbfounded.

"Tricia Hudson. She's their number one agent. I'm sure she'll be happy to provide you with training."

"Oh, right." Pete was silent for a few seconds. "Well, it's been nice chatting with you guys, but I need to get going."

Jacques touched his arm. "It's kind of strange that you left the agency right after Tiffany was killed."

Pete ran a hand through his bushy, black hair. "What are you talking about?" His voice was tense.

"I'm talking about the fact that Tiffany stiffed you out of a really nice commission, someone murdered her, and you left the agency, all in the same day."

Pete's face turned ashen. "The cops have already talked to me. I don't need to explain anything to you guys."

"I was there when you threatened her." Jacques folded his arms over his chest. "I don't blame you for being mad. God knows, she pulled that crap with a lot of people."

A drop of sweat ran down the side of Pete's face, and he didn't answer right away. "I—I didn't do anything to her."

"When was the last time you saw her?" I asked.

"That night. Uh, I mean, when we were all in the office."

My ears pricked up. "You went by the office to see her? The night she was killed?"

"No, earlier in the day."'

I figured I'd test the waters. "We have a witness who saw you there later that night. The time was close to seven o'clock."

Pete's eyes widened in surprise. "Who? Who saw me? Oh my God, I can't believe this is happening." He slammed his fist against the porch railing.

"Do you happen to own a dark-colored SUV?"

All the color drained from Pete's face. He glanced with uneasiness at the front door and then gestured for us to move away. We walked off the porch and stood by Jacques' car.

Pete stared at the ground, his hands in his pockets. "I didn't do anything to her, I swear." Then he glared at me. "But I wanted to. I wanted to kill her. Do you know how much I was counting on that money?"

"I do know. You're allowed to be angry. She stole a listing from me the same day as she did you."

"She did?" His tone softened.

"Yes, and I was upset, too," I admitted.

"What time did you go by the office?" Jacques asked.

He wrung his hands together in frustration. "My wife can't find out what happened. She doesn't even know I left Hospitable Homes. She'll kill me if she figures it out."

I raised one eyebrow at Jacques. It was evident who was in charge at Pete's house. "We won't say anything to her. You have our word."

Pete closed his eyes and groped for words. "I think it was about 6:30. I didn't stay long." He paused, remembering. "She was alone. I went upstairs to her office and told her I wanted my share of the check. But she laughed and called me a fool." He clenched his jaw, and his eyes turned black as coal. He leaned over to grab his mailbox and threw it violently to the ground.

I must have jumped at least ten feet in the air. Jacques moved in front of his car's side view mirror, in case Pete decided to go for that next.

"Wha-what did you do then?" I asked with trepidation.

"I—I kind of went wild. I grabbed her by the throat."

Jacques and I glanced at each other in alarm.

"She started screaming and tried to scratch me. I told her I had to have that money. I'm two months late on my rent." His eyes took on a vacant expression. "She kept screaming, and I begged her to stop. Then she kicked me with those big pointy heels of hers."

"Stilettos," I offered.

"Whatever."

Jacques frowned. "Where'd she kick you?"

When Pete's face turned crimson, I got the message. Huh. Seems like Tiffany and I did have something in common after all.

"Dang," Jacques shook his head. "That must have left a mark."

Pete nodded. "It still hurts a little. I wish I'd never gone."

"What happened after that?" I held my breath.

"She was yelling at me to get out of there before she called the cops. I pretty much crawled down the stairs and out the door to my car. I'm not even sure how I managed to drive away, but I was afraid the cops would be looking for me. Then I went to a bar and got drunk before I came home."

Jacques narrowed his eyes. "Nice."

"I was scared," Pete said. "I heard Tiffany on the phone with someone before I could get out of there. I thought for a second it was the police, but then I knew it wasn't."

My interested piqued. "What do you mean by that?"

"Well, she obviously knew the person. She kept saying, 'You need to get over here. Pete just tried to kill me.'"

"You didn't hear her call the person by name?" Jacques asked.

Pete's face contorted with anger. "Don't you think I would've told you the person's name if I'd heard it?"

Jacques and I both backed up a bit, and I tried to reassure him. "Of course you would have."

"You can't tell my wife. She'll divorce me."

I found myself wondering if that might not be the worst thing that could happen to Pete, but refrained from saying so.

"It's our little secret," Jacques promised. "Did you—did you tell the cops about this?"

Pete clenched his fists. "No. And you'd better not tell them either. I'll just deny everything."

Jacques put his hands up. "Hey, no problem there, buddy."

Was he telling us the truth? I had my doubts. "Do you remember what time it was when you left?"

"I couldn't have been in there more than ten minutes. Yeah, now I remember the car radio definitely said 6:45."

I chewed at my bottom lip. "And you didn't notice any other cars outside?"

Pete shook his head. "Only Tiffany's hotshot Jag. I thought I saw someone in my rearview mirror when I left. I might have imagined it though. I was in a lot of pain."

Jacques mouthed the word "Leslie" to me.

We heard the front door creak open. Pete's wife stood there, hands perched on her broad hips. "Pete, I need you."

Pete froze in terror. "I'll be there in a minute, honey."

"I said *now*."

I observed the woman, intrigued. She had long, dark, straggly hair with a beefy frame. She wore a bib apron and red bandanna around her head. She met my gaze and shot me a surly look back.

"I need to go." Pete started toward the house, then turned back to us again. His deep voice took on a warning tone. "Like I said, you'd better not tell anybody."

CHAPTER NINETEEN

We drove back to Starbucks in silence. Upon reaching the parking lot, we sat quietly in Jacques' car, trying to absorb what had just happened.

Finally, I cleared my throat. "It's got to be him."

This time, Jacques was on the defense. "I'm not so sure, Cin. I mean, he's got some crazy tendencies, but I don't think he's a killer."

I couldn't believe my ears. "He grabbed Tiffany by the throat. Did you see the glare in his eyes? He looked like a lunatic."

Jacques nodded in agreement. "True, but did you also see how afraid he was of Attila the Hun—oops, I mean his wife. I don't think a guy who lets his wife boss him around like that is capable of murdering somebody. Hey, maybe his wife's the killer. Now that I can picture."

I grimaced. "My mother always said you can't trust the quiet ones."

"After we head over to Tiffany's house tonight, we need to sit down and figure out where we are with our investigation."

"Nowhere. That's where we are."

Jacques gazed at me, puzzled. "What's with the attitude?"

"I'm running out of time. If it turns out the vase is gone, along with Ken, I'm done for. The police will be questioning me again. Donna will figure out a way to pin it on me. They'll put me in jail." A wave of panic rolled over me.

Jacques patted my hand. "Try to think positive. I have a feeling we're close—like the murderer is right under our thumb."

"I hope you're right." I sifted through my purse for my car keys. "When I get home, I'm going to call some auction houses. Maybe Ken brought the vase to one of them."

"If it is Tiffany's vase."

"Oh, I'd bet on it. But we'll know tonight for sure."

"Seven o'clock sharp," Jacques reminded me. "I'll pick you up at your house. Be ready."

After a quick stop at the grocery store, I arrived home at about three o'clock. I didn't know how I'd manage to wait around for another four hours. Impatience was already getting the best of me. I jumped every time the phone rang, afraid it might be the police.

I decided to try to keep myself busy. The twins and I took the puppy for a walk. Afterward, we went back to the house, and they lured Greg into playing a game of touch football in the backyard while I started dinner. Darcy helped me vacuum and dust. While my chicken and potatoes casserole cooked in the oven, Darcy joined Greg and the boys outside. I decided to check the auction houses online that Randy had mentioned earlier. My heart skipped a beat when I saw a link for antique vases on the main page. I scrolled through the listings. On the second page, toward the bottom, was Tiffany's vase. There was no mistake—I would have known it anywhere. I found the contact information page and dialed the phone number provided for the company.

After a brief time on hold, a female voice came on the line. "How may I assist you?"

"Is it possible for you to give me information about a certain vase on your site? It's from the Ming Dynasty."

"If you like, I can put you through to speak with a specialist," the woman replied. "They should be able to help you further."

Again, I was placed on hold, and the wait seemed interminable. Finally, a man's voice answered. "Scott Sultan. How may I assist you?"

"I'd like to inquire about a particular vase that's scheduled for auction next week. It's from the Ming Dynasty, black-and-white porcelain with an unusual design."

Scott coughed in reply. "May I ask your name?"

"Cindy York."

"I do happen to remember that piece. It will be made available to the highest bidder next Thursday, May sixth."

I clutched the phone tightly. "Can you tell me who you got the vase from? I believe it might have been stolen."

Scott was silent for several seconds. "Do you have any proof?"

"Well, nothing concrete yet, but I'm positive it was stolen."

"We don't deal with stolen goods, ma'am." It was obvious from his tone that Scott was not taking me seriously. "Everything that comes in here has the appropriate paperwork to accompany the item. I'm afraid I can't tell you anything further. If you'd like to bid, the auction will begin at one o'clock sharp. If you can't be here in person, you can arrange to phone in a bid as well. Thank you for your interest."

"Wait a minute."

I was too late. The phone line went dead.

"Damn." I sat there, staring into space for a moment. I sniffed at the air and then hurried into the kitchen to check on dinner. The casserole was perfect, so I turned off the oven, then went back to the computer and pulled up the listing on Tiffany's house, clicking through pictures in the tour until I came to Tiffany's bedroom. I breathed a sigh of relief when I saw a photo that contained the grand piano. The vase was in perfect view. I printed the picture and put it in my purse. This might come in handy later.

There was no possible way I could wait five more days for the auction to occur. Who knows, maybe I'd be in prison by then. Even if the vase was located, Donna might still accuse me of stealing it. I prayed that my theory was wrong and that the vase still remained on top of Tiffany's piano.

I went outside to call everyone in for dinner. Almost show time.

During dinner, I caught Greg watching me suspiciously. "Baby, is something wrong?"

I shook my head and smiled. Underneath the table, I crossed my fingers. "Everything's fine."

His eyes searched mine, unconvinced, and I looked away in a hurry. "Stevie, please stop feeding Rusty under the table. He's going to get fat."

"But he wants to be fat." Stevie giggled.

Greg continued to stare at me as if he knew something was up. He was momentarily distracted by the sight of Darcy jumping to her feet. She started stacking the dishes in the sink without either one of us even asking her to.

"Somebody's up to something." Greg winked at me.

Darcy laughed. "Not me, Daddy."

"You might as well spill it."

She turned to me for help. I remembered about the prom and smiled reassuringly at Greg. "Darcy's been invited to prom. I figured we'd go shopping for a dress after her punishment is over. We'll take the one from the dance back and get credit toward a new one."

Greg forked a potato into his mouth. "That's nice, honey."

Darcy and I were both bewildered. I had been positive that he'd give her the third degree. Apparently, she'd thought the same thing.

"His name is Ryan," Darcy said, a lilt in her voice. "You'll really—"

I shook my head and shot her a warning look. She got the message. I didn't want to deal with the issue of her date's age right now. Darcy started on the dishes while the twins grabbed the puppy and headed into the living room to watch television.

The time had come to tell Greg the truth, so I followed him into the den. "I need to go back out tonight."

Greg whirled around from the desk. "Why?"

"Jacques's coming by in five minutes to pick me up. We— we're going to Tiffany's house." There, I'd said it.

Greg appeared thunderstruck. "Are you nuts? Do you really *want* to get arrested?"

"I'll be fine. Like I said, Jacques's going with me. We'll use his code to get in. Donna will never even know I was there."

"What if they have a security camera rigged up? Did you happen to think about that?"

Actually, I hadn't. I tried to act casual as I brushed his comment aside with a wave of my hand. "Oh, it would've been mentioned in the listing."

"Don't be so sure. What if Donna had some installed?"

I laughed. "Why would she do that? It's not even her house!"

Greg gave me a worried look. "Don't underestimate her, Cin. She's not going to be happy until you're behind bars."

I didn't want Greg to know how nervous I was because then he'd never let me leave. I put my arms around his neck and kissed him. "Please don't worry. Jacques will be with me the entire time."

"He'd better be."

At that moment, we heard a car horn out front. I ran to the door, signaled to Jacques, and hurried back to grab a jacket.

Greg still sat in the den, his face masked with concern. "Maybe I should go with you."

"It's all going to be fine, honey. Really."

"Please be careful." Greg observed me with a pained expression. "Promise me you won't do anything stupid."

"Your confidence in me is overwhelming," I teased.

The look on his face was troubled, causing my heart to flip-flop in my chest. "Cindy, I mean it."

I swallowed hard. "All right, I promise."

"I love you."

"Love you too." I blew him a kiss and shut the front door with a shaking hand.

While I was scared to death to think what would happen if Donna found me in the house, it was even more frightening to imagine the implications if I didn't go through with this. I ran to Jacques' car before I could change my mind. I'd barely sat down when he zoomed off.

In a panic, I clutched at my seat belt. "Jeez, slow down. I'm nervous enough as it is."

Jacques chose to ignore my comment. "We'd better park down the street from Tiffany's. We don't want the neighbors to see us pulling into the driveway."

"They'd probably think you were showing it to a client—me. It's dark, so hopefully they won't be able to see or remember our faces."

"You don't know Donna like I do. I bet she's already gone around to the neighbors and told them there's no further showings so that they will let her know if any strangers are lurking about."

I blew out a breath, thinking this through. He might be right. Donna was so meticulous about every little detail. Maybe she'd given the neighbors a description of me as well—aka the murderer.

Jacques drove to the side street where I'd parked earlier this morning. Before we could get out of the car, his phone rang. He glanced at the screen. "What's up?" He listened, and his expression immediately changed to one of annoyance. "I told you that car was a piece of junk." An angry male voice, which I assumed belonged to Ed, shouted something through the phone. "Okay, okay, I'll be right there." He disconnected the call in a hurry.

"What's wrong?"

Jacques spoke in an irritated tone. "It's Ed. His car won't start, and he's got to get over to his sister's. I've been telling him for months to get rid of that crap pile, but he refuses. I think he does this on purpose to annoy me."

I managed to hide my smile.

"I need to go right over with my jumper cables. He hates to be kept waiting. Can we come back later?"

"Doesn't he have AAA?"

Jacques started the engine. "Honey, I am his AAA. The guy is too cheap to spend any money."

I couldn't stand to wait any longer. I had to know *now*. "Give me your eKEY and code, and I'll go in myself. Then I'll wait inside till you get back."

The sky was eerily dark, with only a sliver of the moon showing.

He pursed his lips. "I don't like leaving you here alone. If anything happens to you, Greg will kick my ass."

"I'll be fine as long as Donna doesn't show up. How long will you be?"

"Shouldn't take more than twenty minutes. Oh, and I talked to Donna about an hour ago. She wants to meet with me on Monday. She thinks she's convinced me to stay. It'll be a bit of a surprise when I show her my new lease." Jacques chuckled. "Anyhow, she said she was on her way to the movies with a friend, so we're in the clear."

"Awesome. That's a huge relief."

"Amen. I'll call when I'm on my way back so that we can make a quick getaway. It's going to be kind of tough as it is, explaining to Donna why I've been in a house that's not supposed to have any showings."

"You'll think of something. Try to hurry back."

His phone buzzed again. "You see what I mean. Like an old lady, that man. He can't wait two lousy seconds." He picked up the phone and screamed into it while I covered my ears. "I'm on my way, keep your pants on."

I chuckled. "Wow. You guys act like an old married couple, and you haven't even had your first anniversary yet."

"Yeah, well, if he keeps this up, we won't make it to our first anniversary." Jacques reached into his coat pocket for the eKEY and handed it to me. "The pass code is my birthday, 0515. Remember, it's coming up very soon." He winked.

"Thanks, you're the best." I opened the car door.

"Cindy, please be careful."

"Don't worry. I won't let anything happen to your stuff. I'll guard it with my life."

"I'm not worried about the eKEY. I've got a spare anyway."

I grinned at him. "Always so prepared."

"I was talking about you. Don't do anything risky. I'll be back as soon as I can." With a brisk wave and squeal of the tires, he was off.

I proceeded toward the house with caution. The only audible sound was my heart, pounding furiously away. The house and lawn were both submerged in complete darkness. I was surprised the outside lights didn't have automatic timers, unless Donna had shut them off on purpose. She could still allow showings on the house, but it seemed as if she now wanted everyone to forget the place existed. Why?

The ringing of my phone startled me. I took it out of my pocket and leaned back against the side of the house, fearful someone might see or hear me. It was Jacques.

I whispered into the phone. "Don't worry, I'm fine."

"I'm glad to hear that but wanted to let you know Linda just called me back. She didn't know anything about Tiffany having a boyfriend, but—"

"Well, shoot." Another idea that didn't pan out.

"Wait a minute, I'm not finished. She remembered a guy calling last week when they were both in the office late one evening. Shortly after that, she went up to Tiffany's office to hand her a fax and said Tiffany was giggling away on the phone like a schoolgirl. Said she heard her tell the guy she couldn't wait to have her way with him later."

Ew. "I really didn't need to hear that. Did Linda happen to mention the conversation to the police?"

Jacques snorted. "I doubt it. You know Linda. Her mind is a blank slate unless you ask her something straight out. She'd forgotten all about him until I mentioned Tiffany's calls. Said she only remembers him phoning once, so she didn't think it was a big deal. However, the name stuck in her head because it was the same as her brother's."

My pulse quickened. "Anybody we know?"

"Nah. Some guy named Chuck Samuels."

CHAPTER TWENTY

*I*t had started to rain. I remained standing perfectly still, my body pressed up against the vinyl siding, water dripping from my hair. I barely noticed the discomfort as Jacques' words registered with my brain. The cell slipped from my hand into the wet grass below before I had a chance to stop it.

As I fell to my knees to retrieve it, Jacque's anxious voice filtered through the phone. "Cin, are you there?" he asked. "Cindy!"

"Here," I managed to squeak out. "Chuck is—"

"Listen, girl, I just drove past a cop and don't have my hands free. I've got to get off. Be back as soon as I can."

"Jacques, wait—"

The line went dead.

I was finally able to put together the truth. Ken had been having an affair with Tiffany, using an alias, and now Tiffany was dead. He'd killed her, and it was for the vase. While my gut instinct told me my theory was correct, I still needed to see for myself that the vase was really gone. And why did I feel like there was still another piece missing from this puzzle?

With zombie-like motions, I entered Jacques' code and inserted the key into the door. I walked through the foyer, climbed the stairs, and then couldn't even remember doing so. I headed straight for Tiffany's bedroom. With every step I took, my heart knocked louder and louder against the wall of my chest. I flicked on the light switch and glanced toward the piano, then sucked in some air. There was no vase to be seen. Big surprise.

Hands shaking, I reached for my phone as a metallic click sounded behind me, and I whirled around.

"You should've made sure the door locked behind you. I guess you're not a very good agent."

Ken stood in the doorway, pointing a gun directly at my head.

Play dumb. "What are you talking about? Is another agent showing you the house? I thought you were going to buy it from me."

"Forget the house bull." Ken moved closer to me as I in turn took a few steps backward. "You couldn't leave well enough alone, could you?"

"I—I guess not." I forced my gaze away from the gun to stare at his handsome face. Eyes that had resembled dark pools of melted chocolate the other day were now as black and cold as the night. "Ken, you don't have to do this."

He chuckled, the gun never wavering in his grasp. "Little Miss Detective. I knew you'd try to make trouble after the stunt you pulled the other day, so that's why I followed you around. I saw you go into my shop. Who do you think you are?"

Think, think. "I decided to take your advice and sell some jewelry. I need the money badly."

His eyes glittered and for an instant focused on my chest, then back to my face. "Correction. Not a very good agent *or* liar."

My heart thumped faster. *Okay, try not to make him angrier.*

"Yeah, I got top dollar, like you said I would. Now if you'll excuse me, I need to get home to my kids." I took a step toward the door.

He pushed me back roughly by the shoulder. "Nice try. But you're not going anywhere, and you'll never see those brats again."

The bile rose in my throat while he stood there shaking his head at me. "Don't start blubbering, Cindy. It won't work with me. I'm not one of those men who gets all upset when a woman cries. Actually, it kind of turns me on."

Anger rose from the pit of my stomach and threatened to erupt like a volcano. "Looking at you makes me want to vomit. You're not a man, you're scum."

I may have gone a bit too far with my speech. I watched as the phony smile disappeared from Ken's face, and his eyes filled with venom. He didn't say a single word as he nonchalantly drew his arm back and punched me in the face. I saw stars and fell backward in a confused state of agony onto one of Tiffany's Persian rugs. My entire head throbbed, and the pain was so intense in my right eye that I couldn't open it for a few minutes.

When I finally managed to focus, Ken was standing over me, an evil smile twisting at the corners of his mouth. "And if you really want to vomit, I'll help you along." He kicked my stomach sharply with the toe of his shoe. "There. A little payback for the other day."

That did the trick. I lay on the floor in a fetal position, writhing in pain. I turned my head and began retching onto the rug. Ken's laughter roared in my ears, and the room started to grow dark. As the walls began to close in, I desperately fought against the urge to black out.

Don't faint now. You can't. Thoughts of Greg and the kids made me want to weep. No, I couldn't give up without a fight. I owed that much to my family.

One thing was for sure. If help didn't arrive soon, I was a

goner. Ken wouldn't hesitate to use his gun on me. I had to get him talking again and try to stall until Jacques showed up.

Ken tossed me a handkerchief. "God, you're pathetic. Clean your face up."

I tried to mop up the mess. "You and Donna used me to get into Tiffany's house so that you could grab the vase. That whole story about your mother looking for a house was a lie. And then you took the vase and put it in your car while I was in the bathroom." I remembered him steering me toward the other bedroom afterward so that I wouldn't know it had disappeared.

"Well done, Nancy Drew. Almost correct on all counts. But dumb Donna didn't know about the vase's worth. And you won't get a chance to tell her."

"She wanted me to take the blame for Tiffany's murder though."

"I do like brainy woman. Too bad you wouldn't sleep with me. Did you know you're the first woman to ever refuse me? I should've known there was something off about you from the start."

"Why—because I have morals?"

Me and my big mouth again. My latest snarky comment cost me dearly as Ken pulled his shoe back and kicked me in the side this time. My obvious misery made him chuckle, and he leaned down to whisper in my ear. "I'm starting to enjoy this. Maybe I'll continue to torture you until your gay, little friend comes back. Then you can watch me kill him before I take care of you."

Jacques. Bone-chilling panic swept over me. He'd be no match for Ken. I bit my lip to fight back tears. "Please don't hurt him. He didn't do anything. You're angry at me, not him. Please, I'm begging you."

I stared into piercing dark eyes devoid of emotion and realized my words were falling on deaf ears. I was never going to see my husband or kids again. I couldn't let Jacques die too.

Laughter erupted from the doorway as another person joined our party. I stared helplessly at our newest guest.

"Donna! Your husband killed Tiffany."

She shook her head and smiled sadly. "Oh, Cindy. Why did I ever hire you? You're not as smart as I thought. As usual, you have everything wrong."

Could she really be this stupid? "I know you don't want to believe it, but—"

Donna squatted down next to me and breathed into my ear. "Ken didn't kill her. *I* did."

A wave of nausea and confusion passed over me. "But why? She was your friend. And she made you a *lot* of money."

Ken scratched at his head with his free hand while keeping the gun pointed at me with the other. He turned slightly to address Donna.

"What are you doing here?" He didn't seem pleased to see his bride.

She looked at me drooling away on the floor. "I got an email alert that someone had entered the house. Jacques' code came up, but I knew it had to be this nosy witch." She got to her feet, but continued to taunt me. "You wanted to sleep with my husband, didn't you?"

I paused to catch my breath, still afraid I might pass out. "Your husband's got his hands full in that department already. He's been lying to you. He only wanted to get in here and steal Tiffany's vase. Then he was going to dump you."

"Vase?" Donna asked. "You mean the one Tiffany kept in here? That's *my* vase. Everything in this house is mine. Daddy was supposed to leave everything to me, not *her*."

There was the missing piece to my puzzle. I remembered my earlier conversation with Jacques, and my mouth dropped open. "Holy cow. Tiffany's your sister."

"*Was* is the operative word." She made a face. "And she was only my half-sister."

I couldn't believe what I was hearing. "She was your flesh and blood—and you killed her! Why?"

"She shouldn't have threatened to leave the company. I made her one of the top agents in the state, and that's how she repays me?"

I couldn't wrap my brain around this logic. "But she was your sister," I repeated.

"This house should have been mine. I'm the first born. I couldn't believe Daddy would leave it to her. Of course it's worthless now, but that's all right. Her jewelry and other personal effects will be enough for me. Not to mention any antiques Daddy left her." She smiled at me. "You walked right into my trap. I knew she was meeting you that night. When I called Tiffany to ask her to split the Hunter listing, she told me how you'd threatened her. It was the break I had been looking for."

With that, Donna turned to her husband, voice barely above a whisper. She compressed her lips together in a fine, thin line. "How did you know about the vase?"

Ken didn't respond as he continued to wave the gun at me.

Recognition slowly dawned on Donna's face. "Oh my God. You've been here—with her."

"He was having an affair with Tiffany. Your own sister." I spoke as gently as I could.

Ken glared at me but thankfully didn't touch me again.

Donna gripped the bed post between her hands. "I should have known. You never really loved me, did you?"

He snorted and gave her a look of repulsion. "Please. What's to love? If I'd met Tiffany first, I would have married her instead. Then the vase would have been mine, and no one would have had to get hurt. But you—oh, no. You were so jealous of her. It was pitiful to watch."

Her eyes filled with tears. "That's why you haven't slept with me since our wedding night."

Ew. Way too much information for my ears.

Ken burst into laughter. "You're lucky I didn't put a bag over your head."

I couldn't let this one go. "Now that's cold."

He leaned over and kicked me in the side again. When would I learn to keep my mouth shut?

Ken tossed me a pencil and a piece of paper from his pocket. "You're going to write a suicide note and say you're sorry for killing Tiffany."

It hurt for me to speak, but I managed to spit out a few words. "My husband would never believe that, and I won't do it."

"You don't have a choice." He clicked the hammer on the gun.

"Where's the vase?" Donna demanded, looking toward the piano.

Ken waved the gun and flashed an evil-looking smile at her. "That's for me to know and you to never find out."

Donna stared at him, the color draining from her face. Then it dawned on me that Donna's life was as much in jeopardy as my own.

She seemed to realize this as well. "But—you said she was ruining my life."

"Well, she was," Ken growled. "And now you're ruining mine." He moved the gun away from my head and pointed it at Donna.

She gasped. "It was your idea for me to kill Tiffany. You said it was better that way. I could take over all of her listings, keep her personal items." She turned to me. "He talked me into killing her. When I found out you were meeting Tiffany to talk about the Hunter house, everything fell right into place. I told Ken, and he said you could take the blame for both of us. No one would ever know."

Ken moved the gun closer to her. "You need to shut your fat trap now."

Donna wiped her eyes. "It wasn't fair. She was so gorgeous.

Every guy who met Tiffany wanted her. Look at me. I didn't have a date for almost three years."

Ken laughed. "Gee, I wonder why."

Tears ran down her cheeks. "I can't believe I actually thought you loved me. You only care about yourself."

Ken shrugged. "Well, pretty much. I needed money, and there you were—desperate Donna, longing to be loved. Then I discovered your sister had even more money than you. Plus, she was way better looking. Too bad she had to go, but it all worked out for the best anyway. Now me and my vase can live happily ever after."

"God, how stupid I am. How much is the vase worth?"

"About two million," I said.

Donna gasped out loud. "And you weren't going to tell me? You bastard."

"Tick tock, tick tock." Ken aimed the gun at me. "Your time has run out—now." He motioned to Donna. "Then you're next, old ball and chain."

Donna began sobbing hysterically. "You were going to take off with the vase and not even tell me. I bet you stole her jewelry too, didn't you? Where's the diamond necklace that was worth about twenty grand?"

The necklace I'd seen Randy with earlier. I was confident that was the one Donna spoke of.

"You need to shut the hell up." Ken smacked her across the face.

Donna started screaming and tried to tear the weapon from his hands. Furious, he smacked the gun against the side of her head. She fell backward onto the hardwood floor and lay motionless.

My hands flew to my face in horror as the scene unfolded before me.

Without missing a beat, Ken turned his attention back to me. "Sorry, Cindy, say good-bye now. See you in the afterlife."

Think, think. "Okay. Just let me finish the note for my husband."

He examined his watch. "Hurry up. You have thirty seconds."

My cell phone started to ring from inside my jacket pocket. Jacques must be on his way back. He'd be worried when I didn't answer. It was a realization that left me both hopeful and terrified. I didn't want Jacques to get hurt because of me. I had to do this on my own.

Ken smiled. "Don't even think about answering that."

At that moment, the ringing stopped. With a trembling hand, I picked up the pencil and purposefully pressed the tip hard onto the paper against the floor. The point broke instantly.

"Nice going," he said. "Well, I guess George doesn't get a note now."

"I—I have a pen in my pocket." I reached inside my coat before he could protest and held the ballpoint pen for him to see. "Speaking of notes, did you send the others to me?"

"Of course. We were trying to pin the murder on you. I was hoping you'd go to the police with the picture, especially after they found out you were in Tiffany's house. I'm sure you would've been popular." His eyes glittered with anger. "But, of course, you didn't cooperate."

I glanced at Donna, still lifeless on the floor behind him. "What are you going to do with her?"

Ken's face brightened. "You know, this might actually work out to my advantage. I'll kill you and then Donna. I'll make it look like you both killed each other. After all, you did come in here without consent. The police will guess you were trying to cover something up. Donna found out you were here and came to confront you. An argument ensued, you killed Donna, and then yourself." He clasped his hands around the gun like an eager child. "Yes, this will work out just fine."

There was nothing to stop him. The last glimmer of hope left my body as I tried to prepare myself for death. I thought of my family and prayed silently that they knew how much I loved them.

At that very moment, one of Donna's eyes flickered open. Ken was focused on me and didn't see the quick movement. He lowered the gun so that it was level with my chest. "Do you have any last words, Cindy?" His lips twisted upward into an evil-looking smirk. "Did you tell George how much you love him?"

"Lowlife," Donna moaned.

Ken turned around, surprised by the sound of her voice. It was the split second I needed.

"His name is Greg, you jerk!" Ignoring the pain in my side, I leaped forward and thrust the ballpoint pen into Ken's thigh with such force that it actually stuck there for a moment. He screamed in agony as the gun clattered to the floor.

Ken and I both leaped for the weapon at the same time, but I managed to grab it first. As I wrapped my fingers around the trigger, Ken gathered my hair in his hands and pulled as hard as he could. My upper body snapped backward from the pain. Meanwhile, Donna had grabbed my pen and crawled forward, hitting Ken in the calf with it. He cried out and released his hold on me, falling to the floor. I somehow managed to get to my feet and faced him as I wobbled, the gun shaking in my hands. Paul's face appeared before me, and I gasped, flinching as I tried to force the mental picture away. *Oh no. Not now. Please.*

My voice cracked in a hoarse whisper as I aimed the gun at Ken, unable to stop my hands from shaking. "Don't move."

Ken roared with laughter as he staggered toward me. "Please. You don't have the guts."

I observed him as he grew closer, his face mocking me. I sucked in a sharp breath, closed my eyes, and began to squeeze the trigger. A loud, almost deafening, blast startled me. I lost my balance, falling onto the floor and letting out a grunt of pain as my side connected with the hardwood.

I looked at Donna who in turn was watching Ken, horrified.

He held his hands over his stomach, blood seeping out at a furious pace. Ken stared at us with a vacant expression and crumpled to the floor, eyes closed. I stared at the gun between my hands in amazement. It hadn't been fired. Donna stared in shock at something past me, and I turned my head, bewildered.

There was Jacques, holding a pistol in one hand and his phone in the other. "9-1-1? I need the police, please. And an ambulance. Yes, 55 Riverview Drive."

"Thank God you're here," I managed to croak out.

Jacques disconnected the call, then knelt by my side. He removed the gun from my still-shaking hand and stared down at me with concern. "Are you okay, love? You're white as a ghost, and your poor eye is swollen. What else did that slime do to you?"

The pain in my side was agonizing, and Jacques' face danced in and out of focus. I tried to sit up. "Where—where did you get a gun?"

Jacques gently eased me back down. "Lie still, darling. I got permission to carry a while ago. Too many real estate agents have been victims of crimes lately. We need to protect ourselves." He stared at Ken with a look of disgust on his face. "I'm only sorry I didn't kill the bastard. If I'd been here a second later you might have though."

He held my hand as Ken lay bleeding and moaning in pain with Donna sobbing by his side.

My heart overflowed as I smiled at my best friend. "I guess we'll never know for sure."

Jacques spotted my Hospitable Homes pen lying on the floor next to me and reached out to grab it. He grinned. "Did you use this on him?"

I managed a small chuckle, despite the pain in my ribs. "A real estate agent always has to be prepared."

Then everything went black.

CHAPTER TWENTY-ONE

*T*he next few hours passed in a blur. Police cars arrived within minutes, along with an ambulance for Ken. Shortly afterward, another one arrived for me. Jacques phoned Greg, who arrived in a panic while the paramedics were loading me into the second ambulance. They allowed him to ride to the hospital with me.

Donna confessed to the murder of Tiffany Roberts and was taken away to the police station for booking.

Jacques also went to the station for questioning. I remembered him hugging me and saying he'd be over to see me as soon as he could break away.

I was in and out of consciousness all the way to the hospital. Along with my black eye, I had two bruised ribs. The doctor wanted me to stay overnight for observation. This was becoming an all-too-familiar scenario for me.

Greg insisted on staying with me. Helen agreed to watch the kids and even asked Greg to send her love. I couldn't help but wonder if my husband made up that part. I talked to each one of the kids on the phone and told them I loved them, so at least they knew I was okay.

Ken had severe abdominal injuries but was expected to survive. Fortunately, he'd been taken to a different hospital and would be under constant surveillance until he was well enough to be moved to his new home—a jail cell.

I found it somewhat sad that Donna was probably going to spend the rest of her life in prison while Ken, who had obviously brainwashed her from the beginning, might serve a lesser sentence.

"It's scary," I said to Greg, after I was all settled in my hospital bed, his arm around me. "What if he decides to come after me?"

"That won't happen, baby. He's going away for a long time. You never have to see him again."

"It's amazing to think a smart woman like Donna was duped by him. And Tiffany, too."

"You and Jacques said it yourselves. Donna was so desperate for a man, she'd do anything. Even though she's the one who pulled the trigger, Ken's far more dangerous than her."

My voice trembled as I reached for Greg's hand. "He was going to kill both of us. I didn't think I'd ever see you or the kids again."

Greg kissed me tenderly. "Thank God for Jacques."

As if on cue, my best friend appeared in the doorway, bearing a large bouquet of yellow roses.

Greg stood up to let him hug me. He'd once confided to me that it made him uncomfortable to be around Jacques. The thought of my two favorite men being unable to get along always saddened me. Now none of it mattered anymore. After Jacques finished hugging me, he turned around to see Greg standing there, hand outstretched. Jacques extended his as well, while I grinned from ear to ear.

"Oh, what the hell." Greg pulled Jacques' arm forward and captured him in a hug, his voice choked with emotion. "Thanks, man. You saved my wife's life. I'll never forget this."

That was more than enough for Jacques, who suddenly

looked misty-eyed. "My immense pleasure." He sat down in a chair next to the bed to fill us in on the details.

"How come no one ever knew Tiffany and Donna were sisters?" Greg asked.

I waved my hand in the air. It was one of my few body parts that didn't hurt. "Hospitable Homes doesn't allow relatives to work in the same office branch. In this case, it mattered even more because Donna was the manager, and she distributed the leads."

Jacques' voice was heavy with sarcasm. "I guess we know why Tiffany had them all. Plus, Donna was getting a share of Tiffany's commission on the side. When Tiffany got her license, she came to Donna and asked her for a job. Donna made Tiffany sign a contract stating she'd give her fifteen percent of every sale she made in the next two years."

"I knew it. When did you find this out?"

"Right after you fainted—when we were waiting for the police. I couldn't shut Donna up."

"Darn. I always miss the good stuff."

Jacques grinned and went on. "Of course, it was totally illegal, but Tiffany was just starting out and desperate for sales, so she agreed to it. Donna probably never expected Tiffany to become number one in the entire state but must have been thrilled when it happened. After her career took off, Tiffany became resentful and wanted to go out on her own. The two-year agreement was up last month, and Donna knew Tiffany planned on opening up her own brokerage firm. She couldn't afford to have Tiffany leave and begged her to stay put for a while."

"And how did that slime Ken fit into the picture?" Greg asked.

"Donna said she met Ken a couple of months ago. By the end of the first week, he had moved in with her and told her his life wouldn't be complete until she married him."

Oh brother. I wrinkled my nose. "Until he met Tiffany, that is."

Jacques snorted. "Well, let's be honest. If you were in his shoes, who would you have chosen? A gorgeous, young woman who's making money hand over fist or a middle-aged woman with a Raggedy Ann hairdo who's so desperate that she places personal advertisements in the newspaper?"

I groaned. "Please don't say middle-aged. Donna is only a couple of years older than me."

"Sorry, love." Jacques winked. "By the way, you look fantastic."

Greg and I laughed.

"Personal ads, huh?" Greg smiled. "No need. She should have come to me. I know this one mechanic who'd have dated her."

I put my finger to his lips. "I'm guessing Ken had an alibi for the night Tiffany was killed too."

Jacques was lapping up the attention. "Of course. He was at some gold and silver exhibition out of town, Donna said."

"He made sure to cover all his tracks," Greg commented.

I scoffed. "He knew Donna didn't know the value of the vase. He listed it with the auction house and was getting ready to leave the country. Donna would've never seen him again."

"No great loss there," my husband remarked.

"Donna didn't know, and neither did Tiffany. If she had, she would have sold that baby on the spot, I guarantee." Jacques shook his head. "My guess is Ken must have found the paperwork when he was helping her go through the junk in the basement."

I yawned. "I think Tiffany and Donna believed everything he said. Sounds like they treated him like he was some type of god."

"Freaky, isn't it?" Jacques asked. "And see where it got them. Remember, I did tell you it was all about the looks, darling."

I smiled. "For some people, I guess. Ken and Donna decided I should show him the house because it would make me look like the guilty party. He didn't want Donna to know about the vase, so it was a perfect time to grab it and then trot off to New York City, papers in hand. Of course, when the vase was discovered missing later on, Donna would think I'd stolen it."

Greg frowned. "He followed you around today. When you went to the pawn shop, he knew you were up to something."

I sighed and leaned forward. "You both tried to warn me not to show him those houses. Everything would have been simpler had I listened."

"Hon, you got off easy." Jacques stretched and crossed his legs at the ankles. "Tiffany paid with her life. And look at how he used Donna. Now she has no life—because of him."

Greg rubbed my back gently. "Hard to believe such a shrewd woman like her turned out to be so stupid."

"She was blinded by lust," I said.

Jacques shook his head at me. "She was duped by a con artist. I'll bet he was going to have the money wired to an overseas bank account when the vase sold. He probably planned to take off tonight."

"Well, the only place he's going now is up the river," Greg said.

Jacques got to his feet and glanced at the clock on the wall. It was after one o'clock in the morning. We'd been talking for over an hour.

"I hate to be a party pooper, guys, but I'm beat." Jacques leaned over to give me a kiss on the cheek. "And you need your rest. Be ready for work on Monday morning, missy."

I was confused. "And where am I working now?"

Jacque placed his hands on his hips. "Girlfriend, what am I going to do with you? I told you earlier I signed the lease for my new office space, so I'm hiring you as my first official agent. I'll draw up a formal contract for you to sign."

I could barely contain my excitement. "But what about Hospitable Homes? Couldn't you take over as manager there?"

Jacques dangled his car keys. "Probably, but I don't want it by default. Anyhow, I've always dreamed about having my own agency. I wouldn't be surprised if this branch went under now. By tomorrow there'll be too much bad publicity surrounding the place. No one is going to want to be associated with the agency now, thanks to Donna."

I hadn't thought of that. "Well, this is great for me, but I feel bad for everyone else."

He laughed. "They can come along too, if they want. But you'll have the place of honor, an office right next to mine. I even have your first listing ready."

"Get out." I was immensely pleased. "Where?"

His eyes gleamed. "Tiffany's house."

"What? But how?"

"When Tiffany died, Donna was designated as backup agent on the listing. She then took it over and listed me as backup. We'd worked together in that capacity before. This way, if she wasn't available, people could always contact me about seeing the house. Since Donna can no longer act in that manner and is in no position to change anything, I'll take over the listing. And I've decided to give it to you."

To say I was thrilled was an understatement. "You don't have to do that."

"I want to. I know you'll do it justice."

Despite the pain, I suddenly felt like break dancing. "I can't wait to go to work Monday. Gee, I never thought I'd say something like that."

Jacques blew me a kiss and shook hands with Greg.

Greg cleared his throat. "Hey, as soon as Cindy's feeling up to it, we'd like you and Ed to come for dinner."

"No thanks."

Greg's eyes widened with surprise.

Jacques grinned. "This girl needs a night off from cooking.

We'll all go out—say, night after next? My treat to celebrate the new business. You can even bring the little monsters."

I beamed at my two favorite men. "That would be great."

"Okay, I've got to run. See you soon, lady."

"Bye, boss."

After Jacques had left, Greg got back into bed and hugged me close to him. "He's quite a guy."

"Took you long enough to find out," I teased.

Greg silenced me with a kiss. "I don't know what I would have done if something had happened to you tonight."

I buried my face in his chest. "I have so much to be thankful for. You, the kids, and even your mother. Let's stop at the florist on the way home tomorrow and get her some flowers as a thank you for taking care of the kids."

Greg's arms tightened around me. "You're wonderful, baby." Then he chuckled. "Guess what I found in Mom's purse tonight?"

"What?"

"Our good silver."

"Oh, cut it out."

Greg laughed. "Yeah, that was bad, I know."

"I'm serious. I'd like to do something nice for her. I don't want any more fighting. Life is too short. I realized that tonight."

Greg cradled my face in his hands. "You're right about that. And I intend to make the most of every moment—with you."

"Same here," I whispered, kissing him.

CHAPTER TWENTY-TWO

*D*espite pain killers the hospital had given me, I did not sleep well that night. A police officer arrived early the next morning to ask me a few questions. This time, it wasn't Officer Simon. I secretly wondered if he might have been too embarrassed to come, but there was no way of knowing for sure.

Greg slept like a dead man next to me, and it took several nudges to awaken him and stop his snoring so that the policeman could hear my responses.

Officer Tomlinson listened while I told him what had transpired in the house. I showed him the picture of Tiffany's vase I'd thrown into my purse. He wouldn't reveal any details about the case but mentioned that a call had been placed to take the vase off the auction house's schedule. It was being held as evidence and eventually would become part of Tiffany's estate.

After Officer Tomlinson left, breakfast arrived. I was busy getting my caffeine fix on when my cell buzzed. Jacques. "Hey, you."

"Morning, love. How are we feeling today?"

I winced as I shifted positions in the bed. "Sore, but I'll live."

"Apparently, Donna's been placed on suicide watch. She's due to be transferred to a correctional facility downstate sometime later today."

I gasped. "How the heck do you know all this? A policeman was just here and wouldn't tell me anything."

Jacques spoke with authority. "I have a friend over at the station."

"You have friends everywhere. I'm getting jealous."

"Yeah, but you're at the top of the list."

I grinned. "I'd better be."

At that moment, a nurse walked into the room with my discharge papers. Greg got off the bed while she placed them in front of me to sign.

"Hang on a second, it looks like I'm being paroled." I scribbled my name down and handed the paper back to the nurse. "Can I call you when I get home?"

"Sure thing. Ed and I will stop by later, if you're feeling up to it," Jacques said.

"Definitely. I can't wait."

Jacques cleared his throat and hesitated. "Cin, there is one other thing. I've got some news that won't make you very happy."

"Uh-oh. What's up?"

"I talked to Marcia Steele, and it looks like Tiffany's house has to come off the market."

"Please tell me you're joking."

"I wish. I'm not positive, but if Tiffany didn't have a will and no living relatives, besides Donna, there wouldn't be a new owner to sign any contracts for a listing. It may have to be turned over to the estate to see if any other relatives file first. If they do, we may be able to list it again in the near future."

While I was disappointed, this wasn't totally unexpected. One thing I had learned in the real estate business was that nothing was ever a sure thing—similar to life. I tried to make

light of the situation. "Well, that's just the way the deal crumbles,
I guess."

Jacques chattered on. "I know you're disappointed, dear. I'm
sure it'll come back to us at some point." A buzzing noise came
from the phone. "Oh, that's Tricia Hudson calling back with
another counteroffer. Too bad for her that my client's not
lowering their price. God, I love making that chick's life rough.
I'll call you right back."

He clicked off, and I sighed. Same old story. The big sale had
slipped through my fingers once again.

"Baby, what's wrong?" Greg frowned.

"Tiffany's house has to come off the market. Something to do
with the estate."

Greg took my face between his hands. "Hey, you still
have me."

"Yeah, and you're better than any old house." As I gazed at
my adorable husband, I knew I was the luckiest woman alive.
Our money problems were still there, but we'd make it, with or
without Tiffany's house. I sensed that working for Jacques
would be the best thing to ever happen to my career as well.

Greg chuckled and helped me out of bed. "Let's get you
home. The kids will be happy to see you."

"I can't wait to see them too." I scanned the room. "Where are
my clothes?"

"I hung them in the closet last night." Greg brought the
hanger over that held my jeans and blouse. "Do you need any
help?"

I shook my head. "No, I should be able to get them on okay."

"Good. Because my area of expertise is taking clothes off, not
putting them on." He swatted my behind.

"Gregory!"

He laughed. "Come on, baby, let's get out of here."

"Oh." I hesitated for a second. "Jacques said he and Ed would
like to stop by later. Is that all right?"

"You don't even need to ask me that."

My heart swelled as Greg dug the car keys out of his jacket. "I'll go pull the car around and be right back." He kissed the top of my head and left the room, shutting the door behind him.

I removed the hospital gown and sat on the bed to pull my shirt on. That part was easy. In slow motion and with great care, I started on the jeans, wincing the entire time I pulled them around my stomach. I left them unbuttoned, which helped a little. I felt as if I'd just come from an all-you-can-eat buffet, but I'd manage until we got home and I could change into a pair of comfortable sweats.

My phone buzzed again. I looked down and smiled when I saw who it was. "Yes, my hero?"

"Hi, darling." Jacques sighed. "Sorry to leave you hanging before."

"No problem. You almost missed us. We're on our way out." I had to sit down again. I couldn't believe how unsteady on my feet I still was.

"That's what I wanted to hear." He paused. "I'm glad I caught you before you left. I know you're still under the weather, but I'm wondering if you could do me a small favor today."

I snorted in disbelief. "Gee, I happen to owe you my life, so I think I can manage one small favor."

"Well, do this for me, and we're even. I've got this woman who's really anxious to sell her house and needs an agent right away. Could you and Greg stop by on your way home from the hospital?"

I blinked, not sure I'd heard him correct. "That's terrific, but I don't have any paperwork with me. Not even a business card."

"That's okay. She's got a contract already there waiting."

"I'm also having a lot of trouble walking."

"Ah, you and Greg had some fun today, huh?" Jacques teased.

"Stop being such a smart aleck." My curiosity piqued. "Who is this woman? Can't she wait until tomorrow?"

Jacques sounded horrified. "Oh, no. It's today or nothing. She's moving this week and needs to put the place on the market before she goes. I promise it'll only take ten minutes."

A sale is a sale. I sighed, longing to get home to the kids. "Nothing like waiting till the last minute. All right, what's the address?"

"Well, since you obviously haven't figured it out," Jacques said in a smooth tone. "I'll give you a little hint."

"That would be so wonderful of you."

"Please do not address your new boss with sarcasm," he admonished. "For starters, she lives on Partridge Lane, and she's eighty years old."

I burst out laughing. "Mrs. Hunter? And you say she has a contract ready to go?"

"I dropped a new one off to her yesterday. It's waiting on your signature."

"Tell her I'm on my way."

"Thanks, Cin, I knew you'd come through for me." Jacques sounded pleased with himself. "Oh, and there's one more thing."

"Now what?"

"Can you swing by the market and pick up a can of salmon first?"

I grinned. "Sure, I'll take care of it."

ABOUT THE AUTHOR

USA Today bestselling author Catherine lives in Upstate New York with a male dominated household that consists of her very patient husband, three sons, and several spoiled pets. She has wanted to be a writer since the age of eight when she wrote her own version of Cinderella (and fortunately Disney never sued). Catherine has a dual major in both English and Performing Arts. Her book, For Sale by Killer, won the 2019 Daphne du Maurier award for Mainstream Mystery/Suspense. She loves to read, bake and attend live theater performances.

Printed in Great Britain
by Amazon